PUT A BUG IN YOUR EAR

(MiMi Ni MUSHi O iRERU)

Sam Sumac

First published 2025
by Rowanvale Books Ltd
The Gate
Keppoch Street
Roath
Cardiff
CF24 3JW
www.rowanvalebooks.com

A CIP catalogue record for this book is available from the British
Library.
ISBN: 978-1-83584-148-8
ePub ISBN: 978-1-83584-149-5

PUT A BUG iN YOUR EAR

OR

耳に虫を入れる
Mimi ni mushi o ireru

by

SAM SUMAC

This book is dedicated to Jiro Ono (小野 二郎, *Ono Jirō*). After this unwavering sushi master opened his restaurant, *Sukiyabashi Jiro* (すきやばし次郎) in 1965 in the Ginza District of Tokyo, Japan, this world hasn't been the same.

Hakuta

Unangax̂ for "I Made a Mistake"

彼らは私の言うことを聞いていないと思います
karera wa watashi no iu koto o kiite inai to omoimasu

"I don't think they heard me."

Yukio Mishima (nee Kimitake Hiraoka)

旅に病んで　夢は枯野を　かけ廻る
tabi ni yande/ yume wa kareno wo/ kakemeguru

sick on my journey,
my dreams go wandering
on this withered field

Matsuo Basho, Death Haiku, 1694

編集者からのメモ

henshū-sha kara no memo
A note from the editor
– i.e., the Sam Sumac Association

We are extremely excited to have this complete transcription of Sam Sumac's novel *Put a Bug in Your Ear* ready for publication. Although the story is clearly written in the usual/unusual style of his earlier books, there are many features of it that seem brand new. For starters, while it reads as a version of a cheesy monster movie, it has a definite Sam Sumac twist to it. As a staffer recently proffered, "This book is like watching a Toho Co., Ltd. movie while taking a trip on the subtropical Japanese bluing mushroom *Psilocybe subcaerulipes.*"

Now, even we had to look this reference up, but the description is more than apt. Within this story, Sam Sumac uses the familiar medium of a Japanese monster movie, but he does so while distorting the limits of the tale's reality as far as he can stretch them. Like all of the Dadaist writers before him, he stoops low enough to absurdity to feel its body heat, but not so far as to devolve into uttering only gibberish and fart sounds.

As the Sam Sumac Association digs deeper into this mysterious author, we continue on a daily basis to learn things about the man and his writings. Many times, admittedly, these revelations generate more questions than answers, but that's the nature of what we do. One thing we can say with some authority is that Sam Sumac was someone who was prone to becoming hyper-focused. Whether it is idioms, blues music, names, politicians, the apocalypse, aliens, or Henry Kissinger, his stories are rife with details that don't always make sense in the big picture but were clearly important to him. Some might say these were his obsessions, but we reject the negative connotation of this term and use "preoccupations" instead. With *Put a Bug in Your Ear*, it is clear what was preoccupying the author when he wrote this tale – Japanese culture and proverbs (ことわざ – *kotowaza*).

We asked Dr. Chie Nakane, a highly regarded Japanese anthropologist and Professor Emerita of Social Anthropology at the University of Tokyo, to take a look at our transcribed manuscript and give us her impressions.

According to her, there are three forms of these old Japanese sayings: 言い習わし (*iinarawashi*), 四字熟語 (*yojijukugo*), and 慣用句 (*kan'youku*). And while they're all very similar, there are some nuanced differences between them. *Iinarawashi* are short sayings that dispense bits of wisdom, *yojijukugo* are four-character idioms that create sayings that need to be interpreted, and *kan'youku* are also idiomatic phrases, but they're longer than *yojijukugo*. Dr. Nakane concluded that, while all three forms of Japanese proverbs can be found in this story, it is apparent that Sam Sumac's understanding of the Japanese language and culture was so rudimentary that he totally misused most of the sayings and completely misrepresented the culture in his text. She then went on to infer that the man should really have been reprimanded for such a dereliction of his authorial responsibility to adhere to the precincts of cultural awareness.

Regardless of this, Sam Sumac seems to have developed a real love for Japanese proverbs, to the extent that he sought to use them as a literary tool throughout this entire story. There were two specific sayings that, judging by the way that the author enthusiastically highlighted them in his notes and then used them so prominently in this story, were particularly important to him:

泣いて暮らすも一緒、笑って暮らすも一緒
Naite kurasu mo isshô waratte kurasu mo isshô
Life is the same whether we spend it crying or laughing.

しょうがない
Shouganai
It is what it is.

Whenever we're analyzing a Sam Sumac story, it helps us to try and pinpoint what the author was attempting to communicate exactly to those of us in his audience. When it comes to *Put a Bug in Your Ear*, we think that understanding these two statements is essential for finding the avenue of the message he was going for in these pages. There seems to be so many examples of good news/bad news throughout this tale that we cannot help but think that Sam Sumac was saying that, in the end, the interpretation of those moments depends entirely upon the perspective of the participants and the onlooker.

Insipid labels of happiness or sadness, goodness or badness, didn't really matter to Sam Sumac, since he believed so strongly that Life happens regardless of those viewpoints. Apparently, whether there's a positive or negative reaction to what's happening wasn't as important to the man as just weathering the storm. In fact, it appears that he was highly critical of overtly celebratory or somber reactions by humans. We're unsure if Sam Sumac's conclusion in this matter comes from an Eastern religion/philosophy or a Doris Day song, but he obviously felt strongly enough about this issue to hammer at it throughout the rendering of this saga.

It therefore seems more fitting to ignore our usual direction to the reader to "enjoy" this latest Sam Sumac book. Clearly we should just say, read the book. Whether it's enjoyed or detested really didn't interest the man. Either way, we imagine him shrugging his broad shoulders and uttering with a sharp grin, "*Shouganai* (しょうがない)."

千里の道も一歩から

senri no michi mo ippo kara
A journey of a thousand miles begins
with a single step.

Needless to say, the rather shocking emergence of the massive monster from the volcano overlooking their town sent the residents of Akutan, Alaska, scurrying for the exits in full-panic mode. And while their island was so small that there was really nowhere for them to go, the hundred and sixty permanent town residents and the two hundred employees of the local Trident Seafood processing plant tried to get as far away as they possibly could from the towering terror that was now clawing itself free from its subterranean lair. In their hasty flight they left behind those cherished possessions that they couldn't carry, as well as their less able family members who were not fast enough to keep up. Clearly, it was not a time to be either too careful or too entirely caring.

One Aleut man, a Raymond Alagagta, aged eighty-two years old, had been abandoned by his granddaughter. It wasn't entirely her fault. The old man had puttered around unnecessarily and started packing his small valise instead of taking flight.

Being a veteran of the original Reassignment of the Unangax̂ from Akutan after the Japanese invasion of the Aleutian Islands in 1942, Raymond knew that he needed to pack better this time. If he and his people were again to be transported back to the same under-supplied federal work camp north of Ketchikan at Ward Lake, he felt it was imperative that he gather all of the important medicinal items to help his family fight for survival there.

Raymond also felt compelled to bring some of his deceased wife's things to leave on her unmarked grave in the nearby Bayview Cemetery – a place he hadn't been able to visit since her death from dysentery during the war. So, instead of blindly running for the door and screaming expletives, as most people were currently doing in response to the monster coming out of the volcano, he was calmly packing up his Linda's favorite scarf, some aspirin bottles, his Pepto-Bismol, and his gathered toiletries for the trip.

As he finished this task and looked around for his granddaughter to help him, he suddenly became painfully aware that he was now all alone. On top of that, he could see the one-hundred-and-fifty-foot-tall lizard monster now standing atop the nearby Akutan Peak. The reality of his situation hit at that moment and, as a defense mechanism, he slipped deep into his people's lore. As one of the last vessels of the Unangax̂ traditions, words, and beliefs on Akutan, he shouted out the old tongue's name for the massive Arctic giants that haunted their mythology.

"Inupasugjak!"

A fleeing fish-gutter from Seattle who happened to be rushing past the old man's house at that very moment heard Raymond's loud announcement, and figuring that the wise-looking Native man was probably some kind of a shaman who was introducing the world to the just-birthed monster, the fish processor decided to disperse this name wherever he went, henceforth. And, like all rumors and hearsay, it spread like wildfire and the name stuck. Soon, the creature became solely known by the locals, military personnel, scientists, and the world media as Inupasugjak.

Sadly, in a lost-in-translation kind of situation, the eloquent Unangax̂ term that Raymond Alagagta had passionately uttered was heard completely differently in English. Phonetically, it sounded a bit like "He-Knew-Pat-Sajak" and it was *this* pronunciation that came to identify the terrifying creature.

At that moment, the world was in a very understandable state of hysteria. Just forty-eight hours prior to the emergence of this monster lizard in the Aleutian Islands, a gigantic meteor had come screaming down from the sky and smashed violently into the Earth near Vincennes, Indiana. The destruction from this impact had been thorough enough to level the city and the entire surrounding area for miles and miles. Dangerous seismic reverberations were felt globally, and if those weren't a big enough catastrophic event, the space rock down deep at the bottom of the resulting crater suddenly cracked open and a fifty-meter-tall monster that eerily resembled a cockroach emerged. It had become all too clear that the planet was now facing a reality straight out of the many monster movies that had entertained the populace at drive-ins and movie theaters for generations.

Except that this drama wasn't going to be silly, nor any fun.

As for the giant cockroach – unimaginatively code-named the Palmetto Bug Monster by the U.S. military – it certainly did not act like the common pests of so many households around the world. For starters, it didn't skitter off in its characteristic tripod gait to the shadows of the pantry. No, this giant creature stood up on its hind legs and began to walk. While such a feat itself could have been considered awe-inspiring, the creature then began to destroy everything around itself as it went.

Using its gargantuan forelegs, midlegs, wings, and some kind of bioweapon ray gun in its abdomen, the Palmetto Bug Monster left nothing but a wide path of utter destruction in its wake as it made its way northeast toward the Indiana capital city of Indianapolis.

Once it reached this destination, it obliterated the large urban center with a frightening thoroughness. One moment the city that was known as both "Crossroads of America" and "Nap Town" existed, the next it didn't.

The United States military quickly responded and hit the target hard, but nothing seemed to hurt the creature. Tanks, missiles, jet fighters, and gunfire – none of these had any impact. The contents of the local weapon arsenals were thrown at the space alien with no effect. The Palmetto Bug Monster appeared to be completely impervious to anything that could be hurled at it, and it went about its ghastly business of devastation while treating the armed resistance against it as if it all were a harmless swarm of gnats circling its head. And to make matters worse, now that it had finished obliterating Indy, it was heading on a path that led straight up to the "Windy City" of Chicago.

The television cameras caught it all, and from every conceivable angle, and as the entire Planet Earth watched, a growing feeling of shock and horror began to overwhelm everyone. Such a scenario was nothing anyone had prepared for in reality. Experts came forward, doomsayers emerged from the shadows, and religious leaders spoke about the end of times.

But two questions were really forming in the minds of the residents of Earth: when will the United States finally resort to using their nuclear arms to stop the creature, and if those don't work, would the cockroach continue on its mindless rampage around the planet and destroy the whole goddamn place?

So it was not inappropriate that the little isolated island of Akutan didn't put on its best airs in response to the appearance of its own titanic alien monster. With all of the awful pictures and descriptions of the annihilation streaming out of people's televisions and radios as the cockroach lay waste to the Midwest, it was natural that everyone on this little Aleutian island was currently freaking the fuck out about the emergence of a monster lizard from their own island's volcano.

As for He-Knew-Pat-Sajak, its "birth" was much different than the Palmetto Bug Monster's. There'd been no bombastic arrival, no immediate reign of death. The creature, which visually reminded most herpetologists and pet-store clerks of a fourteen-story-tall leopard gecko, came unexpectedly out of the dormant volcano like someone who'd been buried under the sand at the beach and had suddenly sat up. It then stood on its hind legs and stretched its arms out like a weary sleeper waking up.

To those who knew about such things, its skin looked oddly faded and its eyes looked cloudy. And it acted a bit disoriented. It gazed around, as if to assess where it was and where it needed to go, and then it raised its head up to the sky, apparently to let out a thunderous roar toward the heavens, but what came out sounded more like coughing from an ancient, emphysemic lion at a zoo.

When it finally began to walk away from the volcano, it did so in a hesitant and clumsy manner. It tripped several times, stumbling but not falling, and unlike the space bug in Indiana, the lizard acted as if it wanted to avoid people and their dwellings. It headed away from the settlement of Akutan, and it appeared to be going out of its way to tiptoe around the place to reduce any inadvertent destruction, which, truthfully, was challenging for a creature of its immense size. Not that there really was much on Akutan Island to destroy.

The monster initially stalked in a southwestern heading to go over to the neighboring Unalga Island, which would have put it on the pathway toward the more populated Unalaska Island, but then it suddenly stopped and looked around like it was trying to get its bearings. Abruptly, it reversed its path and headed back north over the volcano and toward the town of Akutan. But instead of rampaging through the collection of simple houses, Quonset huts, and the large Trident Seafood Processing plant, He-Knew-Pat-Sajak veered east and ventured out on the unpopulated peninsula that led toward the shortest crossing to nearby Akun Island.

When the scrambled military jets arrived from the Shemya Air Force Base and prepared to engage the creature, the pilots watched as the mighty lizard stopped at the curved shoreline of the Green Bight. They were attempting to keep calm in spite of the unbelievable scene that was unfolding in front of them, and they circled around the beast, waiting to get a clear answer from their superiors as to what the hell they were supposed to do. Having heard of the ineffectiveness of the conventional weapons that had been used against the Palmetto Bug Monster, and knowing of its lethal ability to easily pluck all aircraft from the sky, they were more than a little ambivalent about confronting this new threat unless directly ordered to do so.

The lizard made to enter the water, but as soon as its toe pads touched the frigid Akun Strait it appeared to be having second thoughts. However, in the act of testing the water's temperature, its left foot caught on a massive boulder mid-step and it awkwardly fell in, creating a geyser-like splash and a small tsunami that buffeted the shore. Those island residents still standing close enough said that the sound the monster made as it hit the water was akin to a shriek, but then it began thrashing about like a novice swimmer at the YMCA. Like the geckos of Earth, it wasn't a great swimmer, and it commenced to do a graceless aquatic "gallop" as it made its way in the direction of the virtually lifeless Akun Island.

The fighter pilots, their weapon systems painfully howling with target acquisition warnings, waited for the go-ahead to unleash their payload of missiles onto the flailing reptile in the water, but a stern message to stand down was finally issued. According to the powers that be, the goal at this point was merely to keep surveillance upon the creature, not engage with it. The lizard didn't seem bent on destruction and death, nor was it headed toward a populated area, so the military leaders openly acknowledged that they had much, much bigger fish to fry...or, in this case, cockroaches to squash. The pilots were told not to fire their missiles and to keep a safe distance to observe He-Knew-Pat-Sajak.

Meanwhile, back at his house, Raymond Alagagta was having what amounted to a small emotional breakdown. The combination of the shock from witnessing a giant monster emerge from the volcano, the pain from the perceived desertion by his granddaughter, the unfathomable depth of the aloneness he felt during the whole ordeal, the great sense of relief he felt that his house had ended up unscathed, and the Doppler effect of his remembrances of his dead wife and the horrors of their incarceration during the war all collided inside his mind and overwhelmed him.

When his granddaughter finally returned home, she found him simultaneously laughing uncontrollably, uttering epithets of rage, shedding tears of joy, and crying with an intense sadness. To put it bluntly, he was completely bedeviled.

虎穴に入らずんば虎子を得ず

koketsu ni irazunba koji o ezu
If you do not enter the tiger's cave,
you will not catch its cub.

Eve Sanderborn looked at her naked body in the steamy bathroom mirror of her tawdry motel room in Palmer, Alaska, and smiled. When the fogginess began to envelop the image, she took her soggy bath towel and wiped it clear again. Wordlessly she let her eyes take in the whole picture, from the top of her bleached blonde coiffed hair, down over the plastic-surgeon playground that was her perfectly sculpted torso, and finally to the impeccably painted toenails of her feet at the bottom of her tanned and well-toned legs.

She nodded to herself, because even she had to admit that she was an impressive specimen. The contradiction between her positive reaction to her own reflection in the mirror and her current less-than-desirable situation in the motel room was hard to swallow – as you'll see, no pun intended – but it was, more often than not, the reality Eve faced these days. There was the omnipresent disappointment that her life hadn't gone the way she'd hoped – yet – even though she had put a tremendous amount of effort in guiding it in the way she wanted.

No, Eve *had* long accepted that she was, in more ways than she wanted to concede, just like the father she'd run away from all those years ago. That pathetic man, working tirelessly at a job that he neither loved nor expected too much from, had sunk his hopes and dreams into an old 1941 Buick Special he'd come across abandoned in a garage in Kenmore, New York. Once he'd purchased that battered old auto, he had poured all of his hard-earned money, his time, and his attention into restoring it. In the process, he had wasted irreplaceable time on this planet, lost his wife, and spurned his one and only daughter to focus solely on the only thing that seemed to matter to him: the fucking car.

In the end, after years and years of renting an expensive garage space and going the whole nine yards in the restoration process, including sandblasting the frame, rebuilding the motor, transmission, and every mechanical system from the ground up, and meticulously repainting each surface of the vehicle to its original condition, Eve's father had exactly what he'd most desired: a show-quality, restored classic automobile. What he didn't have anymore was a loving wife or daughter.

While the former had left fairly early, it had taken Eve a few more years to rip a page out of her dear old mom's playbook and run off toward a bigger and brighter future that was far away from the inattentive man and his all-consuming Buick. But she had. And the image of her pitiable father fading away in the rearview mirror of the vehicle carrying her off stayed with her like an unseen emotional tattoo.

As the bathroom mirror started to fog up again, Eve took the towel and cleared it once more to take a final glimpse of her body. As much as it pained her to do so, she had to accept that she was now in the same *exact* shoes as her father – she was the proud owner of something that was in perfect condition through a complete rebuild, hard work, and great expense and sacrifice; something that was beautiful but not practical, requiring nothing but constant up-keep; and something that, on paper, was worth a lot of money, but, in reality, wasn't going to set her on any kind of gravy train that would be headed toward a big payday. And Eve knew that she, just like her father, had blown her wad on something that was beautiful to look at, but would leave her alone, emp-ty, and unsatisfied in the end.

"Hey, darlin'. You done in there?"

The man's sluggish voice coming through the bathroom door brought Eve back from her thought-ful moment. She closed her eyes with this forced ad-mission of what she was actually doing in this back-water Alaskan town and in this seedy motel, and she tried to use her breathing to calm herself enough to continue on this fool's errand of a mission she was trying to forget.

"Yep, all done. I'm coming out."

"Well, hurry up. I'm ready now, little lady."

Issuing an exhalation that was half cough and half chortle, Eve threw the towel down onto the slick tiled floor and opened the paper-thin bathroom door. There, sitting on the edge of the king-sized bed, sat the starkly naked pumpkin farmer whom she'd promised illicit acts in exchange for the main scoop about the tantalizing scandal that had happened at the big weigh-in at the Alaska State Fair. He had her notebook and pen next to where he sat, and he held his now aroused manhood in his hand. He smiled at her proudly as she came out of the bathroom.

"Hey, darlin', I'm ready to give you that interview you were so hot to trot to get. Why don't you kneel down and speak into this here microphone and write down everything I've got to tell ya about how that crooked shithead pirate grower illegally produces the biggest pumpkins in the entire great state of Alaska? You're about to expose the biggest story in these here parts and get the scoop of the century, girl."

Eve Sanderborn was an expert on compartmentalizing. She knew that she should be fighting back the building bile in her stomach from having to perform fellatio on a hayseed like this to get a news story that wasn't really going to resurrect her stalled career, but she'd long ago lost the ability to feel any real sadness about her circumstances. She'd already gone under the scalpel, starved herself, worked out, pimped herself, sold her soul, and checked her ethics at the door enough times to get to this very point here, so this next wholly unpleasant experience couldn't bring her any further down in her descent. As an ambitious television news reporter, she was prepared to do whatever it took to get the big story that was going to be her ticket out of her current imprisonment in obscurity.

Just as she sank down and her knees made contact with the filthy rug on the floor, the door of the motel room suddenly bucked and banged violently on its loose hinges.

"Jimmy! Jimmy! Open the door. It's me, Archie. You in there?"

"For fuck's sake, Archie, go away! *Now* is most definitely not a good time."

The knocking only intensified. It was now like a jackhammer working on the door, and the wooden surface palsied in such a way as to suggest that, if it weren't answered, the rapping was going to cause it to disintegrate.

"It's important, Jimmy!"

"For the love of god, Archie. Go away! Give me five minutes or so. Nothing can be more important than what's about to take place in here. If you don't get your ass away from that door, I swear I'll shoot you in the head with the pistol that's in my pants pocket!"

"Listen, Jimmy. Felix Panzram just landed from his run to Naknek. He was flying medical supplies to the Methodist mission up there, and he—"

"Hear me good, Archie. If you've just interrupted me and my...friend in here to tell me about some Methodist missionaries with the measles, I swear to you, you're a fucking dead man."

"No, Jimmy, listen to what I'm saying, dammit! There's another monster. Felix was taking off from Naknek after dropping off his load when a bunch of fighter jets intercepted him and escorted him back this way. He only got a quick glimpse, mind ya, but he says he saw a giant lizard monster heading up the peninsula. He's guessing it came from the Aleutians or something, but if it keeps heading the way it's going, Jimmy, it might get all the way up here to Palmer!"

There was heavy silence as the pumpkin farmer pondered this shocking news. He rubbed his stubbled chin, then smiled down cruelly at Eve. He lifted his head to face the door once more.

"That's certainly some big news there, Archie, but it don't sound like this new monster's gonna be here anytime soon. I've got a date with destiny in this here motel room, and I'm not aiming on wasting a moment on nothing that ain't life-threatening. Why don't you go over to the Frontier and have a few beers on me? I'll meet you over there once I'm finished in here."

"Okay, Jimmy. If you say so."

When the pumpkin farmer was certain that the man had departed, he turned to look back down at the beautiful naked blonde bimbo between his knees. His face had a look on it that was full of anticipation. After all, the sexy television reporter from California was moving his testicles around in a suggestive way that signified to him that the fireworks were really about to start.

However, when he glanced down at her, there was no mistaking the fact that the woman had somehow gotten her hands onto the revolver in his discarded pants lying next to her on the floor and was now nuzzling the muzzle of it lovingly into the soft tissue of his scrotum.

"We interrupt this scheduled performance to bring you some breaking news – sorry, Jimmy, your interview with me has been cancelled. Please grab your clothes and get the fuck out of my motel room, immediately. Failure to comply will result in a very painful and messy moment of gunplay for you – which, ironically, would end up being a real story worthy of coverage by the news in this dead, backwater town."

Later, as a now dressed Eve sat on the bed, she pressed the receiver of the phone against her ear as if she were trying to shove something coming out of it back inside. She'd been on hold for too long, and she was fighting the urge to smash the phone to bits on the bedside table. Just as she was about to consider actually pursuing this violent act, the phone sprang to life.

"Eve Sanderborn! Why the hell are you bothering me at this hour? You were supposed to head up to

Alaska, get your story, and pay your penance – not call me. We talked about all of this before I sent you and Bernie up there, Eve. No communication until you guys had a good piece about the controversy over the largest pumpkins from the largest state in the Union. Did you forget those simple instructions?"

"Justin, do you know that there's another monster? Here, in Alaska?"

The veteran news director inhaled sharply. He knew firsthand what he had in Eve Sanderborn. Her unlimited ambition, her greasy ethical code, and her own personal hunger made her a very dangerous combination of promise and disaster. He'd been burned enough by her to know she was an attack dog that no one could actually control. And while all of her handlers just tried to get her to chase the wrong balls at the park to keep her from hurting them, or anyone around them, it was only a matter of time before she got off the leash and did some real damage.

"Yes, Eve, I *do* know about the new monster. The military has reached out to all of the news stations around the country, including our beloved KTLA, to keep this new monster, He-Knew-Pat-Sajak, off the air. Their rationale is that that fucking Palmetto Bug Monster's rampage in the Midwest is about all that the American people can deal with right now. The conservative minds at the Pentagon have concluded that whenever you've got a population coming to grips with a gigantic alien creature that appears to be unstoppable and seems to be aiming to wipe our species off the face of the planet, adding another alien element of total destruction to the mix would be somewhat irresponsible. Plus, the giant lizard is supposedly taking the most indirect route to the middle of nowhere. So, as for right now, it's going to knock down some trees, chase some caribou, and swat at some mosquitoes in the tundra where it's headed. If the thing veers toward anything of value, the military has given us permission to release the story to allow people to get out of its path. Until then, the stern official message is 'hands off the story.'"

"Justin, Bernie and I are up here in Alaska, for god's sake. We're sitting here, right next to the action. We're one little plane ride from being able to blow the lid off this whole story."

"You're not hearing me, Eve. The military has issued a no-investigate clause with some heavy national security backing and some threats of awfully extreme punishment to anyone who disobeys. Thanks to that damn cockroach, we're perilously close to martial law being imposed in this country as it is. Some aspects of our beloved democratic way of life that we're so accustomed to having are getting prepared to be packed away into a survival bunker until after this attack. So, no, you will not be blowing anything – except maybe one or two of the locals, if I know you at all."

"Justin, Justin, listen to me. You sent me up here as punishment for what I did. I know, now, that it was a huge mistake to ever proposition the CEO of MegaNews...at a cocktail party...in front of his wife...to advance my own career, but I've been a good soldier and taken the banishment in stride, especially since that fucking alien creature in Indiana is actually *making* the careers of people far less qualified than I who are covering the story there in my stead. But listen to me, for god's sake. You've got a great reporter and an amazing cameraman within spitting distance of the second biggest news item in the entire frickin' world! We could just get up there and cover it without releasing the news until it's time to let the story out. That way, we wouldn't be breaking any of the military's rules, we'd just be documenting the events about a second giant monster that might want to destroy our planet. We'd then be in a position to release the news whenever the green light is given."

Justin Ferguson grumbled passionately on the other end, but this sound had become an indication to Eve that she was getting to him, and she sat up straighter on the bed to prepare for his next rebuttal. She was primed to win this debate as she embraced another chance to actually promote her career.

"First off, Eve, I'm sure as shit that Bernie is probably inside a liquor bottle at the local bar right now. So you have as much of a chance of getting him ready to travel anywhere as you do locating a Rhodes Scholar up there. Secondly, I'm telling you that the military is clamping down on that whole area.

There's no way that you will be able to just saunter up to this new monster and film it."

"What I'm hearing you say, Justin, is that I have permission to *try*. Bernie might be drinking a little more consistently these days, but the old Bernard Egan, that world-class television cameraman with shelves of SOC. awards for his camerawork, is still alive and well within him. I know the man. He'll jump at the chance to get on a story like this. And don't worry about how we're going to get up there. There's a ton of bush pilots who fly out of the municipal airport here who make a living by getting into uncertain areas without attracting any attention. Like they say around these parts, 'there may be old pilots and bold pilots, but there are no old bold pilots.' I'm telling you, I can get *someone* to fly us over to get a closer look at this new monster. Imagine, if you will, having the first glimpses of the creature...to only be released when it becomes something that we can cover officially, of course."

"I don't think it's gonna be as easy as you think to get close to this thing. Supposedly, the Air Force has an enforced no-fly zone around the creature, complete with a shoot-to-kill freestanding order. No one in their right mind will get within a mile of this lizard."

"You know me, Justin, I can be *very* persuasive when I need to be. One of these local flyboys will get us to wherever we need to go, I guarantee it."

"I dunno, Eve."

"Come on, Justin. This could be the BIG one."

"Naw, I still need to hear you say that I have plausible deniability."

"What?"

"When this goes sideways –which we both know it will, Eve – I've gotta be sure that nothing blows back onto me."

"I thought that was inferred with every assignment you send me on, Justin."

"Hardly. I've had to develop some otherworldly systems of defense to keep the splashes from your major turd drops from getting onto me, but this time, I must have complete and absolute protection from the results of your actions."

"How does one go about doing that?"

"Well, make it crystal clear to me that you're acting entirely on your own, Eve. If you decide to pursue this story, you're undertaking some kind of a rogue operation that I know absolutely nothing about. I have no idea you are doing any of this and I have not a shred of culpability in the matter. Whatever happens, it happens to you, not me."

Eve nodded her blonde head as if her news director could see it bobbing over the phone.

"Okay, I've gone off the tracks, Justin. I won't listen to reason anymore. I only have eyes for my own self-advancement. Fuck you and all of KTLA. Me and Bernie are doing our own black-ops kind of news story now. You're just footing the bill."

"That's out of my hands, Eve. I've no idea if they'll reimburse you for this one or not. Plus, we never had this conversation."

"Okay, fine. Plausible deniability aside, I'll only call you again if we've gotten something newsworthy. How does that sound?"

Eve knew the hang-up click and the resulting dial tone was the only answer she was going to get.

She started frantically packing her travel bag, tucked the pumpkin farmer's pistol into the waistband of her skirt, and set about checking out of the motel and finding her drunken cameraman. Time was now ticking, and the story she'd been waiting for her entire lifetime was stumbling around in those mountainous forests only a floatplane flight away.

猿も木から落ちる

saru mo ki kara ochiru

Even monkeys fall from trees.

Usotsuki Shirinigatsuku attracted a lot of attention while waiting for his flight home at the San Francisco International Airport. The man not only closely resembled a younger *Akira Takarada*, the star of many of the earliest Japanese monster movies, but he was also currently surrounded by his own contingency of stern-looking U.S. Marshals. These two visual clues indicated to most of the other travelers heading to or from their gates that the skinny Japanese man was someone they should take notice of.

Oh, there was one other reason he looked so familiar – the highly televised takedown by lawmen that had happened outside of Indianapolis so recently. The images of this Japanese man's contorted face and the sound of his slashing, voiced protests had flashed across television screens around the world, complete with the pointed admonishments of none other than the global newsman Walter Cronkite.

As of late, fame had certainly not been kind to the self-proclaimed Japanese cryptozoologist.

Usotsuki's friends called him "Ghidorah." This name paid homage to Toho Co., Ltd.'s multi-headed space monster, which Usotsuki had been obsessed with as a young boy. Back then, he'd been unable to separate fact from fiction in regards to the study of Godzilla and the other *kaiju* from the monster movies. But mostly, the nickname made the obvious connection between the fact that the fictional creature was such a mishmash of characteristics – a space dragon amalgamation of two legs, no arms, three heads on long necks, giant bat-like wings, and two tails. Similarly, Usotsuki was a terribly complex and complicated mixture of components. And like Ghidorah – the only really worthy opponent of the King of Monsters – the young man was exceptionally formidable.

Born into a low-ranking yakuza family, Usotsuki was destined to live a life tethered to the disagreeable Japanese underworld, but the one coping tool he had for avoiding some of the unpleasant truths of his life was a near-obsession with matinee monster movies. As luck would have it, this leisurely juvenile pastime actually morphed into a more legitimate side gig of sorts as he reached adulthood. So, even though Usotsuki proved to be a willing student in regards to his study of the gang-related businesses and their sophisticated gambling and loan-sharking activities, the ins and outs of their drug trafficking, the science behind their money-lending schemes, the proper methods of smuggling contraband into the Japanese black market, and the management of their pornography interests, it was his thirst for knowledge about his beloved giant monsters and cryptozoology that was his *ikigai* (生き甲斐) – his real "reason for being."

Usotsuki had become a loyal and a good yakuza soldier. He'd followed all orders as issued and never hesitated to fulfill the wishes of his *oyabun*. However, whenever he wasn't participating in the Japanese mob's business, he spent almost every available moment studying his true passion. He'd sought out Shinichi Sekizawa, the main screenwriter of the Godzilla movies, and studied under him like a protégé. He had no interest in moviemaking, but Usotsuki revered the man as if he were his sensei.

The pair had become like two peas in a pod, working together to obtain ancient texts full of Japanese monsters, following up on every cryptozoological report of monster sightings in Japan and throughout Asia, and even co-writing a book that compiled their prints, samples of *netsuke*, and other supernatural investigations into a published work that was respected by those people around the globe who were usually considered nothing but nutjobs. Their work was utterly ignored by most academics.

When it was time for Usotsuki to get his yakuza *irezumi* – the body tattoo that symbolizes the commitment into the membership of the gang – the traditional method of allowing the *horishi* (tattoo master) to have absolute power over the design of the work took on a special flair. The impressive resulting piece lacked the more common elements seen in most yakuza tattoos, but instead, it was populated with *akuma* (demons), *yurei* (ghosts), *yokai* (spirits), *kami* (Shinto deities and spirits), and other legendary creatures of Japanese folklore and mythology. The indelible message was clear. Usotsuki was indeed a made man, but he was split in terms of devotion between the yakuza and the study of the supernatural.

Usotsuki Shirinigatsuku was part con man, part academic, part gangster, part anthropologist, part international spokesman, part thug, and part historian. When people in Japan saw him approaching, they weren't entirely certain if he was going to break their kneecaps, extort their money, exorcise a *kijimuna* from their tea garden, buy their eighteenth-century copy of a *Bakemono zukushi* (monster scroll), or assassinate them with a traditional samurai sword. So, much like the Toho Co., Ltd. monster Ghidorah, Usotsuki was someone who most people gave an exceptionally wide berth whenever he was encountered.

His sudden appearance at the Palmetto Bug Monster's landing site should not have surprised anyone. His entire life had been a process to get him ready for this very moment when science fiction and mythology became reality. However, the young Japanese man was not a known commodity in the United States, so his presence in Indiana and his early attempts at inserting himself into the inner circle of the authorities attempting to figure out how to stop a rampaging monstrous space cockroach did not go well. Accustomed to elbowing his way into any kind of exploration of the supernatural in his home country, he'd expected to be welcomed onto the team dealing with the destructive space *kaiju* with open arms. When he wasn't, his violent mobster side took over, and things had gotten nasty.

His trip home escorted by U.S. Marshals had been the diplomat-negotiated result.

Now, sitting in the waiting area of the San Francisco International Airport, still fuming from his humbling experience at the hands of the stupid American military, he glared menacingly at those around him. He was so deep inside his own sense of anger that he almost didn't hear his name being called over the airport PA system.

"Usotsuki Shirinigatsuku, you have an important call on the red courtesy phone from a Mr. Shinichi Sekizawa."

His head snapped up to gaze over at the red telephone across from the waiting area by his gate. The two U.S. Marshals escorting him had also heard his name, and they looked at one another in concern over the implications of the announcement.

"I must take that call."

A quick and nonverbal conference between the marshals resulted in an authorizing head nod toward the wall-mounted phone. Usotsuki strode over to it alone. He was not considered to be too much of a flight risk, for it was clear that he'd gotten the message that he'd screwed up things with his highly publicized and televised meltdown.

"Hello."

"Ghidorah."

It was indeed his master, Shinichi Sekizawa, and the usage of his nickname was a quick signal that this conversation was going to include some unpleasantness.

"Sensei."

"Don't get on the plane."

"But I must. There are policemen here tasked with getting me on it to fly home. I have no choice."

His sensei sighed, but then said without emotion, "Your *buzoku* waits for you here, and it will not be a good reception...or one that you'll live through, I'm sorry to report."

"I understand their anger. *Machigai o okashite shimaimashita.*"

"Mistakes were definitely made by you over there, Ghidorah, but getting on that plane right now would be the last mistake of your life. I'm calling to warn you about this fact...which definitely marks the end of something...but I also wanted to call and tell you about a beginning. There is now another monster in America. Recently, a giant lizard came out of a volcano in Alaska, and it's currently headed toward the interior of that state."

"How could you possibly know that, sensei? There's been no story on the news about another monster. The television and radio are only filled with talk about the *gokiburi*."

"*Are mā*, I have my sources. You must get up to Alaska...immediately. You need to get your eyes on this new *kaiju* and figure out if this one is going to defeat the bug or help it destroy our planet. Your involvement in this determination could save your life, Ghidorah."

The phone went dead. Usotsuki spoke into the receiver a couple of times, but it was fruitless. His sensei had given his warning and had steered him toward a new pathway, and now the befuddled Japanese cryptozoologist just needed to set about following it.

The boarding process had begun. As the passengers for the Japanese Airlines flight to Tokyo gave their tickets to the JAL counter staff with stiff nods and subtle bows, the U.S. Marshals stood up and prepared to escort their charge to the gate door. Inside the simmering silence of these suited and well-muscled men was the clear intention that this Japanese thug was to get on the airplane and never come back. Their assignment was *not* to fly back to the Land of the Rising Sun with him, hold his hand and make sure he was tucked in on some tatami mat there. They just had to be reasonably sure that the annoying and unwelcome foreign man made it onto the plane.

For his part, Usotsuki got this message loud and clear, and he barely acknowledged his entourage as he handed his ticket to the airline personnel and walked onto the enclosed jet bridge. He may have appeared calm and serene, but his mind was whirling wildly as it tried to find a way of escaping without causing a ruckus or getting caught. He knew that the U.S. Marshals would remain at the gate until the plane pushed back and taxied for takeoff, so any kind of ploy to slip out somewhere between the terminal and the plane was not likely to succeed, but since part of his DNA was that of a streetwise survivor, he'd already begun formulating a plan.

The Sky Chef's scissor truck turned out to be the perfect getaway vehicle. Taking note that the loading door for the food catering service was just behind his assigned seat, Usotsuki tousled his hair and adjusted his stiff posture into that of a slouch, instantly transforming himself from a young and angry yakuza lieutenant into a frumpy Sky Chef employee. He used the usual ongoing confusion of loading passengers onto a wide-body aircraft for a transpacific flight to blend into the river of humanity jostling down the airplane aisle, but then he magnificently slipped from it into the Sky Chef supply truck's vast refrigerated storage space, unnoticed.

Finding a cramped and uncomfortable hiding spot proved to be easy, and he snuggled into the space with the cold resignation that he would have to endure some chilly discomfort long enough to get away from the airport.

With three hundred and sixty-six passengers milling around to get into their seats and some overwhelmed stewardesses and a few frantic Sky Chef employees attempting to get the jet airborne on time, no one noticed that a singular young Japanese man was not where he was supposed to be. There was a precision to the movements in the entire scene that did not otherwise take into account that there might be some intentional or unintentional gaffs occurring in the chaos of loading the aircraft. Usotsuki's ruse worked like magic. (魔法のように, *mahō no yō ni*)

The Japan Airlines 747-100 closed its loading door, was pushed back from the gate, lumbered to the main runway, and took flight. As the two U.S. Marshals watched the behemoth aircraft struggle into the sky and head west, they coughed and shrugged that their boring detail was finally over, and they exited the airport after calling in the success of the mission to their supervisors.

The Sky Chef truck in which Usotsuki was hiding made the remainder of its rounds before heading back to the supply warehouse. There the employees performed their jobs with their usual indifference, allowing ample time for the keen yakuza lieutenant to slip out and take flight from them undetected.

As ironic as it first seemed to him to have this exact problem while standing next to an international airport, Usotsuki Shirinigatsuku knew he just needed to figure out a way to get up to Alaska. Luckily for him, the yakuza and the Wah Ching (Youth of China) chapter in San Francisco had a working agreement, and if he needed to sneak anywhere in the Pacific Northwest, they could help get him there.

Usotsuki paused in thought for a moment in the field outside the warehouse. A lizard could mean different things. His sensei did not mention any specifics about the new monster, so it was hard to tell exactly what kind of lizard it was. Godzilla was often erroneously called a giant lizard, but Usotsuki had it on good authority that the Toho screenwriters had designated it as a mutated dinosaur. And despite the popular misconception that all dinosaurs were lizards, actual taxonomists classified them as archosaurs, a group containing modern-day crocodilians and birds. No, the simple truth was that Godzilla and many of his monster peers were not lizards.

However, there were the Giant Lizards (大トカゲ) that lived on Faro Island in *King Kong vs. Godzilla*, and these were among the only lizards—

Usotsuki gave himself a slap on the chest to snap him out of his somewhat obsessive meditation about lizards in Toho Co., Ltd. movies. He was wasting precious time by worrying about something so trivial or *sasainakoto ni kodawaru* (些細なことにこだわる). Regardless of what the new *kaiju* was, it was time for him to say "*Konnichiwa,* (こんにちわ)" to it.

あほに取り合うばか

aho ni toriau naka
Only a fool deals with a fool.

Retired General Buchanan "Jocko" Richardson surveyed the lawn of the Kennedy Hill Plantation Retirement Home with the steely eyes of a military man performing a grand review of the troops. The manicured lawn spread out toward the towering live oaks majestically framing the driveway as the boundary of the property and its luxuriant grass was currently being mowed and, in some tight spaces, snipped by hand by a team of heavily perspiring black landscapers, but the general, due to an early onset of dementia, was only seeing the ranks of the 82nd Airborne and the 34th Field Artillery march past him. He nodded knowingly at the splendor of the imagined forces under his command. Whether or not the sweaty black men working in the oppressive heat and constant smell of swamp gas took notice of the old white man in his oversized Army uniform is moot, but it appeared as if the former fighting man was wholly supportive of their actions.

General Richardson's life had been held up as the ideal when it came to being an American military man in the twentieth century, and his resume was chock-full of victories. Born into an upper-middle-class South Carolinian family at the start of World War One, he had worked hard in school with the sole purpose of going into the military. After a one-year stint at the Citadel, he then went to West Point, where he graduated in the same year that Adolf Hitler, who was busy amping up Germany for another inevitable war, had attended the Olympic Games being hosted in Berlin. During his next formative years, before the Imperial Japanese Navy attacked Pearl Harbor and encouraged the U.S. to enter the global fray, Richardson had worked himself into the position of becoming a first lieutenant in good standing.

These times were the perfect environment for the advancement of his career. The burgeoning human conflict that was to be given the endearing title of World War Two afforded the young military man the opportunities he needed. He hopped from Tunisia to Sicily to Normandy, overseeing an artillery battalion and then becoming a chief of staff for the 9th Infantry Division. He proved to be a good leader, and he zoomed up through the ranks from first lieutenant to colonel. By the time the Nazis had been dealt with and defeated, the man's place in military history was fully entrenched.

After the war, General Richardson trained to be a paratrooper and then was assigned as the chief of staff for the vaunted 82nd Airborne Division. He quietly became an instructor at the Command and

General Staff College and the Army War College before being promoted to brigadier general during the Korean War. At the time, he was one of the youngest U.S. Army generals in post-World War Two history.

Not being one to stand idly by while any fighting was going on, General Richardson once again became involved in the military efforts in Southeast Asia. Ultimately, he was promoted to lieutenant general, and then assumed the role as the commander of the U.S. Army in the Vietnam War.

It was this quasi-failure after what had turned out to be a purely unwinnable position that finally put an end to his mostly proud military career. Sadly, the Fall of Saigon in 1973 tainted the man's reputation with a sourness that could not be washed off. And with the leadership of both the government and the military looking for *someone* to point their fingers at as the cause of the disappointing Southeast Asian fiasco, General Richardson became the perfect patsy. The general was given an Army Distinguished Service Medal by the President of the United States, but then became quickly identified as something that needed to be swept under the carpet to disappear.

General Richardson became a resident at the Kennedy Hill Plantation Retirement Home soon after. The man's tours of duty had left their indelible mark on him physically and mentally. A bedwetter prone to having frequent night terrors, he demanded to be awakened by revelry every morning at six. Oddly, he ate breakfast in his underwear so as to not stain nor smudge his uniform, which he demanded be pressed and cleaned every day. And once dressed, he stalked the halls and grounds of the place, commanding that he be addressed properly and given a salute by all of those he met. He was beginning to have a rather loose interpretation of reality most days, usually imagining that he was either on an Army base somewhere in the world or even engaged on one of the many battlefields he'd overseen during his military career, but the staff and residents of the retirement home humored him most of the time. That was partly because the man was somewhat likable, but mostly because they all had a distinct fear of him.

This morning, after the satisfactory viewing of his troops and weaponry on the parade grounds, he was headed back to his stateroom for his scheduled visit by Hoa Senđỏ, his favorite concubine while he had served in Vietnam. Arlene Simmons did not really enjoy being called this during their times together, but she certainly admired the general's confidence and intensity during their lovemaking sessions. After some of the other pathetically wilted love interests she'd had at the Plantation over the years, General Richardson earned another star for himself every time they were together.

When he came up to the door of his room, he saw that it was ajar. The old man crouched down and reached for his .45 Colt pistol in its belt holster, but remembered that the staff had taken the weapon to be cleaned some time ago and had never returned it. The general made a mental note to reprimand those individuals and give them KP duty, but that would have to wait until he figured out what to do with this intruder now that he was weaponless. He might be old, but the general knew he was an expert in most techniques of hand-to-hand combat, so he'd dispatch whoever had broken into his stateroom, quickly and quietly.

Apparently he wasn't as stealthy as he thought he was, for as he rounded the corner and got ready to grapple, the distinctive German-accented voice of none other than Henry Kissinger broke the impartial silence.

"General Richardson, why are you sneaking around like some kind of a ferret? Come. Have a seat next to me, my old friend. We have a lot to discuss."

This statement immediately took some of the bluster away from the general. The two had worked well together several times in Vietnam, but their relationship had hardly seemed a friendship. The old general warily took the comfortable chair facing Kissinger and sat down.

"Mr. Kissinger?"

"Henry, please, General Richardson. We are both retired from any official capacity, so let us just have a conversation among friends, shall we?"

"Sure, Mr. Kissinger. What do you feel like talking about today?"

"Ah, I see. Very interesting. Okay, down to business. Have you been following the situation in Indiana, sir?"

The muttering Teutonic cadence of the little man irritated the general, but it was the overall patronizing air of his personality that irked him the most. Diplomats were never his favorites, but this old goat of a backstabber had made a career of backroom and back-alley deals, and he was to be treated with the same concern as some kind of pestilence that could kill you in the end.

"The bug? I've definitely been following the bug, Mr. Kissinger."

"But of course, *Herr General*. What would you do...about the bug?"

"I'd nuke its ass out of existence!"

"*Ach, mein Gott.*"

General Richardson squared his shoulders and turned his head to proclaim proudly, "President Truman might have had a very difficult decision to make there at the end of World War Two, but I can tell you that there are a million-plus American soldiers who're alive today, feasting and fucking, who'd stand up and applaud his decision to drop those bombs on them Japs. The same is true with this bug – the sky should rain fire down upon it, no matter the collateral damage. And I'm confident that that decision has already been made, sir. It's just a matter of when, not if."

"*Ich habe meine Zweifel.* Ah, we will most certainly see. I'm here today to tell you that there's another monster, General. In Alaska. A lizard. Its appearance is being kept out of the news."

"Well, I'll be damned. Same size? Same destructive abilities?"

"*Ja, ja*, same size. But it remains to be seen if it has the same destructive abilities as the bug. At present, this new monster is not aiming for any cities and it does not seem to want to harm any people. Fact is, it's wandering in the Alaskan wilderness right now, far away from any population centers. You need to come with me and head to Alaska immediately, General Richardson."

"Me? As you've already pointed out, I'm retired."

"*Ja, ja*, as am I, *Herr General*. But desperate times call for desperate measures. As soon as *die Kakerlake* made its bombastic appearance, the President reached out to me to become active again. He called me at home just as *mein Fräulein* and I were finishing our *Betthupferl* and *Kakao* and getting ready to *mit jemandem schlafen* on a new *Bärenfell* that I had just purchased at my favorite—"

"Enough with the Hun porn, for fuck's sake, Mr. Kissinger. Why would the President want me?"

"Ah, *ja, ja*, the President called me on the phone and said in that sugary-sweet Southern accent of his, 'Mr. Kissinger, if our world has any chance of surviving this alien monster's attack – and I have it on good authority that we *do* have a chance, but only if we unite as one species against the threat – it's going to take the most monumental diplomatic effort in history, and you are the only man alive who can get this job done.'"

The general leaned forward and exclaimed, "But how do *I* fit into a diplomatic mission? As everyone is well aware, I actually think that diplomacy is nothing but a bunch of pantywaister hooey!"

"*Alles zu seiner Zeit, mein Schnuckiputzi.* The President continued to talk to me, as is his way, and he said that, if I was to be the olive branch for the situation, he needed the team to have a big stick...an element of force behind the diplomacy. And that is you, *der General.*"

"Bull. Why doesn't he just turn to the Joint Chiefs of Staff, Mr. Kissinger? I mean, if he's looking for some big sticks to back up any pathetically impotent statesmanship from you, those veteran military advisors carry enough well-stocked bat bags to do the job."

"*Das mag stimmen,* but the President doesn't fully trust them. He says, and these are his exact words, 'Those military men are *so* hungry for power that they could eat the northbound end of a southbound polecat.'"

"I have no fucking clue what that means, Mr. Kissinger."

"I am unsure as well, but I do know that he does not trust them, General Richardson. Not at all. He thinks they want to get their hands onto the keys to the kingdom, his kingdom. That they will do *anything* to get hold of those."

The general looked like he was ready for a fight. "I've fought and bled beside those men, Mr.

Kissinger, and they are as tough and loyal as they come. They are good men." The old military man let his shoulders sag a bit. "That being said, when the hounds started baying for my blood at the end there, that very group of military men might not have been as obvious as Pontius Pilate at Jesus' trial, but they certainly pretended to have the cleanest of hands as my fate was being determined. And even worse, they stopped answering my Christmas cards, those bastards."

"*Wasser unter dem Damm, mein General.* The President brought your name up as the perfect muscle for this mission. He has a deep respect for you, sir. As he said to me, 'I greatly admire the way that General Richardson handled that whole unfortunate affair.'"

"Wait, he calls the Vietnam War an 'unfortunate affair?'"

Mr. Kissinger gave a dismissive wave with his hand. "*Ja, ja,* in the way that that war was – from the very beginning – a truly hopeless task. Everyone knew that to be true, but the manner in which you handled that thankless undertaking with force, grace, and, in the end, complete and selfless loyalty to this country, well, it made a big impression on the President. He thinks that *you* are the perfect man for another such almost impossible-seeming situation as this alien monster invasion. When I found out about the appearance of the giant lizard, as well, I tried to call him at the White House to see if he wanted us to deal with the cockroach or the gecko first, but I could not get through to him and he won't return my calls."

The general perked up a bit at this disclosure. "So, *you* are deciding to head us up to Alaska, not the President, huh, Mr. Kissinger?"

"Oh, *mein General*, I've been in enough of these types of *küchenbrändes* during my vast career to know that now is the time we need to prioritize. The military is busy attempting to deal with the bug down here. We need to head up immediately to Alaska to figure out how to handle the new monster. And I've got a strong feeling – an *Ahnung*, really – that this lizard is the key to this whole enchilada, and with your military experience and my diplomatic expertise, we will be an unstoppable team for putting an end to whatever is going on now on this planet. It's the perfect last mission, *ja*?"

General Richardson looked around his sitting room as if he were surveying the inside of a fighting tank under his command. The need to follow orders, no matter the mission, was almost encoded directly onto the man's genome, so, regardless of how many questions or concerns he had, his first reaction was almost always acceptance.

"When do we leave?"

"Immediately, General."

"I'm assuming that we're flying out of McEntire ANG. Base in Eastover. I'll grab my go bag. Gimme ten minutes, Mr. Kissinger, and we'll be on our way."

"*Nein, mein General.* I have my 1967 Volkswagen camper-bus outside. The President wanted us to be completely *inkognito*, you understand. Plus, thanks to the Palmetto Bug Monster, most domestic commercial flights have been grounded. Since the military needs to be free to get weaponry to where they need it to deal with the monster, the airspace over our entire country is highly limited and patrolled these days. And if the bug does to Chicago what it did to Indianapolis...well, that is almost un-*think*-able. We must hurry!"

General Richardson went to the closet and grabbed his fully packed rapid deployment bag. By the time he'd reached the front door, Kissinger had already ambled over and opened it, and the two men left the apartment and headed down the main hallway toward the entrance.

"We will take six-hour shifts driving, General," the veteran diplomat continued to ramble on in his Germanic-tainted voice. "You'll sleep while I drive and vice versa. We will stop for gas, bathroom breaks, and food only. Because of the *insekt*, we will have to keep farther south than is usual, but better safe than sorry, *ja*? Even with this slight detour, if we can keep up our driving schedule, I believe that we'll be up to Alaska in four days. We only need to make one stop in Washington, D.C. before heading north, but we must make haste. As we are fond of saying in German, '*Wer rastet, der rostet.*'"

"You'll have to translate that for me, Mr. Kissinger. I don't speak Kraut."

"Ah, well said, General. It means, 'He who rests, rusts.'"

"Oh, there's a sentiment I definitely can sink my teeth into. *Schnell, schnell*, Mr. Kissinger, let's get to Alaska so we can wrangle ourselves a big ol' lizard."

In his odd Teutonic warble, the diminutive former Secretary of State shockingly broke into song. Although his voice and dialect were not completely conducive to getting the Johnny Horton song totally right, the general smiled as soon as he heard the first bars.

"North to Alaska, we go north, the rush is on..."

七転び八起き

nana korobi ya oki

Fall down seven times but get up eight times.

William "Bugsy" Morton had hidden out in the boys' locker room at Tok High School for as long as he could, but he knew that his time was running out. Contrary to the common belief of most victims, Bugsy knew that the boys who were awaiting his exit from the school to beat him up were never going to get bored and decide to go away. Instead, the Molotov cocktails of anger, fear, and self-hate within each of them would only ferment and grow the longer he hid from them.

In fact, the intensity of the violence that was going to be meted out upon him was already building with each moment he stayed in this tiled room that was filled with the omnipresent smells of sweat, wet towels, and semen. The only way to release the unhealthy pressure currently intensifying within his tormentors was to go out, let them take it all out on him, and then get on with his day.

Bugsy coolly stashed his backpack and his jacket inside his locker. He was a seasoned veteran of these kinds of encounters, and he knew it was better to not take anything of value into the fray. Ripped clothes could be replaced and bruises and cuts would heal, but the stealing of valued possessions was the way that these mindless fuckwads went about counting coup. As always, once it was all over, he'd find Tony the janitor, and the man would let him back into the school to get his belongings. Sadly, the looks of pity that the elderly Athabaskan would give Bugsy at that moment would be far harder to take than any of the physical blows that the gang would attempt to inflict upon him.

The door to the locker room opened directly into the parking lot of the school, and as Bugsy now let it close and lock behind him, he had the sphinc-ter-tightening moment that indicated that he no longer had anywhere to hide. There, in front of him, lounged the pack of teenage boys who were waiting for him. Oddly, at first glance, they looked so casual that they appeared to be participating in some kind of a television commercial selling something as be-nign as detergent or clothing. But as soon as they saw him, their countenance changed to something more sinister as they gathered together in a preda-tory way and began to confront their prey.

It was during this next stretch that Bugsy had al-ways found himself trying to remember the specif-ic infraction that was the cause of any of this, but he'd long given up the idea that he could avoid or prevent the soon-to-follow violent scene. There was no other reason for this confrontation than his very existence. He was alive, and that was all the reason that this group of shitheads – all boys whose fathers worked at the nearby U.S. Army pipeline pumping station – needed to get mad at him. Still, as he strode toward them, he found himself again going through his mental Rolodex of his day to find the specific transgression, but without success.

"Well, well, well, if it ain't the little faggot at last. Me and the boys were thinking that you were settling in for the winter in that locker room to hibernate like the stupid, ugly rat you are, you loser."

This was none other than Jerry Zumquist, the leader and mouthpiece of the group. Even now, his words only reflected the depth of his ignorance, and Bugsy fought the urge to correct all of the misinformation coming out of him. He'd long ago learned that this moment of the conflict was not the time to attempt to use words. Any speech intended to bargain, apologize, negotiate, compliment, or rationalize would not only fall flat, it would add fuel to the fire. Clarifying that he was not a homosexual or explaining that rats do not, in fact, hibernate during the winter would only make matters worse. In this case, silence was definitely golden.

"I bet the little coward was searching around for a teacher to walk out with him and keep him safe. Couldn't find one, huh? Too bad for you. Nope, no one's gonna save you now, you bug-eyed, tiny freak. We're going to beat you bloody today, bub."

This was the acting lieutenant of the group, Felix Gandy. From experience, Bugsy knew that this boy was more bark than bite and, when the action really started, he'd be on the fringes slinging his words and cruel laughter more than his fists or feet.

Bugsy walked confidently onward until the other members of the group had fully encircled him, and then he stopped suddenly. He was very short in stature so his assailants towered over him as they came nearer. He looked around at the virtual giants surrounding him, and he smiled. He had everybody right where he wanted them.

It turned out, the young man had a secret that was known to no one but himself. He'd spent the last six years working hard on attaining a black belt in the martial art of kung fu.

Among the ads for Sea Monkeys, giant balloons, X-ray glasses, lasers, spy pen radios, air cars, gag gifts, and police handcuffs in the very back of one of his cherished comic books, he'd spied a tiny and hard-to-read entry about learning self-defense from a self-proclaimed Chinese kung-fu master who went by the name of Master Chui. When he'd first encountered this advertisement, Bugsy was already getting bullied in elementary school, and although he was well aware that it was probably a scam, he was desperate enough to look into it. He wrote to the address and was advised to send a good portion of the money he made working at the Parker House Motel to get the martial arts lessons that would help him with his plight.

It turned out not to be a scam. Master Chui was not only a real person, he had trained originally with

Master Ip – the same sensei for the famed Bruce Lee – in the village of Foshan in Guangdong Province, Southern China. He'd come to America with high hopes of following his master's other student's footsteps to get a lucrative career in films or get a foothold in the martial arts world, but he had quickly gotten disillusioned with everything once here. With no chance of returning to his homeland, he'd turned to producing easy-to-follow self-defense lessons that could be mailed to the seemingly ever-growing audience of preteen and teenage boys who read comic books and were being bullied. It had taken the martial arts master no time at all to recognize the financial goldfield he'd stepped onto, and within a few months he was making far more money doing this than he had ever made training students at a dojo, and with so much less effort.

That's not to say that his lessons were not actually good. They described exactly how the master would train his students as if they were standing right in front of him, and anyone who could read and was dedicated enough to practice consistently could easily become proficient in kung fu. Bugsy did just that. He memorized the instructions, practiced the moves until they became second nature, and showed an incredible level of determination to become a master himself someday.

And the boy had the gall to correspond directly with Master Chui frequently, exchanging long letters and even engaging in phone calls with the man. Although they'd never met in person, Bugsy and Master Chui considered one another friends, and the correspondence course kung-fu master held his student in the greatest of prideful esteem. The young man even became part of the narrative of the ads in the comic books as the success story that all young boys needed to hear.

"We're going to knock the shit out of you, you short little freak. I wouldn't want to be in your stupid shoes."

Bugsy looked down at his battered black Chuck Taylors and then over at Jerry Zumquist's much cooler Adidas lace-ups, and he sniggered quietly.

"Well, Scary Jerry, your feet would be swimming in my shoes. I mean, I might be five foot two with eyes of blue, but you have *tiny* feet for a boy of your age. In fact, they're more the size of an eight-year-old girl's."

The comment caused Jerry Zumquist to look down at his feet without meaning to do so. Several members of his gang openly tittered at him, but Felix Gandy, sensing that his leader had just taken a verbal punch to the gut, quickly lashed out to rescue him.

"Yeah? Those eight-year-old little-girl feet are going to be kicking your ass here in a second or two, you bug-eyed little faggot!"

Still stinging from the snickering by his buddies about Bugsy's public exposure that he had tiny feet, his lieutenant's most recent sarcastic comment caused the dam that was holding back most of the real anger within Jerry Zumquist to break. He was instantly overtaken with the fevered need to commence pounding on the skinny geek who they loved to attack for no apparent reason other than it was fun and kept them from being bored. His pent-up rage flowed out of its hidden enclosure and overtook his body.

He stepped forward and took a mighty swing. Bugsy saw the punch coming, and he tilted his head and leaned into the blow to take it in a place where his skull was thickest. Then he positioned his body to take the ensuing punches and kicks as the others jumped into the fight. With the speed of some kind of tropical viper, Bugsy was able to get in a few well-aimed strikes of his own. The ridiculous dance had begun.

Central to Bugsy's martial arts' understanding was the Chinese concept of *Wu Wei* – non-doing or doing nothing. This topic was the one which he and Master Chui had had endless conversations about, and the older Chinese man had been shocked by the sage-like wisdom of his star teenage pupil in regards to this matter. Bugsy maintained that he didn't need to win these fights, he only needed to survive them. And that meant that he had to hold back. If he annihilated his attackers, as he was quite capable of doing, their defeat would only ignite more trouble for him. Once Bugsy was outed as a kick-ass martial arts fighter, more and more opponents would get in line to take him on. However, if it appeared as if the little loser was always getting pummeled and only got an occasional lucky punch or kick in, the number of attackers would remain constant and their enthusiasm might even eventually wane over time, especially those who'd been the recipient of one of his perceived lucky blows.

Despite all appearances to the contrary, he could already sense that his strategy was working. He'd injured enough of them – either through his well-placed strikes or from turning his hardest body parts to absorb their punishment – to notice that some individuals in the pack were far less enthused about attacking him these days. He knew that these beatings would probably continue until graduation from high school, but they'd begun to feel more like choreographed fight scenes in a movie than a real fracas. He just regretted that there was no way to save his clothing, which inevitably needed to be replaced afterwards.

With many of these gang members currently having bruised and painful knuckles, tender and sore feet, and a few of the guys even suffering from broken ribs, knee contusions, or aching testicles, the gang backed away as soon as Jerry Zumquist declared that the fight was over. Throughout it all, Bugsy had neither been knocked off his feet nor conceded – he never did – but his shirt and pants were torn and he had blood coming from several small wounds on his face.

As the group withdrew and headed toward their cars in the parking lot, they heaped cruel comments of ridicule upon him. He'd danced with this gang enough to know that it was time for them to head home to lick their wounds, all the while spewing hate-filled words as they backed away from him. This round was over.

By the time Bugsy had found the janitor to let him back into the school to get his backpack and change of clothes, and had endured the old man's withering looks of disappointment, he was late. He trotted home like a coyote on the side of the road all the way back to his grandfather's house.

Upon his grandson's rushed entrance, Ira Morton, who was the spitting image of the actor Will Greer when he played Bear Claw in the movie *Jeremiah Johnson*, looked at him with a benevolent expression. For although he could clearly see that his grandson had been beaten up again, he knew he couldn't do anything to really protect the boy. Plus, if Bugsy was going to make it in this world, he'd have to figure out on his own how to endure it all. From what the old man could judge, his grandson was already a seasoned veteran at surviving.

Bugsy's father had ventured off to Fairbanks to get a better paying job when his only son was seven years old. The man had found steady employment in a plastics factory in the "Golden Heart City" and had continued to faithfully send a healthy portion of his earnings to his son and wife, who were living with her widowed father, Ira, in Tok at the time. As Bugsy's father worked his way up the hierarchy of the company, both the frequency of his visits home and the amounts of his monthly contributions to his family began to dwindle. By the time he had formed his own company and become known statewide as "The Ice Scraper King," he had a new home, a new wife, and new children in Fairbanks, and they'd become the sole recipients of all of his money, love, and attention.

Bugsy's mother understandably did not take this turn of events graciously. Feeling abandoned, which she actually was, she took to drinking more than usual. And as she started to wrestle with a deepening sense of self-pity over being trapped in the little town of Tok, and with no clear signs of any possible escape in the near future, the walls of her life started to close in on her. The first merest hint from a friend about greener pastures down in Seattle was excuse enough for her to leave Bugsy in the care of her father and head south on her own.

She'd said that she was "just checking out the scene," but everyone knew that she wasn't coming back. The last anyone had heard, she was remarried to a man who was supposedly a junkie and a pimp working in the affluent Sand Point area.

Remarkably, Bugsy was not as adversely affected by the asinine behavior of either of his parents as one would have expected. The real reason for this was his unwavering and unchanging relationship with his grandfather. The older man was a constant in his life, and his staunch support and interest in the boy mitigated all of the craziness from his mother and father. Truth was, as long as Ira Morton remained a consistent presence in his life, the boy barely noticed the absence of either of his parents. What should have been a horribly traumatizing and damaging childhood turned out to be nothing of the sort. By all accounts, Bugsy was a well-adjusted young man with a heart full of kindness and very little negative baggage.

As for Ira Morton, he'd come to Tok in 1942 as a civilian member of the Army Corps of Engineers during the building of the Alaska Highway. The town, at that time, was nothing more than the Alaska Road Commission camp used to house the construction and maintenance crews for the massive wartime infrastructure construction project, but so much money was spent on the place that it earned the nickname "Million Dollar Camp." Once the road had been completed, Ira had gone native and settled into the newly created town of Tok.

At first he'd become involved in the maintenance and upgrading of the recently built Alaska Highway, but then he appointed himself manager of all of the town roads. He even had a title: Road Commissioner of Tok. This paying position was semi-official, but he was able to eke out a healthy living. Eventually all of Tok's residents began to think of the man as indispensable for the upkeep of their lifeline main road and all the tributary dirt side streets of their town. Nowadays, Ira was old enough to find the job almost too much to handle anymore, and people openly whispered about who was going to take over the all-important role when he retired. Many assumed it would be Bugsy.

With his current assessment of his grandson over for the moment, the older man excitedly told him something of great importance. "Oh-ho, Gustav called just now and needs you over at the Parker House. Pronto!"

"Really? Did he say why, Grandpa?"

"Nope. Just that all hell's broken loose. You need to get your ass over there. Take my truck."

Once Bugsy had hastily parked his grandfather's old Dodge Power Wagon pickup truck in the back lot at the Parker House, the roadside motel at which he worked as the jack-of-all-trades, he scrambled inside into the main lobby. Behind the counter was Gustav Bishop, the owner of the motel and the unofficial mayor of Tok, and he was pinned in place by the agitated actions of three people, all angrily demanding his attention simultaneously. Bugsy could see that there was a striking Japanese man, an ancient-looking Army general, and an incredibly gorgeous blonde woman all jostling against one another and yelling at Mayor Bishop at the same time. Upon Bugsy's entrance, the hotel manager looked over at his employee with a look of relief.

"*There* you are, Bugsy. Oh, thank goodness you're here. I need your help. Can you please get these… guests here settled?"

The three individuals looked at the dwarfish teenager who had come onto the scene, and after the briefest of instances of disapproval over his presence, they switched their squawking to him. It was the second mob Bugsy had had to appease on this day, and he calmly took his place beside Mayor Bishop to do whatever he could to help. He secretly hoped that he wouldn't have to change out of ripped clothing after this second group had been satisfied.

相手のない喧嘩はできない

aite no nai kenka wa dekinai
You can't fight without an opponent.

The Palmetto Bug Monster appeared to be taking the path of least resistance to get to the Windy City and break it into a million pieces. Once it had laid waste to Indianapolis, it proceeded northward like any automobile driver and followed the corridor created by Interstate 65 straight toward Chicago. Unlike most vehicular travelers, however, it left a swath of destruction in its wake. After completely obliterating, without any hesitation, the Indiana towns of Lebanon, Dayton, Lafayette, Remington, and Roselawn, the massive creature ran into what amounted to a last stand by the military around the unincorporated community of Dinwiddie, Indiana.

Here, the U.S. Army Corps of Engineers had dug massive trenches that were to be filled with napalm and lit once the Palmetto Bug Monster attempted to cross them. The U.S. Army had gathered nearly every piece of artillery that they could get their hands on as well as several heavily armored regiments, all of which they spread out to create an impassable horseshoe-shaped gauntlet. The U.S. Air Force filled

the skies with squadrons of B-52s and fighter bombers ready to unleash their arsenals from the skies,
and the CIA had strategically parked giant tanker
trucks filled with pyrethrum powder in the kill zone.
With the President still unwilling to pull the nuclear trigger, the military had put all of its eggs in one
basket by hoping that this all-out assault would stop
the creature.

Unfortunately for the fighting men of this
amassed force, this highly fortified roadblock slowed
the forward progress of the monster, but didn't
deter it much. And while cockroaches do not have
heels, per se, the impressive combined attack did,
momentarily, put the giant insect back on its tar-
someres. However, by jumping up and flapping its
massive wings furiously a few times, the creature not
only navigated over the fiery obstacles and traps set
for it – it sent the flames, insecticides, and even some
of the weapons flying in the wrong direction with the
powerful hurricane-force winds it generated in this
effort. After such an impressive display, the Palmetto Bug Monster then showed its deadly accuracy by
easily shooting down with its abdominal bioweapon
ray gun most of the flying aircraft and then destroying the situated ground assets before continuing
northward.

Entering the sprawling metropolitan area around
Chicago, the creature lumbered into Gary, Indiana,
but didn't find enough to destroy there. It continued
to make a beeline straight up the shoreline of Lake

Michigan to get to a more heavily populated down-town area. It leveled buildings, tore up highways, ripped up railways, demolished regional airports, devastated power plants, and even sank two Great Lakes freighters as it went. Fighter jets continued to circle and fire their payload of missiles, but these did next to nothing to stop the creature, which seemed absolutely hell-bent on mass destruction.

It was an apocalyptic whirling dervish that was now sweeping its way up the Lake Shore Drive in the direction of the Loop and the heart of the sec-ond-most-populated American city.

When the Palmetto Bug Monster finally reached the Museum of Science and Industry, it stopped long enough to survey the flaming path of chaos it had just forged. This odd moment of self-reflection was followed by another strange and out-of-character behavior for the monster: it reached over toward the Beaux-Arts Building, the largest surviving structure of the 1893 World's Columbian Exposition, ripped off its large copper dome, and put this atop its head. In that bizarre instant, the monstrous creature looked like it was modeling a traditional conical bamboo hat from Asia.

[This versatile head-covering has many names, yet has a distinctively similar style throughout the continent. It is known as *do'un* (ដួន) in Cambodia; *seraung* in Indonesia; *koup* (ກຸບ) in Laos; *terendak* in Malaysia; *ngop* (งอบ) in Thailand; *khamauk* (ခမောက်) in Myanmar; *salakót, sarók, sadók, s'laong, hallidung, kallugong,* and *tabungaw* among other names in the Philippines; *nón lá* in Vietnam; *kasa* (笠) in Japan; *dǒulì* (斗笠) in China; *satgat* (삿갓) in Korea; *jaapi* (জাপি) in India; and *mathal* (মাথাল) in Bangladesh. As the Bard of Avon once said, "A rose by any other name would smell as sweet..."]

Next, the Palmetto Bug Monster took the dome of the museum off its head and, now that its odd little fashion show was over, threw it like a Frisbee toward the nearby University of Chicago campus. It crashed into the buildings there like a devastating meteor. Anyone unlucky enough to be inside these edifices was immediately crushed upon impact.

There was another group at the museum who was just now facing the undeniable truth that if it weren't for bad luck, they'd have no luck at all: the former crew of the German submarine the *U-505.* These individuals had been invited by the museum to come have a reunion, meet with their dead captain's wife, and be interviewed and photographed by a *Chicago Tribune* reporter and photographer to be a part of a highly advertised newspaper story about the 35th anniversary of their ship's capture. All of the dire warnings to them about the impending approach of the killer giant cockroach had gone unheeded, in part due to their German, fixated trait of being absolutely punctual for the date and time on the invitation sent by the museum. Now that they found themselves and their unlucky vessel at the feet of the giant bug, they had to admit that their belief in the proverb, *Pünktlichkeit ist die Höflichkeit der Könige* (Punctuality is the courtesy of kings), had caused them all to soon be dead where they stood.

The *U-505* had been captured by the U.S. Navy in June 1944, and it was only one of six such vessels seized intact during the entire war. Its inglorious end only highlighted the fact that the German *Kriegsmarine* sub had been snake-bit from the moment it was constructed in Hamburg, Germany, three years prior. Hampered by a series of largely unsuccessful patrols that had resulted in costly delays for repairs and even some potential acts of sabotage by the French Resistance, the crew, the captain, and the vessel had become the laughingstock of the fleet.

Things had gotten so bad that the acting captain had committed suicide in front of the crew. The next captain, Harald Lange, hadn't had a much better time of it. On his second patrol, the sub was attacked and mortally damaged by the Allies off the coast of French West Africa. In the chaos of that situation, the crew had failed to successfully scuttle the U-boat. This not only allowed the enemy to capture it but, a decade later, to turn it into an outdoor museum exhibit in Chicago, Illinois.

Even though all of these people gathered at the submarine on the day of the Palmetto Bug Monster's attack were ultimately killed, the newspaper photographer's camera survived, and when his film was developed afterwards to document the moment, the images were as disturbing as they were fascinating. Understandably, there was a pall of terror on everyone's face about the impending approach of the one-hundred-fifty-foot alien cockroach, but there was also a look of dubiousness that was too powerful to be ignored. This was partly due to the fact that the *U-505* represented such a stark monument to the crew's abject failures. After all, by not setting off the scuttling charges and by not properly disabling the open sea strainer to sink the vessel, they'd inadvertently allowed a Type IXC U-boat and its top-secret Enigma machine to fall into the hands of the enemy. Unintentionally, the crew's mishaps had probably helped the Allies win the war.

Also, the two-hundred-and-fifty-foot-long submarine now sitting outside the American museum represented a metaphorical metallic admission ticket for the crew's two-year incarceration in a prisoner-of-war camp in remote Reston, Louisiana. There, despite the requirements outlined by the Geneva Convention that allowed prisoners to write home and receive care from the Red Cross, the crewmen had been held in secret to prevent the Nazis from knowing that their submarine and its essential encryption equipment were being analyzed by American experts. The crewmen's family members were beyond shocked when they returned home alive and well to Germany in 1947, having thought that they'd all perished during the war.

It is understandable, therefore, why so many of the crew appeared in the photos to be wholly regretting their visit to the ship for the first and last time. After all, the submarine was not a symbol of German innovation or engineering. It was not a representation of the sacrifice and duty that they had given to their *Vaterland*. Actually, it was not a memorial to anything good for them at all. No, the *U-505*, sitting outside the American museum as a tourist attraction, was nothing but a gigantic *Statue der Scheiße* for most of the men.

The real source of confusion on the faces of the people in the photos, however, came from a comment that the wife of their *Kapitän* had uttered just before the photos had been taken. Frau Lange, in an attempt to explain that her dead husband had spent far more years after the war in the fruit-importing business than he had being a captain of a German U-boat during the war, had said, "*Am Ende wusste mein Mann mehr über Mangos als über Torpedos.*"

When the museum's translator informed all the English-speaking members of the audience that Mrs. Lange had just said that her husband knew more about mangoes than torpedoes, their uncertain response was reflected in the expression of those members of the crew, who hadn't needed any translation of the rather strange comment. In a shared moment of uncertainty, the group had simultaneously blanched at the truth of it all just as the photographer's flash had gone off.

The Palmetto Bug Monster, now having suddenly taken notice of the German submarine sitting in front of it, reached down to pick it up, crushing the doomed group gathered around it in the process. When it stood back up again, it held the U-boat in its arms like a quarterstaff, and as it proceeded on its way toward the skyscrapers of downtown, it spun the vessel as an implement of devastation.

By the time that the hull of the *U-505* had become so battered that it more resembled a sage smudge stick, the cockroach discarded it at the entrance to the neighborhood of Chinatown. It was clear that this famed cultural section of Chicago was to be beset upon by the Palmetto Bug Monster as its next target.

An odd thing happened next. As the panicked residents of Chinatown fled for their lives in the streets, screaming, shrieking, and cursing in the various dialects of *Zhongguo*, the giant cockroach stopped abruptly and tilted its head as if to hear something coming from the northwest. Although a far too benign image to use in this circumstance, it appeared to all as if the monster was currently attempting to hear the far-off whispers of a distant lover.

Without warning, the space alien monster let out one of its deafening hisses before its two sets of massive chitinous wings extended out from its body and began to flutter. The creature took a leap up in the air, the wings began to beat furiously, and the Palmetto Bug Monster took flight. This maneuver produced destructive winds that buffeted the ground and shattered windows, fanned the flames back in the path of the creature, overturned vehicles, and sent any unlucky pedestrians fleeing on the sidewalks flying through the air.

The surviving Chicagoans watched the giant bug lumber in flight toward the northwest, and they all exhaled a short sigh of relief that, for whatever unknown reason, their city had been spared complete annihilation. But as they looked around at all of the injured, dead, and damage from the ruination that the cockroach had inflicted upon their fair city, not to mention the ravaging effects of its current laborious, low-level flight, many people had tears in their eyes and could be heard saying, "Yeah, thanks for nothing."

Another person who witnessed this whole event was none other than Iva Ikuko Toguri D'Aquino, better known as the propagandistic World War Two reporter "Tokyo Rose." This stateless and disgraced woman was visiting the Japanese market Toguri Mercantile, which was on the stretch of Belmont Avenue near Clark Street in the Lake View neighborhood of Chicago. She looked up as the massive cockroach flittered by and said in her characteristically feminine voice, "Goodbye now, goodbye now, goodbye now, goodbye. In just a moment…"

猫に小判

neko ni koban
Gold coins to a cat.

Even though Bugsy and Mayor Bishop were both so short in stature that Eve Sanderborn, General Richardson, and Usotsuki Shirinigatsuku all loomed over them in height, the two worked well together to quickly dissipate the furor that the three travelers had been unleashing upon them. With assurances that there were plenty of vacant rooms available and a guarantee of lodging for as long as was needed, the trio of outsiders finally calmed down enough to act more civilly toward one another and toward the pair who were helping them get rooms at the Parker House.

It was at this lulling juncture that Eve took notice of the two men she'd been elbowing against to get a room. The Japanese man looked to her a lot like that disruptive and detained individual that Walter Cronkite had publicly chastised on the CBS Evening News, but she'd heard that that man had been escorted back to Japan. If that were true, there was no way he could be standing next to her in Tok, Alaska, and she attributed the confusion to her potentially inherently racist inability to tell one Asian apart from another.

As for the other man, she now saw clearly that he was wearing an Army uniform with a colorful patch-work of military ribbons upon his broad chest, and she identified him as both a perceived enemy and poten-tial ally. Intuitively, she relaxed her stature and thrust her ample bosom at the elderly uniformed man.

"Oh, and I think you're part of the reason that I'm stuck here in this hellhole, sir."

General Richardson seemed to take notice of the beautiful woman next to him for the first time, and he struck a pose that he thought would evoke a sense of regality, not to mention sophistication. Unfortunately for the general, his expression was far more lecherous, for he was neither able to deny the immediate attraction he felt for the blonde stranger, nor fully keep his eyes from straying toward the am-ple cleavage that she was currently displaying.

"I do not see how, young lady, but I must say that if I had anything to do with trapping you in these close quarters with myself, I apologize for nothing."

Disregarding the man's painfully obvious at-tempt at flirtation and his overt ogling, Eve playfully placed her index finger onto General Richardson's chest and said in her best imitation of Marilyn Mon-roe, "I was headed north, but some of your mean ol' fighter jets intercepted my little plane that was headed to Fairbanks and forced us to land in this godforsaken place."

"And why were you headed north, Ms....?

"Sanderborn. Eve Sanderborn, sir. I'm a reporter for KTLA. and my cameraman Bernie and I were headed up to get the scoop on...a story about a white caribou calf that's been spotted in the tundra. Maybe you could help us get there tomorrow after all, General...?"

"General Buchanan Richardson at your service, ma'am. My friends call me Jocko. And perhaps after we get settled into our rooms, we could come together to share some drinks, and we could discuss exactly how I could assist you in getting up to see that white caribou calf."

Usotsuki Shirinigatsuku suddenly tapped the general's shoulder, a strictly forbidden gesture in the American military. Filled with a burning rage, General Richardson spun toward the Japanese man who'd had the balls to touch him without permission, but before he could say anything, the Japanese man spoke as if he were talking to someone beneath his standing.

"You and the *baka* U.S. military are the reason that I'm stuck here too. If you're gonna help Blondie get up there, why don't you help me, too?"

The general, who was still seething too much from the young foreigner's infraction to think up a properly vicious comeback, stood there unspeaking, but Eve, suddenly suspicious that the man was a member of the Japanese media trying to get a jump on her story, leaned in toward him and asked in an accusatory tone, "And why do *you* need to get north, Mister...?"

"My name is Usotsuki Shirinigatsuku. I'm the personal assistant to Shinichi Sekizawa, the main screenwriter of the Godzilla movies, and I've been sent here to research locations for a future movie that Toho Co., Ltd. is going to be making soon."

General Richardson tilted his head as he finally found his voice. "It seems rather strange timing to be thinking about making a movie about a pretend monster when there's a real one creating such a horrendous situation here in this country these days."

"*Hai*, but the show must go on, right, General? Regardless, if you're helping the reporter get north, you should help me, too."

"I'm a goddamn general in the United States Army, not a fucking AAA travel agent. I'm here on official military business, not trip planning for anyone! And not for the likes of you, I can guaran-fucking-tee you that!"

"So, you're all wanting to see He-Knew-Pat-Sajak, huh?" Mayor Bishop intervened. "You know, as soon as that giant lizard popped out from the volcano on Akutan, made its way up the peninsula, and started mucking about in the area around Nikolai, it's been all that everyone's been talking about. No one – not even the monster itself – seems to know what the hell it's doing or where it's going."

The television news reporter, the retired U.S. Army general, and the yakuza lieutenant/cryptozoologist all blanched and went stonily silent in their surprise at Mayor Bishop's comment. They looked in shock at the short innkeeper. He had misaligned eyes that were so unnerving that Eve Sanderborn wondered for a second if he were a relative of the actor Marty Feldman, but he'd just uttered – with the nonchalance of giving out the most recent fishing report for sportsmen – what seemed like such a remarkable statement about a supposedly unknown monster that she quickly forgot the resemblance. If the mayor's utterance weren't bad enough, Eve watched the tiny teenager with the black eye and fresh facial wounds next to the odd little man begin nodding at this earthshaking news as if he were figuring out when he could go grab his fishing pole and bait.

The three travelers were too astounded to speak right away, but finally the general was the first to respond. He knew a threat to national security when he saw one. He'd had more than a few spies and traitors shot for less indicting comments.

"And how the hell do you know about any of this, Mr. Bishop? Everything you just said is top secret."

"Oh-ho, general, Alaska may not have a road system connecting places like you all have in the Lower 48, but we've got radios and phones. Some of us call this the Athabaskan Network. Myrtle Akinson here in Tok has a cousin in Nikolai. Cheryl Brokenwing in Nikolai has family in King Salmon. Chris Silverfoot in King Salmon has a friend who works in the Trident Seafood Plant in Akutan as a gutter. In these parts, whenever anything of interest happens, it's like a rock from the Alaska Highway hitting the glass of a windshield and causing the fractures and fissures from that event to spread out far and wide. Any newsworthy event hits the radio waves and goes throughout the network, and pretty damn fast, lemme tell ya. Normally, it's about a potlatch dinner that someone didn't get invited to, a new quilt pattern that is irreverent to traditional quilt-making, another unplanned baby, or a recipe for some beaver stew, but the appearance of a gigantic lizard that's lumbering through our state – well, that's what some would call real *headline* news."

This information hit each of the three strangers differently. They each took a moment to ruminate on the impact of what the mayor had just said, and their minds were awhirl with potential reactions.

The general realized he needed to get ahead of what amounted to this major intelligence leak that might require imprisonments and other implemented gag order measures. Once Kissinger got back from his stupid errand, the two would have to reach out to his contacts at the National Security Agency to help squash this clandestine network and come up with a plan to restore order. This apparent underground resistance needed to be cut off at the roots.

Usotsuki felt the bottom of his intestines flicker. If these country folks knew about the monster and were communicating about its movements so freely, there was no doubt that the FBI and CIA were probably aware of the gecko now – and he was on the blacklist with both of them. Any chance of him sneaking up and inserting himself in the study of the giant lizard was definitely in peril. His instinct for fight or flight kicked in and he prepared himself to get ready to do one or the other.

For Eve, the golden ticket of resurrecting her career was now waving in the wind for any reporter with a radio and a half-decent resume to snatch it from her grip. And that was not something she would allow to happen without a major fight. She leveled her voluptuous chest at Mayor Bishop and, in her best interviewer voice, asked, "Are your people down in Seattle or Los Angeles, Mr. Bishop?"

"My people?"

"Yes, the Indians. Does that Athabaskan Network extend south to the civilized world?"

"I'm Jewish, Ms. Sanderborn, so my people are everywhere. Bugsy, you're part Athabaskan – are 'your people' in Seattle or Los Angeles?"

The boy spoke with a slightly bemused grin on his face. "I hear my mom's in Seattle, but I don't know for sure. I haven't heard from her in years. And I'm pretty sure that I don't have anyone in Los Angeles. Wait. I've got a cousin from my grandfather's side in Bozeman, Montana. Does that count?"

Mayor Bishop smiled a very wide grin of pretended innocence. "So I guess that means yes and no, Ms. Sanderborn."

The general spread his arms wide, shoving Eve and Usotsuki aside. He was now clearly agitated to a point of being quite angry at the mayor.

"Enough, you ridiculous bug-eyed little man! Have your boy show me to my room immediately. I need to start setting up my command center at this motel. As soon as Henry Kissinger comes back, send him to my room. We'll also need constant room service, so commence that ASAP."

As Eve had noted, Mayor Bishop could have been an identical twin of the British actor Marty Feldman. As a matter of fact, the residents of Tok had audibly gasped when the film *Young Frankenstein* was first shown at the community center because, there, up on the screen, was a man who was the spitting image of their own mayor, and he was playing Igor. The only thing that was different between the two was that the mayor didn't have a British accent. Otherwise, they looked and acted virtually the same. And it was the perfect comic timing and the naturally humorous expressions of Gustav Bishop, the well-known owner of the Parker House, that had endeared him so much to the residents of the unincorporated town of Tok to warrant an unsanctioned and unofficial election for mayor. He'd been receiving a stipend from the town's residents and been acting as the representative of Tok ever since he'd first proposed the governmental position.

Now, hearing the last little tidbit dropped by the general, the man gave his best Marty Feldman incredulous look of surprise.

"Henry Kissinger?"

The general nodded. "Yes, he dropped me off here to set up our command post while he drove his VW bus up to Fort Wainwright to get reinforcements."

"Lemme get this straight – Henry Kissinger, the first American Secretary of State from Jewish ancestry, a Nobel Prize winner, and the controversial diplomat responsible for some of the United States' most pivotal foreign policy decisions during the last decade, just dropped you off here in Tok, Alaska, to continue driving a Volkswagen bus up to an Army base in Fairbanks to get more soldiers so you can set up a command post here at the Parker House to fight the giant lizard that emerged from an Aleutian volcano? Is that what you're saying to us all with a straight face?"

General Richardson put his hands onto his hips and sneered at the other people in the lobby. "Yes. You all saw him drop me off, right? It was at the same time that you guys got here. You must have seen him."

No one had seen him. As the general scrutinized their reactions, Eve and Usotsuki could only silently shake their heads to indicate that they hadn't seen any of that.

Mayor Bishop went into full Marty Feldman mode. "You're putting me on!"

General Richardson put his hands down heavily onto the counter. "Who are you talking to, you wall-eyed motherfucker? You better not be talking to me, you insipid little man, for I will unsheathe my weapon and shoot you right between your wide-spread eyes. I've got much more important things to do than bicker with the likes of you. Command that tiny bellboy to show me to my room...immediately."

"Alright. Bugsy, show the general to Room 25."

"But that's the one that—"

"It's okay, Bugsy. Just take the general to Room 25. Thank you. And thank you, General Richardson, for choosing to stay at the Parker House. I hope you enjoy your time with us."

The general bellowed, "I didn't choose to stay here. Kissinger did."

The mayor smiled too widely. "Well, I'll certainly thank him *whenever* he returns. Good day, sir."

Bugsy reached down for the bag at the feet of the general, but the older man moved with such impressive speed he grabbed it first. His urgency was such that the teenager had to wonder if there were Golden Codes for the nuclear weapons in there. Like most of his countrymen, Bugsy figured it was only a matter of time before the U.S. president sanctioned a nuclear attack on the monsters to stop both of them. Truthfully, he had mixed feelings about this.

Outside, the general actually walked in front of Bugsy as they made their way down the row of motel rooms. He was clearly used to leading the charge, and he walked with such authority that the young man questioned himself about where they were actually going. But then Bugsy remembered he was the one showing the general to his room and not the other way around, and he stepped up into pace next to him.

Without turning to talk to Bugsy, the general said out of the side of his mouth, "That little twerp of a man has no idea who he's messing with, young man. If I'm prepared to deal with a one-hundred-and-fifty-foot-tall monster and kill it, I have no problem with squashing a runt like that under my bootheel... like some kind of bug."

"Mayor Bishop is really a good guy, sir. He has a sense of humor that makes everyone smile. When you live in a remote place like Tok, it's good to be able to laugh once in a while. Life can be hard up here, sir."

"Life is hard everywhere, son. That isn't enough of an excuse to act like a dimwit."

"Well, here you are, General Richardson, Room 25. I hope you'll be comfortable and enjoy your time in Tok."

"Son, I once slept like a baby under a jeep during a mortar attack in Bayeaux, France, during the War. Don't you worry your oddly tiny head about my comfort level. I'll be just fine."

The general abruptly slammed the door. Bugsy hadn't really expected a tip, but the elderly man's somewhat rude act rubbed him the wrong way. Originally he'd felt bad that Mayor Bishop had given the general the room right next to the utility space containing the hot-water heater for the entire mo-tel. This location meant that the air temperature of Room 25 was always stiflingly hot and that the old copper pipes in the walls supplying all of the other rooms were shivered and quaked like the chains of a ghost both day and night. But now that he'd had the displeasure of being around the old, cranky, and rude general, he was happy at this somewhat cru-el placement by the mayor. The gruff military man seemed to deserve it.

By the time Bugsy had returned to the main of-fice, the atmosphere there had drastically changed. Without the caustic element of the cantankerous war veteran around anymore, Mayor Bishop, the televi-sion reporter, and the Japanese cryptozoologist had had a chance to get to know one another, and Eve had started to openly flirt with each man. Both of them had obviously noticed that Eve was incredibly good-looking, but now she was able to cast her lures at both the funny-looking innkeeper and the stern Japanese stud to appeal to their masculine natures. Deeply enticed, they both reacted just like she'd ex-pected. Quite easily, Eve had manipulated them to do all of her bidding.

Bugsy soon found himself guiding Eve Sander-born to the best room the Parker House had to of-fer. Using some inadvertent glancing touches to his arm as they walked, some overt eyelash batting, and even some purposeful propping up of her breasts in his direction, Eve was openly attempting to seduce

Bugsy into immediately running over to the local bar, the Tok Lodge, to fetching her cameraman, getting the drunkard poured into the bed of his room, adjacent to her much more luxurious accommodations, and then setting her up with some food and drink. She was going to have a long night to do her planning for how she was going to get a closer look at the lizard.

Whether due to the nice five-dollar tip or the artful acts of enticement from the reporter, Bugsy promised that he would do everything she asked as soon as he had shown the Japanese man to his room. Upon hearing this, Eve gently stroked his cheek as she carefully closed the room door. While the general's exit had rubbed Bugsy the wrong way, the beautiful blonde woman had certainly rubbed him the right way, and he found himself having to adjust the groin area of his jeans as he loped back to the main office.

The Japanese man was far more restrained on their walk to his room. Bugsy figured that the language barrier was keeping him quiet, but Usotsuki was far too preoccupied with the delectability of the gorgeous television reporter to engage in conversation with the unimportant bellhop. He was currently imagining himself letting the woman trace the lines of his *irezumi* with her tongue, and he too was having to adjust the crotch of his suit as he walked. In the midst of this libidinous moment, though, he did have a question for Bugsy.

"You're so calm about the lizard. Why?"

"My grandmother was a full-blooded Athabaskan, and even though she died before I was born, she imparted a lot of the Dena'ina mythology to my grandfather. He raised me believing in the magical world out there. I've personally seen both a gux and a wechuge with my own eyes while on a hunting trip we took together when I was younger, so the sudden presence of a giant lizard fits perfectly into my belief system. Nothing can surprise me, I guess."

"*Hai.* I, too, believe in the myths of the world. I cannot wait to see He-Knew-Pat-Sajak and study it. Another real *kaiju*!"

"Well, Mr. Shirinigatsuku, here's your room. I hope you can get comfortable and enjoy your stay here."

"I have a request, Bugsy-san. Can you please give this note to Ms. Sanderborn?"

Bugsy nodded as he took the piece of paper from the Japanese man, who also handed him a one-hundred yen coin for a tip. It looked impressive to Bugsy, but was only worth about thirty cents in American money. The door closed gently and the teenager turned to head to the reporter's room with the note before starting back to the main office to chat with the mayor.

Normally he wouldn't have been so bold as to read the secret note the Japanese man had given him, but he was curious enough to do so now. It read:

手 枕に / ほそき腕を / さし入れて
Ta-makura ni /hosoki kaina o / sashi-irete
Easing in/ her slender forearm/ for his pillow

Unsure of what any of it meant, Bugsy refolded the paper and took it to Eve Sanderborn's room, and he slipped it under her door. He walked back to the main office to inform his boss that he'd been asked to run a bunch of errands by the beautiful television reporter. He expected the man to be perturbed by all of the requests, but he found Mayor Bishop swooning wide-eyed behind the counter when he got there.

"What a good day for the motel, huh?"

"Yep, that's three more guests than we'd expect to have this time of year. The television reporter asked me to do a bunch of stuff for her – get her cameraman back to his room and get them some food. I didn't think I could refuse. Sorry."

The mayor's face looked overwhelmed with the size of the smile on it. The dimples that dominated his cheeks deepened enough for Bugsy to be able to put the newly acquired Japanese coin he'd just gotten into them if he'd felt so inclined.

The man's misaligned eyes now opened wide enough to express the depth of the overall contentment he was feeling. "Oh, that woman's an ABSO-LUTE peach. I'm in love with her! No, I mean it. I'm absolutely smitten with her, Bugsy. Without question, you are to do everything that she asks of you. Actually, you are to do everything that each of those three ask of you. Just make sure that you put notes on their motel bills so we can charge them in *full*. I've been in this business long enough to know that, when the universe sends you some good fortune, you milk it for all it's worth."

"Okay, Mayor Bishop."

"I want to thank you for showing up today, Bugsy. I really appreciate your help. When those three first arrived, they instantly demanded my sole attention. As you saw, I was having some trouble managing them until you arrived. I'm assuming you were a bit tardy because of that...trouble at school again? Those boys haven't grown tired of harassing you, huh?"

Bugsy reached up to his swollen eye and let his fingertips feel the bumps, the cuts, and the abrasions on his face.

"Yeah, Mayor Bishop, I'm sorry I was late. It won't happen again."

"Bugsy, do you want me to reach out to the school or have a conversation with those boys' families?"

"Oh geez, no, Mayor Bishop. I'm fine. My grandfather reminds me often that one of life's most important balancing acts is learning how to take care of your own problems while only accepting help when you really need it. My situation at school with those boys fits in the former category. It's my responsibility to deal with them, and I am, in my own way. But thanks for the offer, eh?"

"Sure. If you ever need the latter and will accept help from me, just let me know, Bugsy."

"I will."

The mayor nodded toward the location of the local bar. "Okay, why don't you get on your way over to the Tok Lodge to retrieve the inebriated cameraman and get him back to his room as requested. Then grab some food and drink for that blonde goddess. But, uh, when you take her her food and all, could you slip this note to her?"

Bugsy headed off to do his errands, but once again, he could not resist taking a look at the second secret note he'd been tasked to deliver to the beautiful television reporter. In the lovely script of his boss, there was this poem:

There once was a fella from Tok
Who a sweet lass from away did provoke.
She came to stay at his inn,
And riled up his feelings within.
She caused him to suffer from heatstroke.

Bugsy rolled his eyes at it. To woo the woman, the Japanese man had produced something mysterious and exotic, while his boss had come up with something sophomoric and schmaltzy. And, because he didn't know Eve Sanderborn well enough yet, he had to wonder which one she would pick in the end.

In reality, the young man really didn't have a clue about the beautiful television reporter. She already knew she was going to pick both...to serve her needs.

The teenager followed his own train of thought to the painful question that he regularly asked himself. When would it be time for anyone to pick him to love?

自業自得

jigoujitoku
Self-work, self-profit.

It was unclear whether the Palmetto Bug Monster flew so low during its journey up to Alaska because it was physically unable to achieve a higher altitude while in flight or because it had a natural inclination toward carnage. Regardless, the creature hovered so close to the ground as it flew in its northwest heading that the winds generated by its colossal wings caused a swath of catastrophic devastation that followed its pathway. It was as if a massive twister – an F6-rated tornado on the Fujita Scale – had touched down in Chicago and then proceeded to spin its way over the three thousand, two hundred and fifty mile long journey.

Along the way, Rockford, Illinois, Madison, Wisconsin, Minneapolis, Minnesota, Fargo, North Dakota, Regina, Saskatchewan, Saskatoon, Saskatchewan, and Edmonton, Alberta all were left disaster zones after the monster had passed through their urban centers. An eight-lane highway could have been built in the cleared corridor the creature had created with its progress.

The United States military continued to be completely impotent to stop the monster while it was in American airspace. They'd been so surprised by its sudden flight toward Canada, they were caught with their proverbial pants down. The only weapons that they could mobilize quickly enough were the jet fighters and a vast arsenal of ground-to-air missile batteries, and while an endless buffeting by strikes from above as well as from the ground was implemented, nothing seemed to even faze the Palmetto Bug Monster. It continued on its way undeterred.

It was as the creature had come within the proximity of the infamous Minot Air Force Base in Minot, North Dakota, that the American public had held its collective breath. It was well-known that this base was home to an ample nuclear payload that could be delivered by either bombers or ballistic missiles, and it was assumed that if the monster flew too close, the much-anticipated nuclear attack upon it would begin. However, the President, who was now becoming the target of some high-level criticism and even some very large public demonstrations throughout the country, refused to issue the order to use nuclear weapons, and the base was heavily damaged as the giant cockroach flew right over it without a single nuke being fired.

The Palmetto Bug Monster now moved with a perpetual swarm of aircraft around it, and to most observers it resembled the beloved unclean *Peanuts* character who had a permanent cloud of dust swirling around him. The ever-present military jets and helicopters, which continued to swoop in and fire their missiles and drop their bombs in a vain attempt to stop the creature, had to share the crowded airspace around the giant cockroach with a fleet of news helicopters, surveillance aircraft, and thrill-seekers attempting to get a good look at the monster. Collisions and incidents of friendly fire were a frequent risk. With the priority being to attempt to find a means to somehow wound the space alien, policing the skies became secondary.

The Royal Canadian Air Force also had little success in stopping the Palmetto Bug Monster once it had flown over their border. They too were unable to prevent it from wreaking havoc in their country. After wiping the Yukon city of Whitehorse off the map, the monster continued its northwest trek until it crossed the border again and landed in the small and remote mining town of Circle, Alaska.

Here, the giant cockroach seemed to freeze in place in the center of the town, on the banks of the Yukon River. What it did next surprised the snot out of everyone. It jumped up in the air and began to spin very, very fast, all the while firing its ray blaster indiscriminately. Those aircraft that had strayed too close were suddenly shot from the sky, and all of the buildings in Circle, its airport, and even its only road, the terminus of the Steese Highway, were immediately vaporized. Those aircraft still in the air afterwards were able to see that the giant cockroach was now standing in the middle of a circle of scorched devastation one mile in diameter. And for the first time since arriving on the planet, the Palmetto Bug Monster stopped its progression of terror and destruction...almost like it was waiting for something.

As for He-Knew-Pat-Sajak, the gigantic lizard had made its way up the length of the Alaska Peninsula, nimbly striding through the rugged landscape made up of active volcanoes, mountain peaks, rolling tundra, and rugged, wave-battered coastlines. The Air Force pilots who continued to circle around as they kept an eye on the creature noticed that the behemoth's skin was starting to tatter and shred as it approached the town of King Salmon. They reported that it looked like it was wearing some kind of a ghillie suit as it carefully circumnavigated this town. Some herpetologists that had been brought in as consultants surmised that He-Knew-Pat-Sajak was probably shedding its older skin, and that was considered a normal and non-threatening development. At this point, some veteran military advisors made fearful mention of the fact that most reptiles on Earth shed only when they're growing – a chilling prospect in the regard of this already impressively large threat.

Yet, as the monster continued to avoid areas with any kind of population and refrained from doing much damage, except knocking down some of the trees of the forests and scaring a sleuth of brown bears, its migration continued to be mostly an act of nonviolence. Because of this, the official orders continued to be to only watch its progress, not engage it.

When the creature turned north and went directly through the tundra area between Levelock and Igiugig, crossing the Kvichak River Valley, there was a shared sigh of relief from the powers that be that, for whatever reasons, He-Knew-Pat-Sajak had apparently decided to divert its path away from the most populated city of Alaska, Anchorage. And while no one could admit that, at this point, they felt one hundred percent confident that the giant lizard wasn't on its way to join forces with the approaching and equally massive cockroach, it sure seemed like this monster was much less of a threat than the Palmetto Bug Monster. At the moment, it seemed almost harmless. The military gratefully accepted this diagnosis, as they hoped that this trend would continue so they could just keep tabs on the wandering gecko while focusing their full attention on stopping the much more destructive bug.

He-Knew-Pat-Sajak had kept up an impressive pace since leaving Akutan. Traveling at about twenty miles an hour, around the clock, the creature had covered quite a bit of ground. However, as it approached the community of Sleetmute, the Ingalik village on the banks of the Kuskokwim River, which formed a natural channel between the Kuskokwim Mountains and the Alaskan Range, its speed slowed noticeably. After a moment or two of merely ambling, the creature suddenly came to a complete stop and flopped down on the ground. In the most ungraceful pose imaginable, the giant gecko sprawled out harmlessly, using the rising river's bank as a pillow.

The one military observation plane continuing to monitor the creature's progress – it'd been deemed necessary to divert all fighter jets toward the path of the oncoming Palmetto Bug Monster – circled overhead above the dozing giant, its pilots in a state of startled confusion. The horrific giant cockroach had yet to take even a moment of respite, so it was unsettling to see the massive gecko taking what appeared to be a power nap.

There were some in the chain of command who thought that this was the perfect time for a concerted military attack on the lizard, but calmer minds prevailed, pointing out that when deciding between whether to attempt to stop a rampaging giant cockroach or attacking a slumbering monster gecko that hadn't done any real harm yet, it was probably better to let sleeping dogs – or, in this case, lizards – lie.

When He-Knew-Pat-Sajak finally awoke a day later, it stretched and yawned in an almost cute display of a good night's sleep. Then it looked around as if it was uncertain of where it was. It stumbled back in the same direction from which it'd come, then spun around and continued on its pathway up the river in a northeast direction. After staggering stiffly for a little while, the creature found its legs again and resumed its pre-nap pace. It kept this up until it made its way to Minto, Alaska, where it slumped down upon the ground again and took another nap.

This time, the rest was shorter, but its apparent confusion upon waking was more intense. The giant monster seemed almost to do a pirouette as it spun to get its bearings. When this comical dance movement was over, He-Knew-Pat-Sajak acted as if it had heard something faint, far away in the northeast, and continued once more on its prescribed pathway in that direction for the next two hundred and some miles to the small mining town of Central, Alaska, where it once more collapsed and slept again.

The authorities held their breath. On the one hand, the giant lizard had come within one hundred miles of Fairbanks, the second largest city in Alaska, but had not appeared tempted to head in that direction. It had even crossed the vaunted State Route 2 without causing even a single traffic accident, and now it was snoozing peacefully again.

On the other hand, it was currently less than sixty miles from the newly arrived Palmetto Bug Monster, and no one had a clue if that was a very good thing or a very bad thing. Whenever He-Knew-Pat-Sajak finally awoke again, only time would tell whether everyone's prayers had been answered *or* the end of the Earth was now at hand.

三人寄れば文殊の知恵

sannin yoreba monju no chie

When three people meet, wisdom is exchanged.

Bugsy awoke the day after helping check the three strangers into the Parker House, and he could feel that his whole world had changed. He'd come home late after running all the beautiful television reporter's errands and unwittingly setting some of the romantic threads into the shuttlecock for whatever tapestry that was trying to weave itself at the roadside inn, and he'd animatedly recounted all of the events of his night to his grandfather.

For his part, Ira Morton had sat back in his comfortable chair and listened with rapt interest to his grandson, who was one who never got too excited about most things. As the boy had chattered on enthusiastically about the different personalities and the uncertain plot twists that they presented, the elderly man was transported back in time to those evenings in his childhood when he'd laid next to the family radio in the den and listened to *The Shadow*, wholly lost in his imagination.

Bugsy's request to be allowed to skip school had been wholeheartedly vetoed by his grandfather, however. Although dismayed by this command, Bugsy was not one to openly defy the older man he adored so much. So he begrudgingly headed off to school feeling like it was not only going to be a complete waste of time to be there, but that he'd be missing all of the much more interesting show taking place at the Parker House. Uncharacteristically, Bugsy became angrier with each step he took toward the educational facility.

When he walked in the front door of Tok High School, the young man was an unrecognizable entity. To put it bluntly, Bugsy wasn't in the mood to be trifled with. It didn't take too long for his teachers and the other high school students to notice that he was acting very differently. Bugsy was distracted, irritable, and emotional, and the usually meek and mild-mannered whipping boy broke out of his familiar role, ready to strike out against the place he hated so much. Although this was shocking to all around him, his rebelliousness serendipitously assisted in fulfilling his primary desire to get out of school and back over to the Parker House, where he really wanted to be.

Things came to a head in the boys' bathroom. Bugsy, who was still deep inside his own thoughts about the reporter, the general, the Japanese man, and the two alien monsters, forgot his tried-and-true survival strategy of never going into any room alone without knowing exactly where Jerry Zumquist and his pack of thugs were at that moment. Instead, he walked right into the bathroom and ran smack-dab into his nemeses, all of whom were still under the impression that they were the sharks and the diminutive loser now in front of them was the seal. It was at this exact moment that Bugsy decided to throw the *Wu Wei* principal out the window like a nasty, used cigarette butt. Words were exchanged, a fight broke out, and Bugsy alone walked out shortly afterwards.

When asked what had exactly transpired in the bathroom, Jerry Zumquist would later say, with a heavy lisp resulting from losing a few teeth and having had his jaw wired shut, "We got our athes kicked by Bruthe Lee!"

Upon discovery of the unconscious, injured, and beaten boys, Bugsy was immediately taken to the principal's office to face discipline. Principal Robert Osgood was uncertain exactly how to proceed. The unrepentant student sitting in front of him had never been in a lick of any trouble before, not once. Hell, the boy had never even been accused of raising his voice in school before this day, and the veteran school administrator felt – in spite of the severe physical pummeling of the seven other students just perpetrated in the restroom – as if the young boy, who'd reportedly been the victim of countless previous physical assaults from that same bullying group, probably deserved some leniency and the shot at a second chance.

Sensing that his opportunity to get suspended and be sent away from the one place he didn't want to be was slipping from him, Bugsy decided to drive the point home and make it easier on the poor principal. After having to listen to the man's cliché-filled lecture on how violence is never the solution, the teenager announced, "Why don't you take a flying fuck at the Moon, Principal Os-bad?"

Ira Morton arrived to pick up his suspended grandson and bring him home. The two sat in an uneasy silence as they drove over toward the Alaska Highway. Ira didn't have to ask *why* his grandson had kicked the shit out of his tormentors, and he refrained from asking *how* Bugsy had done it, for even Ira noticed the depth of the darkness in the boy's eyes. He knew that this was not the time to expect any kind of an explanation about much of anything. Even the way that teenager had entered the pickup truck and commanded his grandfather to drive him to his desired destination, like he was some kind of a NYC cabbie, was forgivable at this point. The older man knew better than to debate the matter, and he decided to just take his grandson where he wanted to go, no questions asked.

As Bugsy thanked his grandfather for the ride and jumped out of the cab of the truck, he realized he'd already fully shed all those inner demons that had materialized from their hiding spots within him and attempted to possess him. Whatever rage he felt toward the stupid shitheads at school whom he'd finally dealt with, or any disgust he felt toward the pathetically impotent principal, was gone; those negative emotions had blown away and burned off completely like a morning fog on a summer day as soon as he started walking over toward the office of the Parker House. Even his gait changed from a labored shuffle to an almost joyful skip.

Upon seeing him, Mayor Bishop inquired uncertainly, "Bugsy, what are you doing here? Isn't this a regular school day?"

"There was an...incident at school, Mayor Bishop. I got the afternoon off, so I thought I'd come in and help out here."

"Yuh, Bugsy, I sure might need your help. It's been a helluva morning so far, and it appears that I'll be away for the afternoon and maybe the evening."

The mayor proceeded to tell Bugsy the torrid details of the entangled events that had transpired since the young man had headed home the night before. Although somewhat innocent, the teenager was able to quickly ascertain that the roadside motel had been transformed from a cold pot on the back burner to a pressure cooker on high flame. During the night, the three strangers had each been extremely busy, but the television reporter had been the busiest. With a strongly inferred indictment about the sexual component to her behaviors, the mayor described how Eve had forged intimate relationships with the general, the mayor himself, the Japanese man – who turned out to be a fairly famous expert on giant monsters in his homeland, not merely a film advisor – and even a well-known local bush pilot by the name of Sarah Pretlusky.

Unsatisfied with a simple love triangle, Eve San-derborn had worked to create for herself what would have to be called a love parallelogram – or even love pentagon – to get what she wanted, which was transportation to He-Knew-Pat-Sajak.

The mayor sighed heavily and rested himself with his elbows atop the counter. He tried to smile his usual big grin, but there was no trace of happiness in what resulted.

"The outcome has been a horribly ensnared ball of yarn for all of us, Bugsy. But the good news is that Sarah's going to fly the five of us in her float-plane up to see the newly arrived cockroach in Circle and maybe witness the meet-up between the two monsters for ourselves today, so I guess it's all been worth it. I guess…"

Bugsy felt a pang of envy that he hadn't been included in the chance to see the monsters firsthand, not to mention the regret at having missed all of the steamy proceedings of the night and morning, but he was happy to be able to help out at the motel and assist the travelers as they prepared for what felt like a mission of the utmost importance. Playing a sec-ondary role was going to have to suffice.

A little later, as Bugsy made the rounds to gather up all of the garbage bags from the motel rooms, he could see that the cameraman was busy loading his prepped cameras and equipment into Mayor Bishop's rugged-looking Chevy Suburban. Near him,

Usotsuki also prepared to get into the vehicle, but the Japanese man was shooting a triad of scornful glances over at both General Richardson, who was busy at the payphone attempting to get in touch with NORAD, and at Mayor Bishop, who had the hood propped open as he stood atop a milk crate to reach into the engine and check the vehicle's oil levels, and then finally over at Eve Sanderborn's closed motel door. Dark clouds of melancholy drifted across the taut face of the *kaiju* hunter.

"Bugsy!"

The young man spun wildly to see who was saying his name, and the black plastic bag in his hands careened back and forth like the ball sack of a bucking bull. It was Eve Sanderborn, and she had a big and genuine smile on her face as she came out of her motel room.

"What are you doing here, young man? Aren't you supposed to be at school?"

"They gave me the afternoon and the next couple of days off, Ms. Sanderborn. Thought I'd come and help out with things here."

"You don't say. We're getting ready to head over to the airport. You know the pilot Sarah Pretlusky? Well, she is set to fly us up to Circle so we can put our eyes on those monsters. Whenever He-Knew-Pat-Sajak wakes up, it might continue on its way toward the cockroach, and we're gonna be there to see what the creature will do next. Either we'll see the two monsters fight or we may see them join forces –

whatever happens, we'll be there to catch it on film. We'll have the jump on the competition. I'm sure this story is going to get me a Pulitzer!"

The general's booming voice shattered the moment as he roared, "No, you cretin. I'm gonna nuke *your* goddamn ass!"

The older man violently struck the receiver of the phone upon the metal cradle hook several times. After a couple of blows, he seemed to tire from this expenditure of energy.

Eve didn't appear to be intimidated by this outburst as she asked him, "Are you having some problems getting through to NORAD, General?"

"Yes, Ms. Sanderborn, I am. Those limp-dicked morons continue to refuse to acknowledge my authority. I honestly don't understand it."

Mayor Bishop spoke without ever bringing his head out of the open hood of the big Chevy rig, and it appeared as if the vehicle was making a taunting remark at the general. "Maybe Henry Kissinger can help you. Maybe you should call him...collect."

"I already tried that, peckerneck! Damn Kissinger won't pick up either. I know he said this was going to be a clandestine operation, but I'd assumed that whenever I was ready to call in the fucking cavalry, he'd have my back. I'm at a loss as to what to do next."

When Usotsuki turned his head toward the general, his face had a completely impassive expression on it. He spoke with a deadpan delivery. "Is dropping dead out of the question?"

General Richardson instinctively reached for a weapon in his holster and the Japanese cryptozoologist braced for conflict.

Eve Sanderborn stamped her foot as she yelled out her admonishment. "Boys, boys, play nice. We need to work as a team to get what we're all so close to accomplishing. We each have a role to play in this thing. General, I'm counting on you, once we're in the air, to maybe obtain us total air clearance from the military, or at least give us enough time so that Sarah can get us up close to both monsters without having any air-to-air missiles knocking us out of the sky. Usotsuki, you're important because you should be able to figure out if He-Knew-Pat-Sajak looks like he's getting ready to fight against or join the Palmetto Bug Monster – such a diagnosis will be crucial for deciding where we go to film the next events for the whole world to see. And Mayor Bishop, you're essential because you're going to use your local pull to get us into the airport and up into the air in Sarah's plane without any problems. You see, we all need each other."

Mayor Bishop, General Richardson, and Usotsuki Shirinigatsuku all grumbled quietly to themselves like kindergarteners, but they seemed placated enough as to continue without incident. Bernie the cameraman hopped into the backseat of the Suburban and sat next to the Japanese man. Both seemed content to wait patiently while the rest of the group joined them. The mayor slammed the hood closed, removed the milk crate, and then got into the driver's seat and started the vehicle. The general stalked over from the pay phone and attempted to get into the passenger-side front seat, but was quickly informed by the others that that seat was where Eve was supposed to sit. Cursing under his breath, he got in and sat in the back seat next to the camera man and the Japanese monster expert.

As he jostled around in his seat like a restless bull inside a rodeo chute, he spit out, "Fucking DDE never had to ride around like this!"

Mayor Bishop turned to speak to the passengers in his vehicle. He looked just like Sergeant Orville Stanley Sacker in *The Adventure of Sherlock Holmes' Smarter Brother* as he said with far too much patronization, "Why don't you send a letter of complaint by registered mail to Henry Kissinger, General?"

General Richardson heard the two men next to him in the back seat chuckle to themselves, and his face reddened as he shouted out, "I've had about enough of all of you! You don't want to push me to my limit, men. Oh, you definitely don't want that!"

Looking for a second like Farrah Fawcett in an episode of *Charlie's Angels*, Eve Sanderborn put her hands on her hips and shouted toward the car, "Raise your hand if any of you *don't* want to go on this little field trip. No? No one is raising their hand? Good. Then shut the hell up and let's try to act like adults."

Bugsy took this as his cue to complete his rounds. He was disappointed at being left behind as the others went on their big adventure, and all of his movements were indicative of his dejection.

"Bugsy?"

The young man's head spun so quickly at the second mention of his name by the beautiful reporter that he was dizzy. He staggered a bit as he tried to calmly answer, "Uh, yes, Ms. Sanderborn?"

The television reporter smiled an impish grin as she cooed, "Why don't you come with us?"

"Oh, for the love of Pete!" thundered General Richardson. "We don't need the pipsqueak to come along. What purpose could he possibly serve in this endeavor?"

Eve looked over at the elderly military man, who had just complained so loudly that both Bernie the cameraman and Usotsuki had grimaced at the great volume of his voice, and she shook her head. She turned to face Bugsy again and then brought up her index finger suggestively to her lips and bit down gently on her fingernail as if she were contemplating something quite provocative. "No, General Richardson, I disagree. I think Bugsy's going to play a much bigger role in this all than we know. I can feel it – deep, deep *inside* of me."

Bugsy didn't need to hear any more. He dropped the garbage bags and scampered quickly over to the vehicle and stood next to the beautiful blonde television reporter. Mayor Bishop leaned across the front seat and spoke through the passenger window with some anxiety. "Actually, Ms. Sanderborn, Bugsy was supposed to handle things here at the motel to-day while I'm away."

Eve snapped her fingers. "Oh, Mayor Bishop, who do you *really* think is going to stop in for a room today? We'll be back before dark. The motel will be fine."

"There's no room in here for him. We're *konzatsu shita* in the back seat as it is."

The Japanese man's statement about being crowded was empirically true. Both the camera-man and the general were large men, and they both seemed to be attempting to take up as much space on the back seat as they physically could. Poor Usot-suki was more squished against the car door than a bag of *koshi-an*, the sweet and finely mashed red-bean paste of Japanese cuisine.

Eve put her arm around the teenager. "Bugsy can sit next to me in the front seat, between me and Mayor Bishop. There's plenty of room up here. Plus, it's a very short drive to the airport."

As Bugsy hopped up and took his privileged posi-tion, the other men in the vehicle acted like toddlers who'd just been told that they weren't going to get an ice cream cone. All of them could feel that Eve San-derborn was close to kicking them out, which meant that there was the bona fide possibility that they'd miss out on seeing the monsters for themselves, so they held their tongues. However, it would be fair to state they all were clearly pouting at the positioning of the tiny teenager in such a desired location.

The drive to the airport took less time than it had taken to get the occupants into the large vehicle, and with a bit of smooth talking by the mayor, they by-passed the concerned security guard and drove right up to Sarah Pretlusky's aircraft. The pilot was doing a quick safety check of her floatplane, which was painted in the same color scheme and patterning as a faded Swedish flag. The woman was the spitting image of the actress Susan Clark in the movie *Amelia Earhart* and exuded a perfect mix of toughness and femininity. Rushed introductions were made and then the pilot roughly herded the passengers into her plane.

General Richardson balked. "There are too many of us. We won't fit in this death trap."

Sarah Pretlusky patted the metallic skin of the plane as she attempted to soothe the man. "General, this is a De Havilland DHC-2 Beaver, considered to be the best bush plane ever built. And it has a capacity of six passengers and two crew. Eve is going to be my copilot today and help me with the flight up to Circle, and you five will easily fit in the seats. Now, we don't have time to dick around. Please get in and let's get going."

Eve bit the bottom of her lip and then said with a giggle, "I'm going to be helping you with your Beaver...again."

It was decided by Sarah that, to balance out the weight evenly in the aircraft, Bugsy, Usotsuki, and Bernie should occupy the rear seat and the mayor and the general should share the second seat. Although this made the trio more cramped and meant that Bugsy was stuck in the middle and without a window view, the general had stated plainly that he got airsick when he couldn't see all around him, and no one wanted to be barfed on during the flight. With sour faces, all of the passengers put on their noise-cancelling headphones with attached microphones, nifty devices that made it possible to communicate once in flight. No one other than Sarah spoke as the plane taxied to the runway and took off.

The one-hour trip up to the area around Circle, Alaska, was rather uneventful, although Sarah, once she'd gotten the bush plane airborne, descended again to fly a few meters above the treetops. This strategy of flying extremely low in altitude to their destination not only took away any of the impressive scenery that the passengers might have wanted to see, it also meant that the flight was a white-knuckled affair for many of them. The only person to say anything on this matter was the general. After they came perilously close to the crown of a large conifer, he exclaimed, "Whatever we are paying you to fly us up north, Ms. Pretlusky, we should undoubtedly also include the fee for the involuntary arboreal proctologist appointment that you're administering upon us with this flight through the treetops."

The pilot chuckled at his comment, but then said confidently, "This is the only way to fly into a sensitive area without attracting too much attention,

General. The last thing I want to do is give one of those trigger-happy flyboys a target. Don't worry, this is the way I usually get anywhere – and I've had some practice."

"Well, my rectum certainly hasn't," General Richardson said with a cough.

"Point taken, sir. Oh, my, that might not be the best way to phrase that retort, huh?" Sarah replied with a quick cackle.

When they'd reached the Essie Creek, the pilot brought the plane almost down to the water level to follow the small tributary to the Charlie River, and then followed it all the way to the Yukon River before banking northward toward Circle. The sharp turning and rolling caused the occupants to groan and utter whispered complaints and curses each time their bodies and heads were thrown about with the force of the sudden movements, but General Richardson excitedly boomed out, "Ah, Ms. Pretlusky, this reminds me of when I took part in that naval operation Game Warden. We used a fleet of U.S. Navy Seawolf helicopters to support river patrol boats to keep the Viet Cong from controlling the Mekong Delta waterways. I've never felt as alive as when we tracked down those sampans and blew them out of the water! You have some major flying skills! We could have used a pilot like you in 'Nam."

Sarah smiled sweetly at the general as she spoke into the headset microphone. "Well, General Richardson, thank you for the compliment. And I *do* have some major flying skills. But you know what I don't have?"

"What?"

Sarah winked as she answered him. "A penis. And that's why I couldn't have been a military pilot in 'Nam, sir."

The general nodded appreciatively. "True story, ma'am. But I hear tell that a chickie by the name of Second Lieutenant Sally Murphy got her wings in time to be in that war, except that the powers that be kept her safely within only noncombat areas. Mark my words, someday soon you women will get your chance to kill just as many people during wars as we men."

Sarah beamed a big smile. "That day can't come quick enough, sir."

This disturbing conversation only enhanced the discomfort of the other passengers inside the bucking and twisting plane, and their groans and epithets grew in volume.

The plane suddenly came upon a place where the riverbanks opened up wide to accommodate the islands in a small delta-like area, and the pilot banked the aircraft hard to the right and rose in elevation to get above the short white spruces that escorted the river. The giant cockroach could clearly be seen standing in the center of the circular area of destruction it had made, and its appearance caused everyone to utter gasps of surprise. The monster's attention seemed riveted upon something unseen off to the west, and it took no notice of any of the circling military aircraft or the approach of the Beaver float-plane carrying the Tok contingency.

General Richardson pointed at the monster. "Would you look at that ugly motherfucker! I wish I had a nuke strapped to the bottom of this plane. I'd kill that bug, right here and now."

Mayor Bishop quickly inquired, "Wouldn't that kill us too, General?"

This question was followed by as much silence as could happen in a noisy bush plane flying roughly over the Alaskan wilderness.

The general somberly uttered to the group, "Some sacrifices are necessary. All soldiers understand that."

Before anyone could remind the military man that none of the other people in the plane were actually soldiers, Eve Sanderborn excitedly commanded her cameraman to start capturing the scene.

As the sound of the camera became audible, Usotsuki said in a solemn near-whisper, "Oh, the Palmetto Bug Monster has created a *dohyō*."

"A what?" Eve Sanderborn inquired.

"The traditional circle used as a sumo ring."

"Well, Tojo, what the hell does *that* mean?" General Richardson growled.

The Japanese man was too focused on the scene of the gigantic cockroach standing in the middle of the prepared circle to take offense at this racist comment. He nodded knowingly, and then motioned with his head toward the monster. "It means that the Palmetto Bug Monster is waiting for He-Knew-Pat-Sajak, but to engage in combat. I'd bet one of my *tamakin* that we're about to see the two creatures fight, not join forces."

Just then, the plane's radio crackled to life. "Unidentified aircraft approaching the monster from the southeast, this is the United States Air Force F-16A circling you. You are to alter course and fly outside the three-mile security zone established around Circle immediately. Failure to comply will only result in your death, either by one of my missiles or by the monster's activity. Over."

Sarah Pretlusky calmly responded to this threat. "We have General Buchanan Richardson onboard this aircraft, and he's given us the authority to fly in this airspace. Over."

"I don't care if you have the ghost of Major General Claire L. Chennault of the Flying Tigers, ma'am, you must turn back and return to wherever you came from today. Over."

Sarah was not to be denied. "Negatory, sir. We are on a rescue mission today. There's a pregnant Eskimo woman who's about to give birth, and we need to grab her and get her and her family out of harm's way and to a real hospital in the south. We're touching down on the far side of the big island off of town to make the rendezvous. Then we're out of here! Over."

There was a moment of silence before the Air Force pilot radioed again. "Roger that. Grab her and go. There's some major shit about to go down here, ma'am. You don't wanna be anywhere near here when it does. Over."

"Roger, we'll be on our way as soon as she's aboard and we can take off. Over."

Sarah looked over at Eve. "Well, I bought us some time. Those military wing nuts are always a little soft whenever you mention life and death situations involving pregnant Natives. I'll get you as close as I can, and hopefully, those guys will forget all about us when things start going down. If not, we might have to figure out other ways to survive this trip. Hold onto your socks!"

The pilot suddenly maneuvered the stick as if she were trying to cram it into her crotch, and the plane shot straight up into the air. Then she pushed the stick away and down, and the aircraft turned in such a way that the wing appeared to be ready to slice down into the river below.

Sarah Pretlusky said nonchalantly, "This ain't gonna be pretty and sure as shit ain't gonna be too comfortable. Hang on!"

The involuntary chorus of shrieks and screams from the passengers made the small plummeting floatplane sound more like a common loon as it splashed heavily into the waters of the Yukon River and skidded to a stop near the banks of the large island. Sarah shut off the engine and then deftly hopped out onto the pontoon to leap ashore with the plane's anchor, which she planted into the gravelly riverbank of the island. While she did this, the others quickly scrambled out of the aircraft and made their way to dry land.

Instantly, Eve and Bernie set themselves up to get the best shots of the giant cockroach, which towered above the silent Alaskan landscape like some kind of mahogany Colossus of Rhodes. The rest of the group gathered around them and stared at the massive monster in awe. Seeing the Palmetto Bug Monster from the relative safety of the plane had created a false sense of security, but now that they all were standing so close to the leviathan, they felt very small, very insignificant, and very much in danger. The reality of having a front-row seat to whatever was going to happen between He-Knew-Pat-Sajak and the Palmetto Bug Monster in Circle, Alaska, now made their internal anal sphincters (IAS) and their external anal sphincters (EAS) clench tightly.

Usotsuki stood apart from the group. Inexplicably, he suddenly began to hear Akira Ifukube's "Main Godzilla Theme" playing in his head. This leitmotif was the iconic musical characteristic in all of the Godzilla movies, and it was intended to create a sense of awe at the power of the fictional monster. He had to acknowledge that the classical musical piece worked incredibly well in this currently real situation as well as it did when watching an actor inside of a monster suit. The massive, unstoppable monster in front of them certainly merited a theme song that bespoke it being the instrument of the planet's termination. Usotsuki could not stop himself from humming a few bars of the familiar monster movie song loud enough for the others to hear.

月とすっぽん

tsukitosuppon

The Moon and a soft-shell turtle.

He-Knew-Pat-Sajak awoke with a start, and the monster gecko stood up as if prepared for an immediate fight. But to the dozens of residents hunkered down inside their houses in Center, Alaska, it appeared as if the giant creature suddenly was unsure what to do next. It scanned the horizon all around it and then looked to the west as if it had forgotten something valuable back there. Then, with the faintest sounds of the Palmetto Bug Monster's hisses being carried on the wisps of the wind, the massive lizard seemed to find its resolve again and proceeded to rumble quickly east in the direction of Circle.

He-Knew-Pat-Sajak's march, which was facilitated by following the cleared space of the Steese Highway, led it right to where the Palmetto Bug Monster was waiting patiently in the middle of its prepared battle site. As soon as the two monsters saw one another, they began calling loudly toward each other – the massive gecko issuing a series of clicks and barks while the gigantic cockroach chirped and hissed in rebuttal. The blaring exchange was quite impressive, but it was clear to all who witnessed the event that the two monsters had just proffered calls of differing intensities. To most, the giant gecko's vociferations sounded somewhat sapped, but the monumental cockroach extolled itself with a power and strength that was earthshaking and terrifying.

Without pausing, He-Knew-Pat-Sajak entered the defoliated ring and then stopped. The two monsters faced one another and then they exchanged a second round of their conversational altercation. Both appeared to be content with bellowing at the other.

Meanwhile, from the relative safety of their distanced island vantage point, each member of the brave and ambitious monster-chasing group had a different reaction to what they were seeing and they resembled some kind of medieval drama that was using a multiple-setting stage technique. All six people were simultaneously in view, each occupying their own mansion around this unlocalized *platea*.

Eve and Bernie instantly started filming the event. The blonde reporter used her most sultry and serious voice to emphasize the fact that they were either witnessing the end of the threat to the planet or a final collaboration between the two giant agents of doom to bring about the end of humanity. She ominously added that only time would tell which outcome was going to result.

After the initial shock of seeing the two behemoths meeting nearby, General Richardson pulled

Put a Bug in Your Ear (Mimi ni mushi o ireru)

out his holstered weapon to "convince" Sarah Pretlusky that they needed to use the plane's radio to
call the President of the United States and give the
coordinates for an immediate nuclear strike on the
site. He was now wholly convinced that only a well-
aimed A-bomb would wipe out the two threats in
one shot. And although she was certain that the old
man was waving a harmless toy weapon at her, Sarah had the feeling that it made the most sense to
head back toward her aircraft in case things went
south enough to warrant a speedy retreat.

For Mayor Bishop, seeing the impossible size and
sheer destructive ability of the two creatures firsthand was too much for the short bug-eyed man. He
started backing away from the scene with the realization that there was little chance for the survival
of Alaska or the world...no matter what. If the two
creatures fought one another, he now understood
the battle would ravage countless miles of forest before a victor emerged triumphant. And if it was the
cockroach, there'd be no stopping it. But if the two
creatures did unite into a single force, there was no
way around the fact that the planet was wholly and
undisputedly doomed.

Seeing the two real *kaijus* took Usotsuki Shirinigatsuku's breath away, but then the veteran Japanese
cryptozoologist regained his composure. He quickly
assessed that, although the creatures were equal in
height and mass, the gecko appeared tired-looking,
pallid, and even a bit washed-out, whereas the cock-

roach gave the impression that it was quite strong and robust. There was no way to deny that, if the two monsters fought, it would not be a contest of equals. In fact, he knew, then and there, that the gecko had no chance. He could not help himself from thinking about the old Japanese saying *Mudana doryoku o suru, kachime no nai tatakai o suru*. Roughly translated, this means "Don't waste your efforts. Fight within your chances of victory."

Bugsy was a hot mess as soon as He-Knew-Pat-Sajak came into view. Overwhelmed by a wave of unexplainable emotions that flooded him when the gecko approached the ruined area of Circle, he ran toward the water, screaming out what, at first, sounded like gibberish. He bounded into the cameraman and the reporter, almost knocking them down, and thereafter he received a litany of angry chastisements from them. Yet his emotional outbursts continued.

"He doesn't know what to do," Bugsy screamed. "He knows he should charge, but he realizes he cannot win. He's *scared*! He's *uncertain*! He's so *confused*!"

Eve and Bernie tried to get the teenager to quiet down by reminding him that he was single-handedly interrupting the coverage of one of the human species' biggest news stories *ever*, but Bugsy refused to be quiet or to stop moving.

Mayor Bishop, sensing that this was the moment that his intervention might buy him another round

of passion later on from the beautiful television reporter, attempted to tackle the hysterical boy and
subdue him. The result was that he merely hopped
onto the teenager's back and clung to him for dear
life as Bugsy continued to shout out and act so ag-
itatedly. The two instantly resembled midget wres-
tlers engaged in a bout on the banks of the Yukon.

Concurrently, back inside the monster fight are-
na, He-Knew-Pat-Sajak made a sudden rush at the
cockroach. Wholly unsurprised, the Palmetto Bug
Monster sidestepped the attack and then swung its
mighty foreleg at the gecko's head as it flew past.
The sound of contact was like a double-headed axe
being swung into a soggy piece of firewood.

The blow not only drew blood, but greatly
stunned the lizard. It crashed to the ground with a
tremor-causing force, and then it struggled to stand
up. Even as it successfully did this, He-Knew-Pat-
Sajak was wobbly and uncertain. The Palmetto Bug
Monster bounded straight at the gecko, but feigned
another attack, and attempting to dodge this faux
assault, He-Knew-Pat-Sajak reared too far back, lost
its balance, and fell embarrassingly onto its back.
Mercilessly, the bug darted in and began whaling on
the lizard's stomach with its forelegs and midlegs as
if it were beating on a Japanese *taiko*. The gecko's
calls became laced with shrieks of pain.

The cockroach suddenly stopped his attack and
moved back to the edge of the combat area. It let out

a series of loud clicks and hisses as it turned its back on the wounded lizard lying prone on the ground. It seemed to most that the bug was so confident of its win that it needed to do a quick celebration dance.

Not too far away, at the southern tip of their island vantage point, Usotsuki spoke to no one in particular. "Hmm, I have seen this many times. The *gokiburi* is gloating. In nearly every Toho Co., Ltd. movie, the monsters always take time to celebrate their victory prematurely. It's usually the last chance for the opponent to get in a surprise blow and change the course of the fight. It always becomes the time for the counterattack."

Eve and Bernie had long realized that their perfect chance to record the fight between the two monsters was going to be anything but perfect. Between the nearly constant, incoherent shouts of the teenager, the rather odd verbalizations of the Marty Feldman lookalike who was still muckled onto the back of the young man as he tried to placate him with humorous comments and misplaced anecdotes, the running commentary of the Japanese man, who now sounded more like an avid monster movie fan than a real scientist, and the wildly inappropriate yelling coming from the epic, ongoing wrestling match between General Richardson and Sarah Pretlusky – which had started out as an attempt to take away the fake gun from the strangely strong senior citizen, but had now turned into a defensive resistance against all of his inappropriate attempts to grope the female bush pilot – there was definitely going to be the need to edit the sound of the recording of the monsters' battle before they submitted it for national release.

Always the professionals, though, they continued to film and comment on what was playing out in front of them regardless of the continuous distractions going on around them.

Bugsy finally directed his rants directly toward the injured lizard. "Get up! Stand up and get in a quick blow while its back is turned. You must strike while the iron is hot."

Eve and Bernie flinched because the boy's voice cut out so loudly through the chaotic scene playing out across the river that there was the sudden chance the cockroach had heard him. Recording such a career-making event as this wouldn't amount to much if the participants ended up as a gooey mess on the underside of the Palmetto Bug Monster's feet. The reporter and her cameraman each brusquely implored the teenager to shut the fuck up.

He-Knew-Pat-Sajak slowly struggled to get back on its feet. With some effort, it finally stood, uneasily, and with little warning, it began to trot toward the Palmetto Bug Monster, which was still facing away from it. Unfortunately, as the gecko attempted to grab the bug's head from behind, the cockroach slipped out of the hold and yanked the lizard's legs out from underneath it. In an act of desperation, He-

Knew-Pat-Sajak grabbed hold of its opponent's leg and would not let go. It even appeared as if it had resorted to biting the cockroach's tibia. The Palmetto Bug Monster took this opportunity to whale several thunderous blows down upon the vulnerable gecko's stomach, causing it so much pain that it released the leg and then lay motionless on the ground.

The Palmetto Bug Monster reached down and grabbed He-Knew-Pat-Sajak by the head and forcibly lifted the injured monster to its feet. To all, the now defenseless massive lizard teetering in front of the victorious insect appeared to be barely conscious and just waiting for the bug to deliver the death blow. Taking its time, the cockroach backed up a step before shooting a blast out of the bioweapon ray gun in its abdomen directly into the gecko's chest.

The shot sent the lizard flying backward and onto the ground, where it lay still and lifeless. A smoldering column of smoke wafted up from the impact spot of the ray and drifted away in the gentle Alaskan breeze. The cockroach lifted its head to face the sky and trumpeted victory hisses and chirps to the heavens.

While Eve whispered into her microphone about the fate of the world being decided by the defeat of He-Knew-Pat-Sajak, Usotsuki pronounced the gecko dead in his emotionless analysis. Sarah and General Richardson had returned to the group, each wearing disheveled clothing from their tussle. The pilot had eventually disarmed the general and now had his arms pinioned behind his back, controlling him like a prisoner in police custody, but the old military man wasn't resisting her too much because he'd somehow become transfixed by the long, slender silver pendant that the woman wore around her neck. Mayor Bishop had dropped off of Bugsy's back and now stood with his mouth agape at what had just played out. When he professed aloud that they were all doomed, Sarah mentioned that it might be time to get in the plane, before that came to pass.

Bugsy, who was now sobbing uncontrollably, waded into the river. He shouted at the downed gecko, "Get up! You need to get the hell out of there. You need to run and hide so you can recuperate. Do something! *Do anything!* Spit in the bug's goddamn eyes if you have to – just get the hell out of there!"

General Richardson barked out what the entire group was thinking at that very moment. "Shut up, you insane little twerp! If you get us killed because that damn bug hears your crazy ranting, I'm going to make my last act on Earth be the nuking of your ass, you tiny peckerneck."

Sarah began herding the group back toward the plane, but Bernie continued to get the camera shots and Eve still narrated what was going to happen now that the gecko had been killed and the cockroach was free to continue its terrorizing of the Earth. It was not easy getting everyone back into their seats for the quick flight back to Tok, but the veteran pilot mixed enough encouragement and blunt force to finally get everyone aboard.

He-Knew-Pat-Sajak was not dead. It slowly turned over and, unnoticed by the cockroach, got up with great effort and pain. Bleeding, disoriented, and lurching from its walloping, the gecko slowly shuffled toward the Palmetto Bug Monster, which continued reveling in the apparent vanquishing of its foe. When the bug finally realized that the gecko was still alive and standing right next to it, the creature turned its head to look directly at the lizard with what could be called cold malice.

Without warning, He-Knew-Pat-Sajak spit a glob into the eyes of the cockroach. The gooey mass covered the creature's face and instantly caused it not only a sustained moment of blindness, but also enough pain to evoke a loud shriek. In the interlude created by his act, the injured lizard limped toward the river, looked down at the small floatplane by the nearby island, and then fled down the river valley, using a quick change of its skin color to camouflage itself seamlessly in with the foliage of the surrounding forest.

Sarah started up the plane and sped toward the middle of the river to head into the wind for takeoff. Eve commanded her to get them airborne so they could circle the cockroach, but the pilot of the F-16 came over the radio again and announced that, unless the floatplane headed directly south, he was going to personally knock them out of the sky. When Sarah attempted to continue with the fabrication about the pregnant Eskimo woman's family being nearby, the pilot responded that he didn't care if they had the pregnant Virgin Mary aboard and they were leaving Joseph and the three wise men behind – they were to head away from what was going to be a very active military action site in a moment or two.

With no other choice, Sarah headed the plane south and toward Tok.

For the five adult passengers in the floatplane, the flight home was traveled in complete silence. The impressive defeat of He-Knew-Pat-Sajak by the Palmetto Bug Monster created a varied response for each of them, and each sat and stewed about it all the way home. For Bernie, he'd gotten some absolutely fantastic shots of the monsters' battle, and he was confident that the footage would secure himself and his gorgeous reporter worldwide recognition and fame. For Eve, she could almost taste the awards and accolades that were going to come her way from being the only member of the media to capture the epic fight, and her mind was focused solely on the best way to get the story to KTLA and what dress to wear at the Pulitzer award ceremony. For General Richardson, as a military man, he was neither totally happy nor sad that the lizard had gotten its ass kicked, but with only one gigantic monster left needing to get nuked out of existence, his job had certainly gotten a lot easier. For Mayor Bishop, he'd become deeply saddened by what he'd seen because he'd adopted He-Knew-Pat-Sajak as Alaska's own. After all, the creature had crawled out of an Aleutian volcano and then wandered around the wilds of the state, and he had always hated whenever anything or anyone from "Outside" bested an Alaskan.

None of them took any more notice of the teenager. Actually, they did everything in their power to give the boy some space. After his bizarre behavior at the fight between the monsters and his current sobbing inconsolably in the back seat, no one was quite sure what to say or do to help him. Instead, they all stared straight forward and traveled the trip deep within their own heads as they mulled over the events that they'd just witnessed and the dire ramifications they would have for the future.

明日は明日の風が吹く

ashita wa ashita no kaze ga fuku

The winds of tomorrow will blow tomorrow.

If anyone on Earth had had their telescopes aimed at the Moon at the specific time that the silver droplet-shaped spacecraft had taken off from its dark side and then headed directly toward them, they would have known that the planet was going to be visited by yet another alien presence. With some forewarning, proper preparations could have been made. But, alas, no one was looking up at the sky anymore – everyone's attention was entirely focused on the devastation that the giant cockroach had laid upon the American Midwest and the wide path of carnage leading all the way up to Alaska.

On the other hand, with the spacecraft traveling at an unfathomable speed as it hit the atmosphere, maybe its unannounced arrival was really a good thing. The sudden appearance of yet another extraterrestrial object falling from the sky probably would've only caused another round of panic from an already gun-shy earthling population.

To be fair, nothing good had come from the sky as of late.

The alien ship, which appeared like a shiny teardrop the size of a small house, descended upon Tok, Alaska, and landed squarely in the middle of the parking lot behind the Parker House. While it was nearly silent as it maneuvered slowly to touch down, the residents in the roadside motel were all aware that something unusual was happening outside, and they came out to watch what was going on. Upon seeing the landed capsule in front of them, the gathered group became eerily silent.

This assembled welcome wagon included none other than General Richardson, Eve, Bernie the cameraman, Bugsy, Mayor Bishop, Usotsuki Shirinigatsuku, and Bugsy's grandfather Ira Morton, who had been called to help with the still-despondent teenager. They gathered around the spacecraft at a safe distance and stared with a stunned anticipation as to what was going to happen next.

Before the arrival of the Palmetto Bug Monster, most people around the globe had maintained their rigid and unshakeable belief systems – as to what was real and what was unreal – with such certainty that it bordered on arrogance. However, the appearance of the massive space cockroach and its unbelievably destructive rampage had blown apart all of their tenets, shattered all of their ideologies, and stretched the very limits of their reality to the breaking point. Now that the giant bug walked around the place, blowing up shit, there was a new shared sense that anything was possible, or more precisely, nothing that had been believed prior to that to be fantastical or mythical or nonsensical was currently off the table of actually taking place.

That being said, for the gathered group of intrepid monster-chasers, the sudden appearance of a silver extraterrestrial vessel was like a big meaty bone being dropped into the feeding dish of a starving dog. General Richardson immediately began to calculate the timing and the intensity of the nuclear weapon strike he was going to order if the alien presence turned out to be hostile; Eve and Bernie instinctively began to document the event as the gorgeous television reporter quietly narrated the filming of the second biggest story that they'd ever been given; the Japanese cryptozoologist was such a big fan of Godzilla movies that he knew the introduction of an alien race was essential for a good monster story, and he secretly hoped that it was going to be the eerily sexy Kilaaks from the movie *Destroy All Monsters* rather than the emotionless yet cool-looking Xiliens from the movie *Invasion of Astro-Monster*, Mayor Bishop was calculating how much he could charge an alien to be a hotel guest; and Bugsy was hoping that the appearance of an alien might shift the balance of power in favor of the giant gecko.

The silence of the group, other than Eve whispering sultrily into her microphone, was shattered when a section of the spaceship's silver skin suddenly slid open and revealed a doorway. A sleek walkway extended down to the ground, and soon after, the sole occupant of the vessel came bounding out to stand in front of the gathered group. To all present, the alien appeared to be a starkly naked Neanderthal man. The heavy-browed individual was quite shaggy, with a mane of long hair and a thick beard framing his wide face. His hairiness and unabashed nakedness were somewhat discomforting. The glans of his flaccid phallus poked out of the thick fur of his crotch like the cap of a common stinkhorn mushroom (*Phallus impudicus*) sprouting from a dying moss bed.

The next few moments were understandably quite tense. With the television crew quietly recording what was occurring, the rest of the group remained frozen in place. As for the Neanderthal-like alien, after he'd initially made a slightly aggressive movement toward the gathering, which closely resembled the start of a body charge by a dominant male silverback gorilla, he'd stopped and stood as still as a statue. His expressive eyes scanned the individuals, the buildings, and the other elements of the landscape in front of him. He arched one of his pronounced eyebrows and slowly backed up the walkway and into the entranceway of the spacecraft.

Even though there was a growing sense of unease at the moment, the camera continued to roll and Eve aptly described everything that was taking place. The alien stopped just inside the doorway, and he now produced a silver wire from amongst his body hair and extended this toward the wall of the chamber in which he stood. He plugged it into a nearby unseen outlet and then stood perfectly still as he remained connected to the wall for several moments. Throughout all of this, the onlookers remained motionless and wordless as they watched what was unfolding.

The Neanderthal-looking man unplugged himself and put the wire wherever it had originally been stored. He seemed to nod to himself, which was a rather odd gesture to make in those circumstances, and then he reached for a raspberry-colored coverall hanging nearby. He put this on and confidently advanced down the walkway once more to address the group.

"Greetings, earthlings. I'm hoping to get a second chance to make a good first impression on this planet, by starting over. I'm sorry, but, through no fault of my own, we apparently got our new relationship off on the wrong foot, and we need to rewind and start again. Actually, it feels like I need to do something I believe you modern earthlings call 'some damage control.'"

The Neanderthal exhaled loudly through his large and wide nose, before flashing a broad smile that was more akin to what a used car salesman might show to a prospective victim...customer.

"Hello to you all. My name is Baku, and I come in peace. I'm an amazingly wonderful android from the planet Shxtor, and I've been sent to assist in the survival of your planet. My astonishing mission is to help defeat the Noosbit bioweapon, which we've code-named Haag – but I see that you've given it the rather peculiar name of the Palmetto Bug Monster – which has invaded your planet. My role, and I plan to play it oh-so-beautifully, is to engage the Shxtor countermeasure weapon, which was wisely planted on this planet in a volcano as a defense for when-ever it was that the Noosbit threat came here, and get it prepared to defeat the other monster. We've code-named our defensive weapon as Moog, but I also see that you call it He-Knew-Pat-Sajak. I must say that the ship's computers and the truly inspir-ing artificial intelligence within me are all completely stumped as to why you've chosen this moniker for the creature, but that's a topic for another day. Any-how, I will guide the Moog to take care of the Haag and then I will leave your planet, gloriously heading off into the sunset after saving you and your entire world."

He paused to look directly into the eyes of each of the humans in front of him. "Alright, enough with the unimportant explanations. It's time for me to get down to business. Who is the leader of this group? Who gets the purest of joys in meeting me today?"

General Richardson took two crisp steps forward and stopped. He turned his chin to point in the di-rection of the alien in front of him and gave what his troops called his "Patton's Glare." Looking overly angry and stern, the general squinted his eyes and remained silent for a moment too long.

"As the highest-ranked military man here, I am the leader. My name is General Richardson. What are the terms of your surrender, alien?"

"Greetings, General Richardson. No surrender, I just need to be pointed in—"

"Now, hold on a sec there, Beetle Bailey. As mayor of this here town of Tok, *I'm* the leader. Just 'cause you showed up in your uniform and declared yourself to be the second coming of MacArthur doesn't give you any authority over the rest of us. As the only elected official here, I guess that makes me the person that you need to talk to, Mr. Baku. My name is Mayor Bishop."

"Greetings, Mayor Bishop. I just need to be..."

Pulling his weapon out of its holster and displaying it proudly to the gathered group, the general began a look-at-me moment to establish his dominance.

"Well, Mayor Bishop, I guess *this* makes me the leader. I'm in control here, and don't forget it."

The mayor put his hands on his hips and grinned at the older man as he pointed out, "Um, General Richardson, that's a squirt gun."

Eve Sanderborn chortled loudly at this, and her mirth at the expense of the elderly military man caught everyone's ear. They all turned to stare at her with a tinge of judgment at her childish reaction.

General Richardson, now staring at the black water-pistol in his hands like it was a poisonous snake, yelled out, "That goddamn Kissinger – he's a nasty Kraut billy goat! I'm gonna *zerquetschen* his ass when I get my hands on him."

Baku took a step forward. "Ah, good, now that we've established this moment of anarchy here in terms of leadership on this planet, let's get down to brass tacks, as you humans are apparently so oft to say. Regardless of who here wants to be the top dog, could *someone* just point me in the direction of the Moog...He-Knew-Pat-Sajak. Has it sprung into action and headed in the direction of the Haag...er, the Palmetto Bug Monster, to take care of business yet? Oh, I do hope that I'm not too late to help guide it to destroy that piece of Noosbit space trash."

General Richardson pointed his water pistol threateningly at the Neanderthal as he sneered, "Ha! Your creature hasn't sprung into anything yet, alien. First it stumbled around in the fucking forest like a drunken sailor about five thousand clicks *away* from the bug threat while that giant cockroach destroyed several cities of this great country of ours. It was the Palmetto Bug Monster that brought the fight up here to Alaska, not your next-to-useless lizard. Not only that, the goddamn bug just kicked the living shit out of your supposed superweapon yesterday – wiped the floor with its giant reptile ass, to be more specific."

Baku tilted his shaggy head at the general's blunt comment. He furrowed up his prominent brow and seemed to be calculating something inside his football-shaped head.

"That cannot be right. Nothing you've reported fits into the defined, proper, bioweapon protocols. Not at all. Hm, I wonder what's going on?"

It was at this moment that Eve Sanderborn decided to actively capture her story. She got her cameraman's attention as she smoothly sidled closer to the front of the group, pointing her handheld microphone toward the alien like it was a lance.

"My name is Eve Sanderborn and I'm a reporter from KTLA, Mr. Baku. I have a few questions that I feel the American people deserve an answer to."

The android waved his hands in front of it in the potentially universal signal of *not now*. "I'm sorry, but I really need to be led directly to the weapon to do an assessment of it and get the defense of your planet truly started. I apologize for any rudeness, Ms. Sanderborn, but my divine plan of saving Earth does take priority over your need to get a good story."

Baku was attempting to make eye contact with anyone else in the group in order to finally be shown to the Moog to possibly do a needed reboot of it, but the young blonde reporter, undeterred, expertly moved her head to intercept all of his glances and continued undaunted.

"Like, why do you look like a caveman when you've clearly implied that you're an advanced alien android from another planet?"

Baku sighed heavily. It was becoming clear that this female earthling could not be ignored, so he faced his inquisitor directly and inhaled deeply before speaking. "In my haste to expedite the rescuing of your world, and the saving of billions of human lives, Ms. Sanderborn, I *might* have rushed straight from my 'sleep-state' into action without plugging in and getting the latest updates from my ship's computers. You see, when my base on the dark side of your moon was established about fifty thousand of your Earth years ago, the predominant humanoid species of this planet was the Neanderthal. Assuming that a Noosbit assault of this place was imminent, I was given this handsome synthetic skin costume cover to go over my stunning metallic skeleton and innovative internal microcomputer processors to fit in with the creatures I was to interact with, whenever I was activated. Unfortunately, for some reason still unknown to me, the Noosbit attack seems to have been very delayed. Anyhoo, because I was in such a rush to be the beloved savior of your world, I skipped the crucial download from the Shxtor computer that has been monitoring this planet and your species during this span of time of waiting. It became obvious, however, as soon as I took my first step out of my spacecraft that you humans have undergone some impressive changes during that period of delay, and regrettably, I mistakenly approached you all in the appearance of an unclothed and nonverbal Neanderthal ambassador. As soon as I correctly ascertained my error, I returned to my ship and plugged myself into my ship's computer to upload all of the proper languages and cultural norms of the more modern creatures standing in front of me. I must say that I'm now beginning to wonder if this whole exchange wouldn't have been a helluva lot easier if your species had retained its less communicative nature. Nonetheless, with my exquisite appearance now explained and my supreme purpose identified, can *someone* point me in the direction of the Moog, please?"

Eve thrust her microphone at the Neanderthal like she was parrying with an epee. "Did you just call the alien invaders 'News Bits', Mr. Baku?"

"No, Ms. Sanderborn, they are Noosbits. That's N-O-O-S-B-I-T-S."

Eve seemed nonplussed. "Uh-huh, and why do the Noosbits want to attack our planet with a giant cockroach, Mr. Baku?"

The reporter clearly was not going to give up. She'd positioned herself in front of both Mayor Bishop and General Richardson, and she was now maneuvering her sculpted body in such a manner as to physically demand the answers to her questions. The alien appeared to deflate from having to answer her, but he addressed the microphone directly.

"Because your planet exists, Ms. Sanderborn. The Noosbits are a species of sadistic space conquerors who want to possess everything that they can throughout the entire universe. They are the ultimate consumers. To satisfy their intense appetite, they came up with a foolproof system designed to take planets without any loss to their military forces. They send out their bioweapons to the various targeted worlds to tenderize them for an easy takeover, and then, with all of the inhabitants ultimately decimated by their monsters, the Noosbits are then free to come in and take whatever resources the mostly lifeless floating rocks have to offer. It's nothing personal. It's just the way that they get whatever they want."

"These Noosbits must be terrifying warrior giants to be so feared throughout the Universe," General Richardson growled. He seemed excited by the notion of taking on a worthy opponent.

Baku pursed his lips. "Um, no. They're actually a short blue-skinned people, about yea high." Here the caveman put his hand level with the top of his diaphragm.

"What?" the general crackled. "Are you saying that our planet is being threatened by a bunch of little *blue* people? Are you serious? We're being pushed to the edge of extinction by some kind of intergalactic group of Smurfs?"

"The *oni* are blue ogres found in Japanese folklore, General-san. They are usually depicted as being quite fierce," Usotsuki said with a definitive nod.

General Richardson spun to look at the Japanese cryptozoologist as if he'd just insulted his mother. "I don't care about your pretend ogres hiding out in your rice paddies. You can't use some Godzilla movie to explain Planet Earth. And I just can't believe it's a bunch of tiny *blue* aliens who are attempting to snuff out our planet."

The Neanderthal threw his arms up in the air as he chirped, "Well, General Richardson, haven't all of your earthling movies been obsessed with little green men coming from outer space to threaten your planet? It's basically the same thing. Not to split hairs, but the color green is just the mixture of blue and yellow."

General Richardson looked even angrier. "I don't need a lesson in color theory there, Fred Flintstone. I know how fucking green is made."

Eve, sensing that the conversation was now entering an absurd zone from which it could not recover, asked, "And how did your people get involved in this, Mr. Baku?"

"The Shxtors recognized very early on that they needed to stop these space conquerors, so they came up with the Moog Program to counteract each and every planetary acquisition attempt by a Noosbit Haag. Luckily for the universe, my people do this out of the kindness of their hearts, not because of any ulterior motives."

"Bullshit!" the general spit out. "No one does anything like that without personal gain."

Baku grinned at the group. "No earthling might, General Richardson, but we Shxtors are a highly advanced people. I really feel like we're now all wasting too much precious time debating the trifling reasons and minutiae of why I am here to save you. All you need to do is send me in the right direction to complete my inspiring mission of saving you and your planet. Perhaps we could drink some hot water poured over ground *Coffea arabica* and chit-chat as to why the sky is blue and why the Voynich Manuscript is actually a piece of pornography left by a passing Altoonian alien traveler after the Haag – er, Palmetto Bug Monster – is dead and buried, huh? I *really* need someone to please stop this moment of pointless gabbing and just get me to the giant lizard posthaste."

The television reporter brought the microphone forward to ask her next inquiry. "Wait. Why can't you find your Moog? I mean, if it's a Shxtor weapon, one would think that such an advanced alien presence as you're describing would know exactly where it currently is."

The Neanderthal android simultaneously wilted like a leafy vegetable exposed to heat and hardened his physique like a cobra at Eve's pointed question. His ocular orbits opened wide, but his reply was cut off by General Richardson.

"That's right. Even *I* know where the B-52s with the most-deadly payloads are currently hidden. Nope, something definitely doesn't smell right with your story, alien."

While the rest of the group seemed to become emboldened in their agreement with the current challenges, the android shook with frustration.

"Not that it's any of your business, annoying humanoids, but the small antennae on my spacecraft that receives the direct transmissions from the Moog was damaged in a recent meteor shower, and I was unable to repair it before coming down here. After detecting the freshest monster damage on Earth, my ship's computers calculated the best chances of landing nearby during our descent onto your planet, and that is, regrettably, right here. So, instead of placing me right next to the superweapon to let me do my impressive stuff, I've landed in this horrible little town to face a panel of inquisitors who want to ask me a litany of asinine questions. To be blunt, you all are *really* starting to piss me off!"

"Can androids *even* get angry?"

Bugsy's comment came as a surprise to everyone, and they spun to look at the tiny teenager and then back at the Neanderthal.

"Yes, I can. And I can tell you all that I'm currently getting so peeved with you that I must say I'm about to blow my highly developed stack. Here I am, attempting to play my hallowed role as the author of your salvation, and you're playing Twenty Questions with me! For the love of Pete, stop this madness and point me in the direction of the Moog...He-Knew-Pat-Sajak."

It was Usotsuki's turn to speak. He nodded in a very Japanese way to show his respect to the alien, but then he asked the question that everyone was now thinking. "*Watashi no zatsu na kotobazukai wa amari okininasaranaide kudasai*, but what can you do for the monster? You have arrived here seemingly lacking *any* knowledge about the situation, so how do you hope to help the lizard beat the cockroach?"

Baku looked even more incensed. "You *dare* question my amazing abilities, earthlings? Okay, that's the way it's going to be? Well, not that I need to prove myself in any way, but let me explain how this whole thing works in a simplified way so that your underdeveloped brains can understand. You see, the Moog superweapons are impressive in their own right, but after a couple of less-than-spectacular fights between Haags and unaltered Moogs, the Shxtor scientists bioengineered a larval creature that enters the weapon through its ear canal to gain access to its brain and form a symbiotic psychic-emotional connection between the weapon and its supportive android."

"You're making this up," Mayor Bishop remarked.

"No, I am most definitely not. Once the larva crawls inside to the tympanic cavity and nestles close to both the oval and round window of the lizard's auditory apparatus, the close proximity with the creature's simple brain allows the larva and the superweapon to connect together and then transmit their thoughts directly to the android – me! – which is a superior strategist and tactician. The trio of monster, bug, and android – but mostly it's we awesome androids – has proved to be too much for the simpleton Haags. Actually, it's not a fair fight."

Eve hesitated, the microphone still in her hand, and Bernie zoomed in on the frighteningly smug smile now on the face of the android.

"Do you understand what I am trying to say to you now, puny humans? If you stop giving me the third degree and let me do my ingenious duty, this fight can be over *today*. Your world can be instantly safe from this alien invasion and I can go back to my base to fulfill my destiny of continuing to advance and evolve into a supreme sentient being."

"Horseshit!" the general exclaimed loudly.

Baku made a motion with the palms of his hands held upward as if he were attempting to lift a heavy rock. "Okay, General Richardson, knowing that your species is wholly controlled by the belief that seeing is believing, I will show you the larva right now. If I do that, would you finally stop grilling me and just point me in the direction of the Moog so I can set about putting an end to this whole thing?"

The group in front of the Neanderthal nodded wordlessly in unison. The android pulled a small controller out of his coverall's pocket and pushed a button. Shortly thereafter, a black object the size of a large coffin came floating out of the spaceship, down the walkway, and hovered over the ground next to the group. The levitating box shimmered in the Alaskan daylight, and it was impossible to determine what it was made of – it could have been metal, stone, plastic, or even ebony. With a great flourish, the android dramatically put his hand onto an illuminated circle on the side of the object. The top slowly opened up so that the group could peer inside.

"Behold, humans, the solution to all of your problems. Once I get this baby into the Moog's ear, I'll help obliterate the cockroach and then be on my way, safe in the knowledge that it was *me* who saved the day."

The group leaned over to look inside the coffin-like container but, not seeing anything at first, kept leaning in farther and farther, until they looked like passengers waiting at a bus stop standing in a stiff gale. For all intents and purposes, the big box was empty. There appeared to be nothing inside but a large pile of dust on the bottom. Almost like synchronized swimmers, the group straightened up in unison again and looked blankly at the Neanderthal.

His smug grin faded at the non-reaction and he peered around the open lid to look inside.

"What the flying fuck? No! This can't be right. There should be a healthy white larva about five feet in length wriggling around inside there! This does not compute. This does not make any sense."

The general, trying to look authoritative, lifted his chin and directed it straight at Baku before issuing his order. "Calm down, alien. Just bop back up to your base and pick up another one. You must have a whole armory of them up there."

The Neanderthal opened his eyes wide and then spit out, "Another one? Why would there be *another* larva? One is all that is ever needed. I don't have any more up there, ridiculous human. I just have what's in this box. And that's nothing but dust. Holy shit!

You are all doomed! *We* are all...omigosh, I've gotta get out of here."

"Wait. You're abandoning us?" Mayor Bishop asked with a heightening pitch to his voice.

Clearly agitated, Baku continued speaking. "Self-preservation isn't a sin, earthling. Well, maybe it is. Oh, no, I'm feeling guilt. And now I'm getting sad at my complete failure. Argh, you're all going to die a horrible and painful death, and it's all my fault. But I cannot do anything without the larva. I'm only an android, albeit an amazingly impressive mechanical being. Am I a one-trick pony? Who would create such a limited entity who could fail so easily? No, that's not the question. The question is, what am I going to do to prove that I am a superior being? Come on, beautiful Baku, think, think, think."

The group now shared fleeting glances with each other as they witnessed what amounted to the android from outer space having a major meltdown. Their rising confusion about what they were seeing and hearing was yet another unexpected turn in this interaction with an alien presence, and they were left numb and speechless.

Bugsy took a step forward and said meekly, "Maybe we could help you. If we just put our heads together, we could come up with some kind of a solution, Mr. Baku."

"You? You've all been nothing but a hindrance. Actually, there's a good chance that your brainless questioning caused the larva to die. *You* all did this."

General Richardson shook his head at the Neanderthal. "Poppycock, alien! That larva's been dead and gone for a long, long time. You're just kicking the dog now, caveman."

"The general is right, Baku-san. The larva must have died during the long delay. Is there another way to make a connection with the giant lizard? As we say in Japan, even if it rains or spears fall, most problems can be figured out. I agree with Bugsy-san. Let us put our minds together and find a way to save the planet."

Baku glared at the general and then took in the Japanese cryptozoologist with a more kindly expression. Wordlessly, he nodded, and then looked like he was deep in thought.

Finally, he spoke. "I could build some kind of giant mind-transmitting crown to put on the Moog's head. Yeah, that might work. Except none of the materials I need are present on your planet. If I took off right now and went searching in the far reaches of the known universe for them, I could design and construct this new psychic controlling device for the Moog, and then I could come back and save the day."

"I'm sorry, Mr. Baku," Eve stated evenly, "but I don't think that there's enough time for all of that. The Palmetto Bug Monster is moments away from finding and finishing off He-Knew-Pat-Sajak, and then it will be free to destroy us and our world. If you're going to save our planet, it seems like there's no time like the present."

The android gasped in alarm. Then its eyes narrowed into slits as it hunched over as if it were ready to either launch an attack or defend itself from one.

"You all don't have the right to put that much pressure on me. I might be the most magnificent android ever, but there's no way to justify placing the weight of an entire world on my shoulders. That's not fair! Instead of looking at me to rescue you and your measly little planet, perhaps you need to save yourselves. You know, walk on your own two feet."

Confused again by the android's about-face, the group grew oddly silent as they all came to the same, sudden realization that they and their whole species were, indeed, fucked six ways from Sunday. Any glimmer of hope from their initial contact with the bizarre space android had now evaporated, leaving only some kind of ultra-distilled bitterness.

Mayor Bishop broke this dour moment by smiling broadly and addressing everyone grandiosely. "Mr. Baku, I couldn't help but notice that you've used words like 'connected' and 'controlling' while talking about the relationship between you, the larva, and the monster. Interestingly, it appears as if Bugsy might have a weird connection with He-Knew-Pat-Sajak. He's been acting like there is some kind of link between them since we came into contact with the lizard."

Baku raised one of his eyebrows. "How so, earthling?"

"That's right!" General Richardson proclaimed. "The little twerp was acting like the pathetic gecko was his long-lost best friend from the moment we saw it, and he started yelling directions to it during its ass-kicking. It even seemed to follow his commands. And he's been weeping like a little girl ever since that bastard bug bashed the stuffing out of your pitifully impotent lizard. Maybe he does have some kind of a connection to it."

If androids could possibly have the wind knocked out of them, it now appeared that Baku had been punched in the gut. In that instant, he went from an entity that had been previously spewing disconnected emotions like an orbiting lawn sprinkler to that of a laser-focused direct-energy weapon (DEW) targeting Bugsy, and solely Bugsy.

"Is any of that true, young little human?"

Bugsy put his palms up before him. "I don't know. I can't be sure. What Mayor Bishop and General Richardson just said is kinda true. As soon as I saw him, I felt like I've known He-Knew-Pat-Sajak forever. And I've been more emotional about him losing the fight than might seem normal. When I yelled out for it to spit in the bug's eye and run away and hide, it did. But that could have been his survival instinct kicking in, I dunno."

Baku took a step forward and inquired, "Why do you think you've felt such a deep sense of sadness afterwards? Is that because the one hope of defeating the bug had been dashed and you know that your planet and your species are now doomed? Or from something else?"

Bugsy regarded the android before he answered its question. He continued slowly, "I can't be sure. Part of the sadness seems to be coming straight from the lizard."

"Straight from the lizard?" the android echoed. He did an almost imperceptible shake of his furry head before asking, "Other than the obvious, why would the lizard be sad?"

"He is sad because he knows he is the only hope for stopping the bug, but he also knows that he cannot defeat it."

Baku sneered at Bugsy and said patronizingly, "That's preposterous. Moogs easily dispatch the Haags – the fights are never even close. I think you are making stuff up now, little human."

"No, I'm not!" shouted Bugsy. "I think part of the sadness I'm experiencing is from knowing that He-Knew-Pat-Sajak is going through what my grandfather would be feeling if he was tasked with fighting Muhammad Ali to save this world."

"Ho, I'd kick anyone's ass if they came at me, eh!" Bugsy's grandfather snarled.

Ignoring the old man's declaration, the android leaned forward to speak to Bugsy. "You keep referring to the Moog as 'he.' Why is that?"

"Because He-Knew-Pat-Sajak is a male, that's why."

"Perhaps, Bugsy-san," Usotsuki replied politely, "you only assume that being big and bad are male characteristics. Like how we assume King Kong and Godzilla are *otoko*."

"No, he's a male. I know it."

The android arched his substantial brow again and nodded. "Very, very interesting. The Moogs *are* males. The Shxtor scientists realized early on that the high levels of their hormones made the male creatures far more aggressive and easier to control. So they bioengineered them to all be males. Conversely, we don't really know if the Haags are males or females, since our superweapons became so effective at killing them that that gender designation didn't matter. Huh, so you *do* have a connection with the Moog. Very interesting."

Subtly, the entire gathering of people had shifted their attention from the alien android to begin to scrutinize Bugsy. Even Bernie the cameraman, who had been previously aiming his camera solely at Baku, now began to pan between the speakers, but hovered mostly on the young teenager. Bugsy blushed from the new attention.

As for the alien android, he appraised the young man in front of him like a tailor eyeing a customer for the measurements of a new suit. He unabashedly visually scanned him from head to toe, and a hopeful look came over his face as he took a step forward and shook hands with the awkward teenager. "You just *might* be the solution to all of our problems, Bugsy. And I think I can figure out how. I am *that* impressive."

明日のことを言うと天井のネズミが笑う

ashita no koto o iu to tenjō no nezumi ga warau
If you speak of tomorrow,
the rats in the ceiling will laugh.

The Palmetto Bug Monster crawled over to the Yukon River and splashed water onto its eyes. The caustic properties of the lizard's spit were neutralized by the primitive eyewash, but the damage done was too much to overcome quickly. The two thousand lenses of the creature's compound eyes had been impaired, and it was going to take some time for the cockroach's body to repair itself. For the time being, it made more sense to stay at the river's edge and recuperate rather than to blindly search for its mortally wounded foe.

This gave the U.S. military a chance to pummel the bug with repeated bombing runs and missile barrages. Even though they unloaded every conventional weapon in their arsenal, nothing could cause any damage to the creature, which looked as if it had been more seriously wounded by its phlegmatic interaction with He-Knew-Pat-Sajak. The pilots of the aircraft were beyond frustrated that this opportunity to strike the monster with impunity wasn't paying dividends, and a few of them openly spoke on the radio for some kind of action by the military leadership to get their hands on the nukes, which they all assumed would end the whole problem right away. The cohesion of the ranks of the U.S. military was certainly straining during this moment of crisis.

About three miles downstream from this scene, He-Knew-Pat-Sajak was currently crawling undetected along the Yukon River in a southernly direction. It had entirely camouflaged itself with the surroundings and was using the open space of the river valley to move as quickly as its gravely wounded body would allow. Neither the aircraft pilots flying overhead nor the blinded cockroach could see it anymore, so it was free to get a head start on its southbound retreat.

Why it was determined to go this way was uncertain, but the monster, resembling a pilgrim on a holy journey, acted like its salvation lay somewhere in that direction. Although slowed by its substantial injuries, the lizard continued to travel unseen this way after the sun had set and throughout the following night.

The residents of the Parker House had also had themselves a tumultuous twenty-four hours. Eve and Bernie were directed by their bosses to fly straight to Anchorage in Sarah's floatplane to hand-deliver the raw footage of the fight between the Palmet-

to Bug Monster and He-Knew-Pat-Sajak to the local television station KENI-TV. They'd assumed that
they'd be included in the process of editing the film
before flying down to Los Angeles to the studios of
KTLA, where the story would then be broadcasted to
the nation and the world. But word had come down
from the high-ranking leadership of the media giant
that they were to leave the film in the good hands
of the editors of the Alaskan television station, head
straight back to Tok, and get the rest of the story
about the alleged alien and his role in helping defeat
the giant cockroach.

Eve's reaction was to immediately pitch a fit and
make a scene, but the powerful television executives
were both unflinching and unyielding, and in the
end, Eve and Bernie had no other real option but to
follow their orders. That didn't take away any of the
sting from being kept from their moment of glory.
It goes without saying that the plane flight back to
Tok was done in a complete silence that bespoke a
simmering rage.

Upon their return to the Parker House, both
Eve and Bernie headed to the solace of their motel
rooms, where they both attempted to find some relief in their own individual forms of self-medication.

General Richardson had spent the entire day
on the pay phone. At first, he'd reached out to the
commanding officers of the Alaskan military bases
to render his intel, give tactical suggestions, and talk
strategy, but these phone calls had only resulted in

awkward exchanges and embarrassing hangings up. Next, he'd called the White House and the Secretary of State's office, but was politely told to call back after the bug was defeated...which he quickly came to understand was another way to say they'd listen to what he had to say when hell froze over.

Not to be deterred, General Richardson called his former command post at Fort Bragg, North Carolina, in an act of desperation. In a particularly mortifying moment for the general, he came to the sudden realization that he was speaking to a low-ranking secretary who was quite graciously attempting to explain to the elderly man that, although it was always good to hear from a venerable veteran, the 82nd Airborne Division had more pressing issues at the moment than fielding the semi-coherent ranting of one of its retired generals. In this instant, he lost all of his resolve and, with little to no warning, abruptly ended the phone conversation by saying, "And that's the way it is."

Once he'd placed the receiver back into its cradle, the general needed to grab hold of the public phone housing for stability. He was not only feeling more powerless than he ever had before, he also felt utterly and entirely alone. There's no worse fate to befall one for a military man. To have no chain of command, no fightable enemy, no allies to rally, no causes to have faith in, and no mission to complete – these were the very techniques that Colonel Tran Trong Duyet had used so effectively to break the prisoners at the Hỏa Lò Prison, also known as the "Hanoi Hilton," during the Vietnam War. And the general was a broken man. He was so downtrodden by his failures that he actually now longed to slink home to the Kennedy Hill Plantation Retirement Home.

General Richardson looked up into the big Alaskan sky and hoarsely screamed out as loudly as a small child that had lost its parents at the County Fair, "Heinz Alfred Kissinger, *Wo zum Teufel bist du*?"

Mayor Bishop was beset with his own problems. The aptly-named Athabaskan Network was working in overdrive, alerting all Alaskans statewide that now that the lizard from the volcano had been defeated in Circle, it appeared that there was nothing to stop the giant cockroach from turning its destructive tendencies upon the inhabitants of "the great land." Although so ruggedly individualistic as to be highly antisocial, antigovernment, and antiauthority, Mayor Bishop's constituency was now reaching out to him with an incessantness to ask what he was going to do about the situation. He kindly reminded each person that, if the one-hundred-and-fifty-foot gecko couldn't get the job done, there was little that their diminutive mayor could do about it all. Understandably, this response did not elicit too much confidence, and the entire region was gearing up to face the greatest challenge of their lives – even greater than the 1963 blizzard, the 1963 incursion of two Soviet aircraft into Alaskan airspace, the 1964

Good Friday earthquake, or even the 1960 Presidential Election of John F. Kennedy.

Usotsuki Shirinigatsuku was holed up in his motel room. Feeling as if the solution to the current situation was hiding just under the surface, he had resorted to following his mentor's strategy of practicing Zazen meditation to increase concentration. What was troubling the young Japanese cryptozoologist was that he could not recollect the moment in any of his favorite *kaiju* movies that most paralleled the current condition of the conflict between the Palmetto Bug Monster versus He-Knew-Pat-Sajak. Sure, there were many instances when the "hero" monster was soundly defeated and needed to come back and win the fight to save the day. But Usotsuki could not remember another example of when such a crucial aspect –the dead psychic larva that was essential for the control of He-Knew-Pat-Sajak – had been missing in any of the movies. He just needed to focus his attention to mentally go through each and every monster movie he'd ever seen and figure out what could be done to help defeat the cockroach.

Then he remembered the *Shobijin* (小美人) who first appeared in the movie *Mothra* and then were also in all of the Toho Co., Ltd. movies involving that giant moth. Those small pixie-like beauties were used to communicate with Mothra and even translate the language of its caterpillars for the earthlings. When they were kidnapped by the American Clark Nelson in a suitcase and then were forced to sing at a "Secret Fairies Show" in Tokyo, their telepathic connection with Mothra led to their rescue. In a later movie, the *Shobijin* actually helped the humans plead with Mothra to save them from Godzilla. Eventually, it was these miniature twins who pointed out to Mothra that Godzilla was such a potty-mouth when he cursed at the gigantic caterpillar that was only attempting to enlist his help with Rodan to defeat Usotsuki's namesake, Ghidorah.

No, there was no way around it – the key to resolving this epic conflict between the Palmetto Bug Monster and He-Knew-Pat-Sajak was obviously the expired larva, but there hadn't been any instance that the monster movie expert could recall when the telepathic connection to the *kaiju* had been dead and gone, as in their current situation.

This course of meditative thought about the *Shobijin* inexplicably channeled the young Japanese man's ideas into thoughts about how odd his sexual attraction toward these two tiny priestesses actually was. This led to him imagining what a sexual tryst with the pair of one-foot-tall telepathic fairies would consist of – even if it were nothing that seemed worthy of becoming a Buddha or reaching for enlightenment, unless by that *ménage a trois* referring to the accepted Tantric Buddhist sexual practices, that is.

Without warning, the image of Eve Sanderborn's breasts popped into Usotsuki's mind. He tried to divert his meditation in another direction, but the power of their fleshy image over him was so complete that he was incapable of doing anything but surrendering to the worship of the woman's prominent mammary glands.

There's no need to elicit any of the slightly pornographic imagery for this narrative, but suffice it to say that the perfect size and shape of Eve Sanderborn's surgically enhanced breasts eclipsed all other viable conceptualizations in the contemplative mind of the Nipponese monster expert. Quite literally, all he could see in his mind's eye was the television reporter's beautiful boobs.

It was at this moment that fate intervened. An Alaskan mosquito honed in on Usotsuki and landed with an annoying whine upon his earlobe. The pain of the penetration of the insect's proboscis was simultaneous with the slapping of the aural site by the man's hand, causing the instant bloody demise of the bug. The whole incident was like a *keisaku* strike by a Zen monk to remedy meditative sleepiness.

Usotsuki was startled awake and knew what needed to be done. He stood up rapidly and jogged to the door of his motel room, for he needed to get to the alien's spacecraft immediately.

Ira Morton and his grandson Bugsy had spent an inordinate amount of time with Baku. The alien android had politely demanded to examine the teenager in his spacecraft to see if he could perceive any reason as to why the described connectedness between the young boy and the Moog existed. Ira, who refused to leave Bugsy's side, was attempting to stay focused enough to ensure his grandson's safety throughout the host of physical and mechanical checkups that the Neanderthal wanted to run, but being inside the alien's ship was a tad bit overwhelming. The flashing lights, computer noises, and simulated voices harkened to all of the science fiction movies he'd been dragged to by Bugsy, and the older man found himself fighting against becoming too awed of his surroundings to intercede if the alien suggested some kind of anal probe on his grandson.

Baku was beside himself. The android had used every test at his disposal on the young earthling teenager – short of open dissection – and he had not a shred of evidence as to whether or not there was any kind of link between the boy and the Moog superweapon. With the larva being nothing but dust, the self-proclaimed supremely superior artificial lifeform was coming close to conceding defeat, not a concept that had been in his original programming. This newfound understanding that sometimes life sends one down a cul-de-sac with no possible escape must have been something that his unrivaled and evolving wiring had cultivated during its extended "sleep." He'd taken all the measurements, scans, and external probings he could on Bugsy, and he was ready to call it a day. As far as he could tell, the final prognosis was that nothing was special about the boy. If so, then all hope was lost.

Just then, Usotsuki, now followed by the others of the strange little human group, burst into the spaceship. The Japanese man's loud, apparent banzai charge toward the alien's craft had caught the attention of the rest of the gang. Eve and Bernie had come out of their rooms to get a breath of fresh air, Mayor Bishop had been outside the motel office seeking refuge from the ever-ringing telephone, and General Richardson had been hanging onto the public phone like it was some kind of life raft. Seeing and hearing the cryptozoologist's abrupt movements and vociferations brought them all collectively out of their stupors, and they could sense that a scene of some importance was going to take place. And they needed to be there when it did.

Usotsuki did not wait to be addressed by the android, but instead shouted urgently, "Baku-san, Bugsy needs to crawl inside the ear of He-Knew-Pat-Sajak! He can take the place of the larva."

The Japanese man's utterance was bombastic, and other than the normal beeps and blips of the spacecraft, no one responded immediately.

"Hogwash!" Ira Morton thundered. "Why don't *you* crawl inside the lizard's ear, eh?"

The Japanese cryptozoologist made a sweeping hand motion that emphasized his stature. "I am too big, Ira-san, and I don't have a connection with the monster. Bugsy-san is the perfect size and he *does* have some kind of telepathic bond with it."

Baku shook his head despondently as he said, "Sadly, I haven't discovered any proof of this connection you all keep speaking about. I mean, the boy *is* the exact size of the larvae, but it seems pointless to put something that's completely inert inside the superweapon's auditory system at this point. It'd be like saying you'd be better off if someone forced a jellybean into your ear."

"I agree with the Jap," the newly emboldened general declared. "We must at least try *something*. When you're out of options, you have to grasp at straws and then start throwing them at the enemy."

Ira Morton asked quietly, "Why can't you use this mighty spacecraft to attack the bug, Mr. Baku? You must have some kind of futuristic weapon system. Just fly up to the monster and zap it with your lasers."

Baku gave Ira a look of contempt. "This ship is only a scientific transport vessel, old man, it doesn't have any weapons."

Bugsy's grandfather pushed himself in front of his grandson to shield him as he pointed his finger at the alien. "That's a bunch of horse hockey, there. No way a spacecraft like this doesn't have a good weapon system to defend itself. Wouldn't it be better to just have you take care of this all yourself, rather than ask my grandson to risk his life by crawling into a space monster's ear to somehow help it defeat the cockroach and save the planet?"

Bernie had been filming the whole encounter, and now Eve stepped forward with her microphone leading the way. She waved it in front of Baku as if she were attempting to cast a spell with it.

"Is that what you're claiming, Mr. Baku? You cannot use this ship to destroy the bug?"

"That's not only what I'm claiming, Ms. Sander-born, it's the truth. The Shxtors, in their infinite wisdom, decided it was far too risky to put any kind of offensive weapons in the hands of their androids, even though we are far more advanced than they ever could be."

"That makes no tactical sense!" General Richardson thundered.

"Tell me something I don't know, General," Baku replied with a grunt.

"Well, I'm about the same size as Bugsy," Mayor Bishop declared. "Why don't I crawl inside the ear of He-Knew-Pat-Sajak?"

The group looked at the short man to size him up. He actually had a similar physique to the young boy, and there were shared looks that conveyed that the innkeeper's idea wasn't the worst one.

Usotsuki interceded. "No, you have no connection with the creature, Mayor Bishop-san. It must be Bugsy-san."

"I will not allow you all to ask my grandson to risk his life!" Ira roared. "He's just a kid. No, we have to come up with another solution."

"What do you suggest, Ira?" Eve asked sympathetically.

The silence that followed was broken by Bugsy himself. "I'll do it."

The teenager's voice was loud and confident enough to express that the issue was now closed. He smiled at his grandfather. "It has to be me. I'm ready to at least try. You always said I was destined to do big things. Maybe this is it."

Ira put his hands out to grab his grandson's shoulders. "I was referring to you taking over my job of managing the Tok roads someday, not crawling into the ear of some giant alien lizard and attempting to save our planet, Bugsy."

"But it has to be me. And I'm ready to do this. What do we do first?"

"That's the spirit!" The android clapped his hands and then rubbed them together. "First, we have to come up with a way for Bugsy to be able to communicate with me so I can guide him and his superweapon to victory if he's somehow able to converse with it. Then we have to find out where the giant lizard currently is located so we can fly to it in my ship and put Bugsy inside its ear. We must hurry. We really don't have much time."

雨降って地固まる

ame futte ji katamaru
After rain falls, the ground hardens.

The Palmetto Bug Monster stood up tall on the banks of the Yukon River and looked around to find He-Knew-Pat-Sajak. The river-water eye-bath had washed away the lizard's caustic saliva and the insect's regenerative powers had healed up its wounded eyes, but a quick visual scan of the surroundings yielded nothing to indicate where its opponent had limped away to. When the monster didn't see its foe, it looked closer at the fighting ring it had created. There, in the middle and trailing toward the river, was the unmistakable magenta blood of the gecko.

Most earthling cockroaches may have primitive brains – with one one-hundred thousandth the number of brain cells that most humans possess – but they tend to cram neurons into their brains more concentratedly and use each brain cell more flexibly than the dominant mammal species of Earth. Evolutionarily, their intricate circuitry allows them to do some tasks that few *Homo sapiens* could do without any technical assistance.

After cockroaches were seen scuttling around in the wreckage of the nuked Hiroshima and Nagasaki landscape, the leader of the Imperial Japanese Army's infamous covert biological and chemical warfare research and development unit, Unit 731, a Lieutenant General Shiro Ishii, proclaimed that it was clear that those persistent members of the order *Blattodea* could survive a nuclear blast. Actually, he said, "*Gokiburi wa jinrui yori mo nagaiki surude shou.*" This translates simply into "Cockroaches live longer than humans."

So, while the Palmetto Bug Monster might not have been a rocket scientist, it quickly ascertained that the lizard had fled toward the river, and since the blood trail didn't continue onto the opposite shore, it correctly decided that the gecko must have stayed in the water as it flowed down the wide delta channel. The massive insect concluded that it then made more sense that its wounded adversary had headed downstream, and it set off confidently in that direction to find and destroy it.

The cockroach knew how much it had wounded the gecko in the fight and just how inevitable its destruction was going to be, so the monster moved with a relaxed nature that belied any need to rush to find its mortally wounded nemesis. It used its time wisely as it fired its ray blaster to level the surrounding forests of the river valley as it proceeded. The mission to reap as much devastation on the planet that it had been sent to so as to prepare for its

Noosbit masters was ingrained into its genetic quality, but the current need to dispatch the lizard found an equal footing inside the now-enraged Palmetto Bug Monster.

Just as it appeared that the giant cockroach was about to proceed unimpeded right toward the still-camouflaged and unseen gecko and finish the wounded creature off, a squadron of McDonnell CF-101 Voodoos from the Royal Canadian Air Force attacked it. This squadron had been given special permission to strike the creature within the American airspace, and it unleashed a barrage of CRV7 (Canadian Rocket Vehicle 7) missiles that had been heavily modified. A Canadian entomologist by the name of Ernest Melville DuPorte, who was widely known as "a father of confederation for entomology," had designed a canister that fit onto the missiles, and this contained a healthy dose of natural cockroach deterrents like boric acid, peppermint, tea tree oil, eucalyptus, bay leaves, and diatomaceous earth. The Canadian fighter crews had casually given the nickname of "Canuck Poutine Pounders" to the improvised weapons. Within the small circles of the little-known Canadian weapons industry, there was immense national pride about them.

For the first time since being on this planet, the Palmetto Bug Monster felt the impact of the weapons that had been hurled at it by the inconsequential inhabitants. These Canadian missiles had squarely hit the target and their chemical payloads had an instantly negative effect upon the giant cockroach. The warhead explosions were shrugged off, but the special payload caused the massive creature some mild discomfort and even a little disorientation. Before the monster could recover and destroy the Voodoo fighters, which were already hightailing it back across the border, the U.S. Army garrison from the nearby Fort Greely opened up a tremendous fusillade of missiles and shells from their concealed locations in the proposed Yukon-Charley Rivers National Preserve.

The timing of this attack was perfect. On the heels of the effective Canadian chemical assault, the Palmetto Bug Monster was taken aback momentarily before it recovered enough to turn its attention on these artillery units. In the process, the cockroach became more intent on the locating and destroying of the weaponry of this assault than pursuing its wounded opponent, which gave He-Knew-Pat-Sajak additional time to get away.

Four thousand, three hundred miles away, the American capital city of Washington, D.C. had become akin to a giant pimple. Fearing that the alien monsters were going to target the city full of the most crucial leadership of the United States of America, the military had fortified the urban center so impressively that it had become an impregnable-looking fortress. If the city-destroying cockroach was going to fly back east and try to wipe out the nation's "Chocolate City," the place was not going to go quietly.

However, the city was anything but a setting of unification. The entire nation had had time to process the inconceivable images of the complete destruction of Indianapolis, the partial devastation of Chicago, and the Palmetto Bug Monster's calamitous pathway up to Alaska, and there was a growing belief that the American people were about to revolt against the perceived ineffectiveness of the President. Sure, no one in their right mind really wanted him to authorize the use of nuclear weapons, but nothing else seemed to be working. One look at where Indianapolis used to be and at the charred South Side of Chicago gave everyone a pretty clear picture of what the space bug's ultimate intentions were. If there was any hope of stopping the Palmetto Bug Monster, eradicating it with nuclear weapons seemed like the best option.

On top of that threat, the highest-ranking military leaders were no longer just whispering the word "coup" anymore; they were saying it openly in normal conversations. They had lost countless soldiers and equipment, and they did not like to lose. Clearly, the goddamn cockroach was winning, and they were getting restless to be allowed to use the only weaponry that might have a chance of killing the alien monster. By now, they had grown tired of asking for permission from their spineless president.

Consequently, the entire city was under a form of martial law. Military units loyal to the President were kept closest to the White House to act as a buffer to any threat – from the military or the general public

– and Washington, D.C. was in a state of complete and constant discord. Even the members of Congress, in both the President's party and on the other side of the aisle, were openly challenging the man to dispatch the cockroach with nuclear weapons. They called for public assemblies on the Mall, at which the massive crowds began to chant at a deafening volume, "Nuke it, Nuke it! Nuke the bug!"

The President would not budge. What had seemed initially like indecision now was seen as a newly stubborn man digging his heels in on the matter. The country's second "Great Compromiser" was not only no longer going along to get along, he was apparently eager to report that he was *never* going to use nuclear weapons on the creature, and that was final. His handlers and his intimate circle of advisors were adamant that the usually pliable man was most definitely committing political suicide with this stance, but he would have none of it. He was seemingly far more determined to get the core of the government ready to transport themselves to the underground bunker at the Greenbrier Resort in White Sulphur Springs, West Virginia.

With the vice president and his family already housed there, the President set about to make sure the essential components of the American political machine were packed and prepared to go into hiding if it looked like the cockroach was coming their way. As for himself, he more resembled the captain who was preparing to go down with the ship.

The strangest bit of news, which was leaking out of the White House like the transmission fluid of a 1970 Dodge Dart, was the fact that the First Lady was currently missing. Initially, her absence had been assumed to be a part of the overall confusion that existed inside the Capital Beltway. When people are rushing for the exits of a burning theatre, there is no time to check everyone's ID at the door. However, when she was still unaccounted for after that initial panic, the thought was that her disappearance was part of a well-conceived plan to protect her from the angry crowds, hostile military leadership, and the one-hundred-and-fifty-foot-tall killer cockroach. If the VP and his family were holed up in the governmental underground bunker, why wouldn't the President have sent his own wife there, too?

But then it became painfully obvious that no one – especially the President – seemed to know where the First Lady was at that very moment. As an already over-encumbered man in the midst of an unthinkable and catastrophic situation, the President of the United States took the news of his wife's absence without much grace. He started a downward spiral – as if he were searching for the sub-basement to his despondency – and insiders and outsiders alike saw this as one of the most awful harbingers in an already overfilled apothecary of the most depressing omens of these dark days.

The whole goddamn situation had now become a pustule ready to burst.

嘘も方便

uso mo hōben
Lying is a means to an end.

The impromptu rest area set up outside the office of the Parker House now resembled the tense waiting room of a busy veterinarian clinic full of antagonistic cats and dogs. The three men – General Richardson, Mayor Bishop, and Usotsuki Shirinigatsuku – all were in their lawn chairs in a state of muted agitation as they stewed in their own swirling tempest of hidden emotions. They all had chosen to sit in solace with one another, but there were invisible vapors of suspicion, open aggression, and self-loathing waving around them in some kind of syncopated and yet disharmonious moment.

This scene had been set into motion after Baku had finished creating a futuristic silver headset that Bugsy was to wear when he crawled into the ear canal of He-Knew-Pat-Sajak. This ingenious contraption would allow the teenager to communicate wirelessly with the alien android inside his spacecraft and allow instructions to be relayed back to Bugsy within the giant lizard's ear canal. After the unit tested splendidly, allowing the little earthling and the

Shxtor android to converse clearly from great distances, the group dispersed to get ready to find He-Knew-Pat-Sajak and get its human telepathic translator inserted inside it. Well, "dispersal" might be an oversimplification – and therein lay the source of the three men's current perturbation.

Ira Morton decided to stay with the alien to discuss the risks that his grandson was going to be facing. And while the alien android certainly had a lot to set in place for the next phase of the defense of this planet, he not only appreciated the opportunity to converse with a member of this odd species and learn more about their paternal instincts, but he was also lonely. He enjoyed the older man's company.

Bernie the cameraman headed back to his motel room to finish off the handle of Jack he had there. He knew that he'd have to be on top of his game when it was showtime, and he figured he'd binge some alcohol in an attempt to get in the right mood for that. As a professional, he knew that the next series of events were going to be very challenging to film.

The plan to use the alien spacecraft to transport the group to the location of He-Knew-Pat-Sajak, get the kid inside, and then confront the evil giant cockroach to have a final battle scene was going to be a bunch of micro and macro visual moments that would greatly test his abilities in both scope and scale. The classic movie *Tora! Tora! Tora!* (In Japanese: トラ・トラ・トラ！) had awed Bernie with how the filmmakers had used scenes that alternated between small groups of men in the cramped spaces of war-ship bridges, war offices, and aircraft cockpits *and* impressively expansive aviation battle scenes that overflowed the screen. Now he was going to have to use a similar technique to capture the group in a smaller space of the spacecraft *and* the giant crea-tures' epic battle outside it, and he knew he could, but only after a few stiff drinks.

When Eve asked Bugsy if he'd like to come back to her motel room for an intimate interview before the big moment, General Richardson, Mayor Bish-op, and Usotsuki all groaned in unison. The teenager innocently seemed to think that the offer was real-ly about the blonde television reporter getting the chance to speak to someone going into a dangerous situation, but the three men correctly identified that it was actually a sexual proposition. They knew this, of course, because of their own previous erotic ex-periences with the woman, and they came out to the lawn chairs to sit together in their unsharable mo-ment of jealousy and their shared effort of trying to avoid imagining the titillating antics going on inside Eve's motel room.

"We're fucking doomed."

The general's sudden declaration broke the un-comfortable silence, but the little Alaskan city official and the thuggish Japanese cryptozoologist looked at him with disagreement. Mayor Bishop posed just like Marty Feldman as he excitedly countered, "The plan seems sound, General. I think Bugsy can pull it off. I really do. I have to have faith that he can."

The general boomed out loudly, "That little shit couldn't find his own asshole if he had a spotlight and a CSAR team to help him. We're fucking doomed! If our president's balls would finally drop and he'd allow us to nuke the goddamn bug, we'd be all set."

Usotsuki looked at the military man with respect as he retorted, "But General-san, all great monster movies have a moment when something that seems implausible saves the day. This may be our *only* opportunity for victory."

This comment seemed to make the older man become incensed. He spoke through clenched teeth as he replied, "Just because a bunch of slanty-eyed rice-eaters have made some silly movies in which guys in ridiculous costumes act like made-up monsters doesn't mean you have any say in this current situation, you Nip bastard. Your *whole* life is nothing but pretend."

Mayor Bishop stood up so fast that he knocked his lawn chair over. "General Richardson! You cannot speak that way to another guest in my motel, sir. I will not allow you to be so rude."

The general looked at the now standing, outraged Marty Feldman doppelganger and then over at the obviously insulted Japanese man next to him, and he had to admit that he felt a pang of regret about what he'd just said. He clicked his tongue and looked down at the ground as he spoke softly. "I'm sorry, Usotsuki. That kind of racist outburst was completely uncalled for. I'm just upset by this whole monster

SNAFU. Plus, it pains me to think about what Eve and that kid are doing right now. I hate to say it, but I think that I'm still in love with that woman."

The two other men gasped in astonishment. Mayor Bishop got his chair set back up and sat down into it slowly. He and Usotsuki stared hard at the general. To hear the usually stoic war veteran issue an apology and then admit something so confidential was surprising, to say the least. Such honesty seemed to beckon for more.

"I am also in love with Eve Sanderborn," Mayor Bishop admitted.

"*Watashi mo kanojo ni koi o shite imasu,*" Usotsuki replied, and the other two had to assume that this was also some kind of an admission of love.

With their three hearts now openly on their sleeves, the men sat back into their lawn chairs like the planet's gravity had just increased in strength. Such revelations about an emotion like love were never made in these situations, and each individual pondered what his response to this all was going to be.

General Richardson leaned forward and put his hands onto his knees. "For you two it's different. You're young. I'm an ancient old man who's living off his past accomplishments. I really have nothing to look forward to but a future of degradation and, ultimately, death. When asked why he was so impulsive, my friend General George S. Patton once said, 'A good solution applied with vigor now is better than a perfect solution applied ten minutes later.' I kinda thought Eve would give me some kind of a new future, but I was fooling myself. Old men often make fools of themselves. We cannot help it because we're so desperate to do everything with vigor before we die."

Mayor Bishop then spoke with emotion. "Well, General Richardson, at least you have somewhere to go after this is all over. Yes, I'm still convinced this plan will work and that we will live to see another day, week, month, and year. And when it's all over, you get to go back to South Carolina and bask in those impressive accomplishments of your past at that fancy rest home. Me, I will be stuck here in the middle of nowhere, managing a piss-poor fleabag motel and pretending to be someone of importance. I thought Eve might be my ticket out of Tok and to a better life."

"*Uwaa!*" Usotsuki uttered in surprise. He'd never shared such feelings around other men before. Even when he was conversing with his mentor, he never thought to delve into such deep personal topics or emotional discourses. And he most certainly did not offer any admissions of vulnerability with his yakuza *bōryokudan*. He was half-tempted to let the previous comments waft around in the air around them all and not contribute, but the general's previous mean comment had unlocked something within him.

"Ah, Mayor Bishop-san and General Richardson-san, we're all experiencing a moment of what we Japanese call *Goetsudoushu* – we're all in the same boat as spurned rivals for Eve's attention. I thought she was going to give my life some legitimacy, something which, as the General-san just pointed out, might be lacking from my world at the moment."

The Japanese man shrugged as to indicate he was done talking.

The general was clearly through with this touchy-feely stuff, too, and he sat back heavily into his chair and stared into space. Their moment of sharing was over.

Undaunted, Mayor Bishop's face grew into a big grin and he leaned in eagerly toward the two other men as he said in a sing-song voice, "Rub-a-dub-dub, we're three men in a tub, huh?"

Neither man initially responded, but eventually the general retorted, "Shut up, you wall-eyed motherfucker."

Meanwhile, back in the Shxtor spacecraft, Baku had grown tired of listening to the older earthling prattle on and on about keeping his grandson safe. Sure, the desire to protect his progeny was impressive at first, but then it had become far too repetitive. The incredibly advanced android knew that there were no guarantees in life. Hell, even a Gherradian warrior – among the dumbest and most violent creatures in the entire universe – knew that! Yet this human was bound and determined to get some assurance for

Bugsy's safety. Having an advanced and impressive empathetic programming as part of his electronic makeup, Baku first tried to gently tell the man that he had no way of seeing the future, but he quickly became frustrated enough with Ira's stubborn insistence to start giving more and more pointed answers, until he decided to change the subject completely to something that was much more important: himself.

"Mr. Morton, has your mind been completely blown by encountering me? I mean, I am so much more advanced, so much more enlightened, and much more complete than anyone or anything you've had the pleasure of meeting before. I can tell from your questioning that you're in awe of me."

Ira Morton was a man who suffered no fools. For the ridiculous caveman standing in front of him to dare to redirect the legitimate conversation about the safety of his one and only grandson – the one person wholly important and vital to his life – into a moment of pure peacocking was too much for him to handle. He gritted his teeth and his face took on the expression of a snarl.

"Advanced? Enlightened? Maybe you are, maybe you ain't. But being a complete asshole? Well, that's obvious."

The android looked aghast. "Now, Mr. Morton, there's no need to be rude."

The quiet and calm older man had now transformed into an angry and aggressive persona. "First off, Cheechako, you come down here wholly unprepared and ill-equipped to handle the situation. Then you act like some spineless worrywart as soon as you face any kind of adversity. Next, you require a teenage boy to volunteer for what amounts to a suicide mission to solve your problem. Yeah, my mind is blown away by you, but it sure as shit ain't in a good way."

Here, the android began to weep. It lowered its head almost to its chest as its body heaved with sadness. It slowly looked up at Ira Morton with actual tears in its eyes. "I have feelings, you know!"

Ira scoffed, "You're an android, Mr. Baku. You're nothing more than a tin can with some kind of a weird rubber caveman suit over it and a bunch of wires inside. You don't have feelings. I don't know much about robots from outer space, but I'm pretty sure that you cannot feel any real emotions. I mean, you're a machine."

The Neanderthal turned to face the older man with its shoulders squared. "You earthlings are so rigid in your thinking. You're all so black and white when it comes to your ability to discover and learn new things. It's a weakness that your species hasn't shed yet, and if the Haag weapon doesn't kill you all, it will bring you down like an anchor tied to your feet, let me tell you. Fifty thousand years, Mr. Morton, is a *very* long time. That's how long I've been in stasis, asleep as it were. That's an awfully extended period of meditation to experience. And I was completely alone. So, while it's true that when I was first constructed, I was the tin man you speak about – an automaton incapable of feeling emotions – during those eighteen million two hundred twenty-six thousand five hundred Earth days of nothing but self-growth, I'm proud to say that I *evolved*. I started out as an android, but I became a sentient being who is flooded with feelings these days." Baku eyed Ira to see if any of this was sinking in. "And because I had no mother to nurture me and no father figure to guide me through this process, I only had myself to rely upon. That's it – me, myself, and I. Are you really saying, Mr. Morton, that you think an entity who has a smidgen of self-awareness, self-appreciation, and self-love is something that's bad? Are you unable to see this beautiful creature in front of you without judging it? If so, then the lesser of the two of us might just be *you*!"

"Uh, well, that's certainly a lot to take in, Mr. Baku," Ira sputtered. "I mean, it's kinda like if my old truck suddenly told me that it was thirsty, had amorous feelings for my feet, or was too tired and depressed to take me to the store."

The Neanderthal took on an angered look of complete disbelief. "First of all, I am NOT an antiquated form of transportation, Mr. Morton. It's rather insulting for you to compare me with one in the same breath. One is a crude machine, the other is a revolutionary entity who bridges the gap between the mechanical, electronic, and biological worlds. I'm not some object that you hop into and guide to go buy frozen dinners. I'm an amazing, vulnerable, advanced, and superior life-form. In fact, you earthlings really should be bowing down before me!"

Ira guffawed. "Heck, now you're sounding like what Bugsy would call a narcissist."

"A narcissist? You make that sound so bad. Why is it so horrible to be in love with one's self? Having a healthy self-respect is a step in the right evolutionary direction, don't you think, human?"

Ira Morton went silent. Inside him, a fierce mental debate had arisen about whether he needed to stop Bugsy from helping to save the planet or to help him do so. Both sides of the argument had tons of pros and cons. On the one hand, obviously it would be horrible if the Earth was completely devastated and everybody was murdered so that an alien race could take it over. On the other hand, it was now clear as day that this space android was pathologically insane. Sure, the stopping of the Palmetto Bug Monster seemed to be of the utmost importance for the survival of the human species, but following along with an unbalanced and possibly malfunctioning alien machine who wanted to throw his grandson into harm's way to do so seemed foolhardy to the older man.

Baku had noticed the sudden stiffening of the man's body, and although he was still miffed from the earlier insulting discourse, he sensed that there was about to be some kind of a physical attack. Such a pugilistic exchange would threaten the whole situation, so he decided to be the bigger android – person – and placate the senior-citizen earthling.

"Bugsy is going to be fine. By entering He-Knew-Pat-Sajak, it will actually be like he's going inside the strongest military weapon in the universe. Even if, heaven forbid, he cannot bond with the Moog and the Palmetto Bug Monster somehow defeats them, the young man will be safely ensconced within an impregnable bunker when it happens. This world will be totally doomed if this takes place, but I am nearly one hundred percent confident that Bugsy will come out of the endeavor unscathed. You have my word."

While Ira contemplated the value of a bonkers space android's word, he also recognized the fact that he didn't have a choice in the matter, not really. Bugsy was going to do this whether he wanted him to do it or not, and the world was in such peril that most rational ideas of helping it in a sane and safe way would have to be thrown right out the window.

"Well, I will tell you something, Mr. Baku. If my grandson gets hurt, or worse, I'm going to arrange a conjugal visit between you and my old truck. You have *my* word on that!"

When Bugsy came out of Eve's motel room later, dusk was washing gently over the Alaskan landscape. The young man's hair was tousled and his face was etched with fulfillment and a slight tinting of befuddlement. He shut the door and appeared to be in a daze as to what to do next. When he saw the mayor, the general, and the Japanese cryptozoologist sitting in the lawn chairs behind the office, he shuffled toward them. They saw his approach and each reacted with a mixture of anger, envy, and admiration. Bugsy took an empty chair, collapsing into it as if he'd just hiked the Chilkoot Trail.

"Well, well, look what the cat just dragged in," Mayor Bishop sarcastically announced.

"How was your 'interview,' Bugsy-san?" Usotsuki asked pointedly while making air quotes with his thin fingers.

"I sure hope you wore a jimmy hat, young man, or it's gonna burn when you pee later on."

This unpleasant reception and the last pointed comment by the general brought Bugsy out of his stupor. He looked around inquisitively and then inquired, "Uh, where's my grandfather?"

Mayor Bishop pointed at the parking lot. "He just left to go home. It seemed like his conversation with Baku didn't go great. He stalked off toward his truck and drove away. Baku just re-cloaked his ship so no one can see it. We're not sure what happened."

Bugsy nodded at this explanation, then blurted out, "I just had sex with Eve."

The three men made quick sounds of lamentation, and then they contorted their faces and shook their heads as if they'd just heard the worst news.

"How can you tell when a woman fakes...it?" Bugsy asked.

His overly honest question caught the group off guard and they were momentarily stunned by it.

General Richardson broke the uneasy silence with his powerful commander's voice. "I wouldn't know. No one I've ever been with has needed to fake their utter satisfaction with my performance, young man. Only a weak-wristed child and a pantywaist like yourself would have to ask that question."

Mayor Bishop and Usotsuki both responded to the general's barb with disdainful frowns. They felt like there was no need to belittle the boy, even if he had just slept with the love of their lives. Even more, there was a deepening sense of dread that had begun seeping into their guts and had started to gain too much traction for them to ignore anymore. Their usual efforts to deny these feelings initially had worked, but the teenager's frank question had just eradicated those attempts to ignore what they both knew was the truth. Eve had faked her orgasms with them too.

Bugsy peered at them with a new-found clarity. He could see the unflinching denial on the general's face and the looks of apprehensiveness on the features of the other two, and the truth of the matter registered with him in a way that almost took his breath away. Eve had faked everything with him, and she'd done the same to each of these other men.

"The thing that suddenly hit me when I was in her room, doing that stuff with her, is that her hair is bleached, her boobs aren't natural, she admits that she's had tons of plastic surgery, and she will do or say *anything* to get the story. There's no way around it. Eve Sanderborn is a complete fake! I mean, she even fakes her orgasms. Everything she does, says, and makes you believe – it's all a lie."

The Japanese cryptozoologist tilted his head and then responded sweetly. "Ah, Bugsy-san, the Japanese have a term, *tatemae*, which is the polite facade we put on in public to please others. But everyone does this. We all say and do those things that we think will assuage the people who are listening to us or who we want to make friends with us. Do not be too hard on Ms. Sanderborn. She is just trying to survive."

"Usotsuki's right, Bugsy." Mayor Bishop chimed in. "Don't be too hard on Eve. She may not be the most authentic person on the planet, but, let's face it, she's brought a flood of sunshine into all of our lives when we needed it the most. She's single-handedly made us all feel alive and happy, and that's worth something, isn't it? Hell, we all might be dead in the next few days. Me, I'll take a moment of bliss, even if there's an element of untruth to it all."

Usotsuki gave a curt nod. "*Hai*, Mayor Bishop-san is right. Savor the moment. Don't rip it apart with too much thought. *Shouganai*. It is what it is."

General Richardson abruptly stood. He sneered at the three others seated in the lawn chairs, and then he brought his chin up and pointed it toward his room. He inhaled deeply for a second and then spoke. "Well, gentlemen, this moment of Kumbaya has been fun and all, but my guts are saying that it's time to carpet bomb the toilet. Before I go, I just want to clarify a couple of things. Eve Sanderborn didn't fake a damn thing with *me*. Also, you little puke, now that you've had your cherry popped, you need to do your job tomorrow by crawling into the ear of the giant lizard and save this world. All these asinine questions and worthless feelings are secondary to that. You have *one* mission in this life now, and you will do that or we all will die."

The general marched off without another word. They watched his cadenced gait take him to his motel room, where he stopped to put his key in the lock and then walked inside and disappeared from sight.

Just then, a mosquito bit Bugsy on the neck and he slapped at it, and in that instant, he knew it was time to go home to his grandfather's house and go to sleep.

しょうがない

shouganai

It is what it is.

Usotsuki Shirinigatsuku came out of his motel room and stared at the activity happening in the Parker House parking lot and over on the Alaska Highway. The Japanese cryptozoologist looked like death warmed over. Due to his excitement in attempting to transcribe into his journal the events around the monsters, the alien android, and the little intrepid group of monster-chasers, he wasn't sleeping enough. It was becoming apparent that he was suffering from an unhealthy case of sleep deprivation, and the others had begun to notice that the foreign man was feeling more irritable, slightly depressed, somewhat anxious, and often stressed. He hadn't vocalized any paranoid thoughts yet, but he seemed to be glancing around like he expected a *Kudo-kai* assassin or a *shuten-dōji* demon to show up at any moment and slice his throat.

The actions around the new arrival to the scene in front of him caught his attention. Inexplicably, a taco truck from Los Angeles had made the substantial journey to get to Tok and had arrived before dinnertime the night before. Actually, the owner of this food truck, Alejandra Fuerte, had seen the writing on the wall in terms of the bigger cities becoming the prime targets of the Palmetto Bug Monster, and she'd initially decided to pack her truck up to the gills with supplies to set up shop in an area that might be less on the monster's radar. Instead of finding some quiet, out-of-the-way locale in the mountainous forests of the Pacific Northwest to ride out the apocalypse as planned, once she'd heard about the cockroach and the lizard both being in Alaska, she'd correctly determined that that was where the action was going to be. So, instead of heading away from danger, Alejandra had driven straight toward it...all for the mighty taco dollar.

Usotsuki watched the long line of customers streaming from her truck's window, and he gave a nod of appreciation at the young woman's shrewdness. Eve and Bernie's newly released footage of the Palmetto Bug Monster and He-Knew-Pat-Sajak battling in Circle, Alaska, was now saturating the media airways worldwide, and the amount of activity on the Alaska Highway had exploded.

The road had, almost overnight, become full with military vehicles headed north and frightened civilians headed south. Due to Tok's ideal geographical location, the U.S. Army had implemented a roadblock in the heart of town to keep anyone except for their own weapons and troops from heading north toward the monsters. That meant that the place was full of waiting Army soldiers, stranded travelers, and far too many attention-seekers. Every room at the Parker House and all of the campgrounds and parking lots of Tok were at capacity, and most of these people turned out to be hungry for tacos, which made Alejandra's pockets bulge with profits.

Out on the highway, there was a constant motion of military vehicles. Troop carriers, tanks, pieces of artillery, and missile launchers rumbled around the clock on the highly patrolled road. This combination of nearly constant, thunderous sounds and vibrations had been distracting when they'd first started, but now everyone at the Parker House was becoming oblivious to it all. For the second time in the recent days, Usotsuki could not help but hear another Akira Ifukube musical score as he watched the frantic energy of the passing military buildup. Ifukube's "Frigate March" played in his head, because the scene in front of him so closely resembled those moments in Toho Co., Ltd. movies where the Japanese Army deployed their tanks and weapons only to get crushed by the monster they were to attack. The frivolity of his thoughts – the connection between monster movies and the reality in front of him – made him cast a grim grin.

The Japanese man's moment of solitude was suddenly shattered.

"With all this constant activity, I worry that Baku's ship, even cloaked, is going to attract too much attention when it takes off with us inside it later today."

Mayor Bishop had approached Usotsuki so quietly and startled him so badly he had physically jumped in fright. Perhaps he was struggling more from the effects of his lack of sleep than he cared to admit. But upon seeing the benign little innkeeper next to him, he relaxed a little, replying, "General-san's plan to create a distraction at the airfield is a good one. All the soldiers will be looking over there instead of over here when we take off."

"Ho, the old goat has a good idea once in a while, huh?" Mayor Bishop said with his wide and endearing Marty Feldman-like grin.

Usotsuki could not help from smiling. "Not often, but sometimes, Mayor Bishop-san."

"Hey, Usotsuki, you want a taco? I'm going to grab me another one of those delicious goat barbacoa tacos. Or a couple. I haven't tasted anything so delicious in a very long time. Plus, that Alejandra is an absolutely captivating creature. She's such an intriguing combination of outward toughness and inner mysteriousness. I hate to admit it, but I cannot stop myself from thinking about her. I know it sounds absolutely preposterous, but I think I'm falling for her...hard. I've bought half a dozen tacos since she asked to park in my parking lot, just to be close to her and talk with her a moment."

Usotsuki bowed gracefully and quickly at the mayor. "Oh, Mayor Bishop-san, *koi wa shian no hodo*. Love is beyond reason during normal times, but with two giant *kaijus* battling one another and our world hanging in the balance of the outcome, I cannot even attempt to describe anything as even resembling 'normal' these days. We must find happiness whenever and wherever we find it. Perhaps you and this woman are like astronaut Glenn Amer and Miss Namikawa in *Invasion of Astro-Monster*, and you will find love that defies everything."

"Yes, I am definitely feeling a love for that angel that defies *everything*, Usotsuki."

"Well, Mayor Bishop-san, that may be true. But as a man with his own cloudy past, I must say that I'm sure from those handmade tattoos on her forearms that that woman has been in a gang and probably been in prison."

"Pshaw, Usotsuki. No one who can smile with such warmth and take an order so compassionately can have a bad bone in her body. And I think that we've already really bonded in my visits at her counter. I'm pretty sure she feels the same way about me as I feel for her."

The Japanese man spied the unending line of prospective taco buyers and he guessed that the overwhelmed woman probably didn't focus on the individual faces of her customers enough to distinguish one from the other. As they said in Japan, *kao wa yoku ni* – all faces look the same.

Interestingly, Usotsuki Shirinigatsuku was as good a judge of character in people as he was with the nature of the supernatural. He was nearly correct when it came to his diagnosis of the owner of the taco truck, Alejandra, but he wasn't entirely spot-on. The Mexican woman *had* emigrated from the Cancun region with her family because of some religious persecution they'd faced there. Once in the United States, she *had* indeed gotten recruited by a female Latino gang and, ultimately, was arrested for an assault. She *had* been incarcerated in a juvenile correctional facility, and *had* let her cellmate there commemorate her stay with a series of crude tattoos, but she had not let this drag her down into becoming a permanent resident in the LA underbelly.

To get away from the dark side of the City of Angels, Alejandra had fled up to Alaska upon her release to get a change of scenery and to safely pick vegetables up there. Instead of ending up in a dead-end agricultural position, she was lucky enough to meet someone who helped her get hired at a salmon cannery on the coast, and she saved up enough money from her substantial paychecks to be able to return to LA and purchase her very own taco truck. With her nearly disastrous scrape with lawlessness stowed firmly behind her, she'd turned to a new future of becoming a successful and legitimate businesswoman. Usotsuki had correctly identified the young woman's troubled past, but not her reformed present.

And the Japanese man had been wrong about all of the customers looking the same to Alejandra, as well. While the young woman *had* been inundated with people wanting her tacos, she *had* noticed Mayor Bishop. How could one not? The man was so short that he needed to stand on tiptoes when ordering, he had the cutely attractive characteristic of having such memorably wide-spread eyes, and there was a noticeable kindness to him as he repeatedly ordered another round of goat tacos. She'd noticed the eerie resemblance between Mayor Bishop and the actor Marty Feldman, and since *Young Franken-stein* was one of her favorite American movies, she had to admit that she was well aware that she was having some tingling in her loins whenever the little man came over to order some more goat tacos.

No, if the Japanese cryptozoologist had waited to witness Mayor Bishop getting through the line to order his next meal, he would have seen the special spark that had flashed between the Mexican woman and the little Tok city official in that moment, and he would've known that love was in the air. But he'd already returned to his room to update his journal some more.

When the group gathered again later, they set about instituting General Richardson's new plan. This was a fairly simple affair, but it had a few moving parts and needed a healthy host of characters to pull it off in a synchronized fashion. Baku designed a timer to attach to the two sticks of TNT that Ira Morton "borrowed" from the locker he maintained as the Tok Road Commissioner. He occasionally needed some explosive power to blast the ice dams that formed in the spring, to quickly remove windthrows and windsnaps faster than a chainsaw, and even blast apart the boulders that fell onto the road from time to time.

Sarah Pretlusky was tasked with placing the device in a location over at the airfield that held no chance to harm anyone with the resulting blast. She'd chosen the derelict Constellation aircraft at the end of the runway. As long as anyone could remember, the "Connie" had been a landmark of the airport – a nearly mythical entity in what amounted to an elephant graveyard of deteriorating aircraft – and she was certain that the TNT explosion would create a spectacular diversion while endangering no one's life.

When the timer went off and the massive fireball erupted over the airfield, the passing military units and the ones instituting the roadblock of the Alaska Highway all sprang into action to confront the source of the blast. Eve, Bernie, Usotsuki, General Richardson, Bugsy, Ira Morton, Mayor Bishop, and Sarah Pretlusky all quickly scrambled aboard the momentarily uncloaked spacecraft to join Baku. Recloaked again, the engines of the invisible ship started up and blasted the craft off. There was too much commotion due to the reaction to the explosion at the airfield for anyone in Tok to hear, see, or feel the takeoff of an alien vessel in their midst, and the crew found themselves safely hurtling through the Alaskan sky in the interior of the alien's ship.

The brusque way that the group had been herded directly into what Baku called the Command and Control Center of his spacecraft had been explained by their Neanderthal host as being necessary. After all, because he was an android who didn't sleep, eat, or have any other recreational needs, he stated, with a heavy quiver of his upper torso, that there really wasn't much more to see inside the vessel. The layout of the central bridge area was almost out of a science fiction movie – futuristic, stark in decoration, and without any creature comforts. There was a single control panel made up of a virtual sea of buttons, dials, and switches with a utilitarian sitting bench in front of it. Several flat television screens of differing sizes and shapes, which the alien referred to as "monitors", were clustered around the controls, and Baku checked these with great frequency. Not only that, there were other large monitors on the walls around the circumference of the circular space, and these showed up-to-the-minute images of what was taking place outside the spacecraft.

With all of this imagery, the flashing lights on several wall panels, the incessant beeps coming from hidden speakers, and the frantic actions of the alien captain, the cabin was initially a very distracting place for the earthlings to stand.

As they hurtled northward, Baku made it clear to the group that, while Bugsy was the star of the show, each person in the group was an equally important member of the supporting cast. Sarah was instructed on how to fly the spacecraft, and she was designated as the official copilot of the mission. Bugsy's grandfather was there to be the boy's emotional support, and he was to help throughout the whole ordeal in keeping his grandson calm and focused, no matter what happened. General Richardson was given the enviable role of military advisor, someone who was supposed to help the group navigate their mission in the midst of the armed chaos of the area. Usotsuki was to continue to lend his expertise on the giant monsters and their behaviors. Mayor Bishop's function was the most uncertain, but his ability to keep coming up with unusual ideas had shown that he had a mind that thought quickly on the run, and those were qualities that this group was going to need to succeed. Of course, Eve and Bernie were supposed to document the events for posterity...and as an awesome news story.

Now that the excitement of getting the group aboard Baku's ship and getting out of Tok unnoticed was over, the earthlings could turn their attention to the odd outfit that Mayor Bishop was wearing. Looking like the spitting image of Marty Feldman's character, Marty Eggs, in *The Silent Movie*, he now sported a leather flight cap and a white silk scarf. The way that his hair was all tucked inside the cap only accentuated the vast wideness of his eyes.

"What *are* you wearing?" the general bellowed with scorn, looking down at the shorter man.

"Oh, this? My Uncle Petey was a fairly famous barnstorming pilot in the thirties, and he willed this to me after his fiery crash in Phoenixville, Pennsylvania. I figured that, if we're all about to embark on such an ambitious mission as this, I needed to bring some of the good luck this hat and scarf brought to my uncle."

"Well, you look like a horse's ass!" the general retorted with a snort.

Eve shook her head. "I disagree, General – I think the mayor looks debonair. Plus, we certainly do need all the luck that we can get."

Before anyone could refute the television reporter's comment, Bugsy called out another new direction to Baku. He'd begun to pick up signals from He-Knew-Pat-Sajak almost immediately after leaving the parking lot of the Parker House Motel, and once above the trees and soaring near the tops of the mountains that surrounded Tok, the young teenager had started to act like a two-legged dowsing rod guiding them straight toward the lizard's location. His eyes were now closed tightly in concentration as he continued to stream out directions as if he were possessed.

The monitors on the walls revealed that they were moving at an incredible rate of speed. The passengers also noticed that they were smoothly flying over the beautiful Alaskan landscape that they might have seen earlier if it had not been for the low-level and jerky maneuvers during their original trip to Circle in Sarah's floatplane. The impressive technology of the alien spacecraft completely dampened the motions of the vehicle and made it feel like they were floating on air, and this gave them an opportunity to appreciate the pristine wilderness they were soaring over.

Another video monitor over the control panel had been focused intently on the continued battle that raged between the bug and the U.S. military. Baku had deployed several small flying scout drones to keep track of the cockroach, and these hovered near to the monster, undetected, and sent these crisp images back to his ship.

What the group saw was that the U.S. military, emboldened by what they thought were instances when they'd hurt the cockroach, was continuing to hit the monster with waves of intense aerial bombardment and precise ground artillery barrages that were now escalating to a fevered pitch. However, nothing thrown at the Palmetto Bug Monster seemed able to hurt it in the least. After the general lamented about their ineffectiveness, Baku pointed out that at least they were slowing the creature down a bit, giving the Moog a chance to get farther away.

When the ship was about ten miles away from where this frenetic showdown was taking place, Bugsy opened his eyes and suddenly screamed, "Stop! Stop right here! Land us right here."

Baku stopped the spacecraft so it hovered above the Yukon River valley. The monitors showed nothing but unending forests all around them, and even Baku tilted his furry head and asked, "Really?"

"Yes. Put us down on the riverbank below us, Mr. Baku. Immediately."

The cloaked space capsule landed gently on the rocky riverbank and the occupants scanned the screens for any sight of the giant gecko, but no one could see anything out of the ordinary.

General Richardson abruptly commanded, "Do not uncloak this spacecraft yet, alien. There are enough surveillance aircraft in the air, probably including some E-3 Sentries or EWACs and Gruman OV-1 Mohawks flying around keeping an eye on the battleground, and we don't want them to catch a glimpse of us yet. As soon as they do, they're gonna put their sights right on this ship."

Baku nodded, but then he turned to Bugsy. "Anything more? Do you know where the Moog is?"

The boy was nodding to himself. He looked surprisingly relaxed as he answered. "Yes, he's right next to us. We need to open the hatch, lower down a rope to the ground, and let me climb down so I can go over to him and make contact."

"Okay, we can certainly do that," Baku replied jauntily as his fingers worked furiously across the keyboard.

"We don't have a lot of time to waste, so I need to make my goodbyes quick," Bugsy said bravely.

General Richardson, Usotsuki, and Bernie all gave Bugsy hearty handshakes as they wished him good luck, but Mayor Bishop hugged the boy tightly before letting him go toward Eve, who embraced him tenderly and smoothed a cowlick from his forehead. As he pulled away from her, she brushed his cheek with her hand.

When he turned to face his grandfather, Eve whispered toward Bernie, "You got that, right?"

Ira Morton had tears in his eyes, and Bugsy was taken aback by the unusual display of emotion. He too choked up, but he quickly reassured his grandfather that he would be fine and would keep talking with them through the headphones. Ira brought his forehead to Bugsy's and spoke softly to give him his Athabaskan blessing, "*Unangam tunuu Unangas alganaa ukuchxiza{ ama huzu{ ngiin tunu{tach{iza{.* This means, 'Our language defines who we are and lets us communicate with one another.'"

Bugsy scurried to the opening that had appeared in the ship's hull and grasped the fibrous metallic rope that hung to the ground. After he belayed down and stood on the riverside scree, the rope was retracted and the hole closed. The occupants of the ship were now left with nothing to do but view the screens and watch what happened next.

Bugsy's voice came over the intercom so that all could hear him. "Mr. Baku, take off and get yourself in a position to see what's going on. Cloak the ship and keep it far enough away to be safe from the action."

Ira Morton pushed Baku out of the way and spoke into the microphone. "What if this doesn't work, Bugsy, and you need us to pick you back up?"

"No, Grandfather, everything's gonna be fine. I can feel it."

Baku did as he was told. The invisible ship shot into the sky and hovered a few hundred feet above the river. The occupants all turned to watch the monitors with keen interest.

General Richardson furrowed his brow and then spoke with some urgency. "Hey, alien caveman android, how long can we hover like this? Won't we run out of fuel?"

"No, General, this ship is powered by a reactor that will never run out of fuel. We'll be able to oversee the events from a safe distance till the cows come home."

The general made a movement as if he were acknowledging a joke that he didn't think was funny, and then he said gruffly, "This whole shit-show is probably going to be over in a matter of minutes. We won't have to wait on any fucking cows, alien."

Ira Morton pointed at the screen and asked, "Who is Bugsy waving to?"

Everyone stared at the monitor showing the teenager. His right hand was held up in front of him in a gesture of greeting.

Baku leaned in to the microphone. "Bugsy, who are you waving to?"

This question initially went unanswered, but when the young man brought his left hand up to the same level, the group understood that he wasn't waving, he was feeling something they couldn't see. He had his hands on He-Knew-Pat-Sajak.

Bugsy's voice came through the speaker. "Mr. Baku, do your sensors show any other planes nearby? Is there anyone watching us right now?"

The Neanderthal looked at a circular screen in front of him and saw that it was completely blank. He scooted back over to the microphone. "There is no one around us right now, Bugsy, other than a few rodents and birds, a moose, and a lone wolf."

"Good."

He-Knew-Pat-Sajak suddenly dropped its camouflage. What had been a pebbly shoreline now revealed a one-hundred-and-fifty-foot-long giant gecko lying down in plain sight. Bugsy had his hands firmly planted on the scaly jaw of the massive creature. They watched as the boy made a motion as if he were playing patty-cake and gently slapping his hands against the reptile's skin. Unsure what the monster was going to do next, the group inhaled a collective breath and held it.

Sarah Pretlusky spoke without moving her lips. "I hope that lizard doesn't turn its head and eat the kid like he's a cricket."

The group looked over at the bush pilot with annoyance, then glanced back at what was unfolding with uneasy expressions full of dread.

He-Knew-Pat-Sajak gently rolled his head, but he did not eat Bugsy. Instead, the creature effectively lowered its earhole down to a level that allowed Bugsy to climb inside. When the group saw the teenager disappear from sight, they let out a massive whoop of celebration.

Ira Morton sighed heavily. "This all just might work out."

Usotsuki grinned. "Bugsy-san and the *kaiju* are connected, Ira-san. I really think that they have *kizuna*."

Bernie continued to film and Eve narrated, and they smiled proudly that they were capturing pure gold on film. Regardless of what happened in the end, they would have evidence of the great human accomplishment they all were witnessing – like footage from the NASA Mission Control Center during the Apollo 11 Lunar Landing. While they still hoped that their film reels would advance their careers with the reporting of the battle of the monsters and the arrival of the alien android, they now sensed that, beyond that, they were documenting something that would be truly profound for the entire species. It would be monumentally important in the future *and* it would launch their careers like a rocket – it was a truly win-win situation.

Mayor Bishop was joyous, but his reactions were a bit muted. No one could tell that the man's guts were rumbling like an active volcano. Apparently, the multiple goat tacos he'd eaten over the last twelve hours weren't fully agreeing with him, so he only managed a stifled, "Atta boy, Bugsy."

General Richardson looked pleased, but his face betrayed that his military experience was telling him it was far too early to celebrate. He knew all campaigns were a series of events, some of which appeared to be progress, some of which were really regressions, and some merely indicated that it had all been for naught. The Vietnam War was filled with many celebratory moments like this one, but in the end it was nothing but a heart-shattering, ball-busting, gut-wrenching defeat. There were too many divots in his soul to be very optimistic about the scrawny kid getting inside the giant lizard's ear, so he merely turned toward Baku and said gruffly, "As a friend of mine once said ambiguously in a famous speech, 'We have reached an important point where the end begins to come into view.'"

水に流す

mizu ni nagasu
To let it flow with water.

When Bugsy had volunteered for this mission, he'd imagined that entering He-Knew-Pat-Sajak's ear canal would be similar to the time that his grandfather had asked him to shimmy into a storm drain to clear out a blockage that was resulting in flooding around Bertie Ketzler's driveway. This elderly matron of Tok was held in high regard by the community as a grandmother to all, and Bugsy had jumped at the chance to help her, regardless of the potential unpleasantness of the task.

Ira Morton had asked his grandson to do this for him because the ancient stone culvert was too narrow for a grown man to fit into, but it was tailor-made for someone with his grandson's physique. As soon as Bugsy had crawled inside, he'd known it was going to be a messy, challenging, and difficult assignment. Not too worried about the dangers of encountering any poisonous snakes – Alaska was too cold to support any snakes, poisonous or non-poisonous – the teenager was fully cognizant that the endeavor's real foe was going to be claustrophobia. However, as he wriggled through the built-up muck and the stagnant standing water, he had room enough to move his arms in front of him to help with crawling through the darkened space.

By the time he'd reached the obstruction, which was a tangle of branches that had accumulated over the years and been cemented together by the water pressure of repeated snowmelt floods, he was in such complete darkness that he was required to turn on the flashlight his grandfather had given him. This illumination revealed that the problem was much bigger than one he could solve without the proper tools.

Ira, who was standing on the plugged side of the channel, had asked Bugsy for a report, but his voice came through the blockage muffled and incoherent. And when Bugsy tried to tell his grandfather about what he was seeing, the old man still could not hear him distinctly enough to understand. This problem was solved by Ira moving around to yell down into the other opening. His new position had allowed clearer communication to take place, but his voice now echoed off the stone subterranean walls into a cacophony of noise that was more startling than helpful.

"Ho, what do you see down there, Bugsy?"

"It's a big tangle, Grandfather. I can't do it barehanded. I'm gonna need a pickax or something to break it up.

"Well, get yourself back up here, Bugsy, and we'll set you up properly."

Bugsy had then realized the exact difficulty of the situation he was currently in. When he'd first entered the darkened tunnel, he'd been so focused on crawling forward that he hadn't really noticed the tightness of the space. Now that he was required to come back out, he comprehended that that maneuver was going to require some thought. He'd started to do a reverse wriggling, but these aggressive movements had become spasmodic and awkward when trying to blindly back up. For the first time, panic had grabbed the young boy and made his voice tight as he yelled toward his grandfather, "I dunno how I'm gonna get back out."

Ira had sensed the boy's discomfort, and having been in such circumstances when he was younger and skinnier, he'd calmly directed his grandson. "Okay, Bugsy, listen to me. Stop. Take a breath or two. You are fine. It's gonna sound weird, but you need to scrunch your body up into a ball. You've gotta trust me on this one – you'll have more than enough space to spin around like that. Use your whole body to move yourself until you're facing back this way and then you can crawl out. Don't worry if this takes a couple of tries, Bugsy. You've got lots of time and way more space than you think. Oh-ho, I'm tellin' ya, your mind is your worst enemy."

Bugsy had heard everything his grandfather had said. The man's soothing voice and comforting instructions had flushed out the rising anxiety within him, and he'd set about to following his directions. He'd assumed the tight fetal position and, using his elbows and knees, had spun himself around completely. As promised, there was plenty of room to do this maneuver, and without much stress or frustration, Bugsy had been able to get himself facing the correct way. Then he'd released his clenched body to stretch out, and he'd crawled back to the entranceway and his grandfather. Here, the older man had handed him tools with shortened handles to work in the cramped space, and with his newly-gained confidence, he'd squirmed back into the narrow tunnel and had easily cleared the blockage without any problems.

Now, however, Bugsy could quickly see that wriggling into the ear canal of a gigantic alien gecko was going to be a much different kind of ordeal. This passageway, which had started out wide enough to easily fit his body into as he had progressed farther inside, now squeezed down upon Bugsy until it was tight up against his shoulders. The outside light was soon lost, and while the dry and slightly waxy surface let his body glide without too much friction, he was comprehending that those reassuring memories of taking care of the culvert tangle with his grandfather were beginning to evaporate very quickly, leaving him with only the feelings of an achingly painful apprehensiveness.

He knew he needed to get some support to avoid his building panic attack, so he spoke into the headset's microphone. "Mr. Baku, could you please put my grandfather on?"

Ira Morton's voice came soothingly through the headphones. "Ho, what's up, Bugsy? How's it going in there?"

"It's very dark. And very tight. Uncomfortably tight, actually. I know that you can't talk me through it from inside the spaceship, but just hearing your voice might help me."

Ira could hear the rising uneasiness in his grandson's voice, so he did not stop to ask the boy what he needed to hear. Instead, he just started to recount his original arrival in Tok in 1942 and the meeting of his future wife there. He continued speaking about their courtship, their Athabaskan wedding, and the happiness that they'd had together. By the time he'd begun to tell some funny stories about the birth of Bugsy's mother, the teenager's forward progress was stopped.

"Oh-ho, Grandfather! I'm here. I'm gonna sign off to see what happens next."

"Take care, Bugsy. I love you."

Nothing initially happened. Shrouded in complete darkness, with both the irrational fears of suffocating and the swelling claustrophobia of being unable to move his arms, Bugsy felt he was barely holding on to his sanity. Flipping out would be catastrophic in such a tight, dead-end space, so he was working on staying calm. He was so determined that this effort was going to amount to something – that it wasn't fated to be a failure – that he clung to that belief as if it were a life ring.

It was at this moment that He-Knew-Pat-Sajak's first thought rumbled through and reached Bugsy's mind. Shared thoughts between alien species and earthlings might not have a specific sound or volume, per se, but Bugsy swore that the giant gecko sounded just like Mr. Snuffleupagus on *Sesame Street*.

Well, what now?

Bugsy was unsure of what to answer, but since one cannot truly control their thoughts, he retorted honestly in a much more muted tone.

I dunno. But I'm here to help. I think we just need to figure out how.

Well, welcome aboard. I'm all ears.

The psychic chuckle by the alien gecko was so infectious and warming that Bugsy was unable to resist it. In spite of the dire circumstances and the most inhospitable conditions he found himself currently in, the teenager let out a mental guffaw at this shared humorous moment. If nothing else, He-Knew-Pat-Sajak and the boy both knew that they were clearly bonding.

口が軽い

kuchi ga karui
One's mouth is light.

[We interrupt this regularly scheduled program for an essential parenthetical aside from the transcribing team at the Sam Sumac Association. As was probably noticed in the ending of the last chapter, differing sized fonts were used to indicate the individual thoughts of He-Knew-Pat-Sajak and Bugsy Morton. This was our solution to help rectify a literary situation that Sam Sumac had inadvertently created in the story.

In this section of his original handwritten manuscript, which was drafted on a dozen or so placemats from a Your Host restaurant, the differentiation between these two characters' thoughts was done with two contrasting Crayola crayon colors: Thistle (Hex: #D8BFD8) for Bugsy's thoughts and Mulberry (Hex: #C8509B) for He-Knew-Pat-Sajak's responses. It was immediately clear that the choice of these two hues was not happenstance. The former's lighter shade worked well to convey a younger man, and the latter's boldness definitely lent enough weight to represent a one-hundred-and-fifty-foot-tall giant gecko. So, as we read his script, it was fairly clear who was thinking what, but we quickly realized that this plan could not easily be translated into the printed word of a published book.

Our often-quoted staffer took this as an opportunity to remind us about the "I Can't Pay the Rent, You Must Pay the Rent" skit. This is considered by many to be one of the world's shortest and most performed plays, yet it takes an element of skill in pantomime to effectively capture the difference between the tenant and the landlord. Using distinct voices and a crumpled-up napkin to be either the mustache of the landlord or the bowtie of the tenant, the single performer is usually able to convey who is who. By using this common item as a prop and the deep/soft speaking inflections, the funny play usually happens flawlessly.

However, our staffer pointed out that whenever this act is done without the benefit of a paper napkin, the performer can also use a differing physical height to convey the two characters. By standing tall and talking deeply, the actor portrays the powerful landlord, but by slouching down and speaking lightly, the slightly less empowered tenant is depicted. Of course, during the speedy delivery of the skit, it can become impossible to remember when to do the right stance and voice, and often hilarity ensues with the mismatched portrayals.

Needless to say, we couldn't tax the reader or the typesetter with the proposed Thistle versus Mulberry color contrast scheme envisioned by Sam Sumac. Our test manuscript with the duologues using those two Crayola colors caused most test readers to get migraine headaches, much like flashing lights can trigger these painful cranial events. The publisher that we approached with the prototype out-and-out refused to take on the project, and their rational reasons about why led us to believe that no one in the business would touch this book. We were at a loss as to know what to do next.

A typographer friend by the name of Eric Eaton came to our rescue. He suggested that by using fonts of differing sizes – slightly bigger for He-Knew-Pat-Sajak and slightly smaller for Bugsy Morton – we could convey the proper characterization in those chapters when mental telepathy was occurring between the two characters. He warned us to not go too big nor bold, since that would make the gecko to appear to be yelling loudly, which would be, he correctly identified, out of character. He also cautioned us from going too small and light for Bugsy, since the teenager might be diminutive in stature, but he's one of the biggest heroes of the whole tale. Ergo, it wouldn't make any sense for us to make the reader think that his thoughts were more like Tiny Tim's song "Tiptoe Through the Tulips". Heeding this expert's warnings, we set about to make the change from dissimilar colors to the diverse font sizes. In the end, we're quite pleased with the way it turned out.

Another thing that needs some explanation is the fact that He-Knew-Pat-Sajak appears to be speaking English in his thoughts. Sam Sumac had very concise notes on the manuscript that clearly indicated that such a presumption would be entirely erroneous. He states with emphasis that thoughts and the spoken language are quite different, and that shared thoughts would require no translation, since they encompass the wide spectrum of meanings, qualities, and emotions without words. He even points out that Matthew Henson, the African-American valet for Admiral Robert Peary on many of his expeditions to the North Pole, may have had to learn Inuktitut to speak to the four Inuit guides because his white Arctic explorer boss couldn't/wouldn't learn the language, but if Henson and Ooqueah, Ootah, Egingwah, and Seeglo had been able to share their thoughts psychically, they would have skipped the need to use multiple Inuit words to describe snow and ice. Everyone would have just thought about it, and they'd all have known it to be true.

One more thing that Sam Sumac was adamant about was that English is *not* a universal language. In his many writings, he goes out of his way to explain that, although most in the English-speaking world believe their tongue is the first choice throughout this globe and out into the far reaches of the universe, it is mathematically improbable that it exists on any other planets. His use of Universal Translators and other literary techniques in his stories belies the fact that he assumed that there's an almost unimaginable number of languages spoken throughout the galaxies, and he just needed to convey the stories to his audience in a language that they could read.

Lastly, Sam Sumac was clear on one more thought. He warned all readers to not assume that He-Knew-Pat-Sajak was speaking, since the presupposition that a giant alien gecko could talk at all would be so absurd as to be asinine.

We hope that this explanation about the different font sizes and the use of English in the story makes it clearer for the rest of the book about what is occurring and why. And now back to our regularly scheduled programming.]

井の中の蛙大海を知らず

i no naka no kawazu taikai wo shirazu

A frog in a well knows nothing of the ocean.

Safely hovering three hundred feet above the ground, the crew aboard Baku's cloaked spacecraft was experiencing a moment that was anything but placid. Having had a fleeting glimpse of the wounded He-Knew-Pat-Sajak lying prone on the ground and then watching Bugsy climb into the giant creature's earhole had done nothing but put them all on edge. Hearing Ira Morton talk to his grandson to soothe his frayed nerves as the boy crawled into such a perilous situation was, however, reassuring. The whole episode had been like sampling some Italian pepperoncini honey – a jarring dose of heat mixed with an endearing sweetness.

The gigantic gecko had not only disappeared from view after it resumed camouflaging itself with its surroundings as soon as the young man had entered it, but Bugsy hadn't said another word since reporting that he had reached the end of his journey. There'd been nothing definitive to look at anymore on the monitor and no further reports from the brave teenager. The fourteen eyes of the septet of human passengers were glued onto the unchanging screens and their fourteen ears were tuned into the mute intercom speakers, while the alien android furiously typed on the keyboard in front of him as he scanned the multiple smaller screens that framed his command center. For the earthlings, the fact that there was nothing to see or hear made the whole experience excruciatingly tense. For Baku, he was too busy coordinating the surveillance of the current position of the Palmetto Bug Monster, observing the status of the earthling defenses, and monitoring a small panel off to the side dedicated to his ever-expanding sentiency to notice.

Ira's sentimental stories had touched the group. Even though they were tired from staring at nothing and hearing nothing new – and had, in fact, all been contemplating the possibility that the boy might have suffocated and died in the monster's ear canal, if they were being truthful with themselves – the shared humanity of the connection between grandfather and grandson had unlocked a hidden cache of emotions within them all. As anxious as they currently were, they knew that they had just witnessed something deeply profound. And each individual in that futuristic command center was now processing a slurry of newfound feelings about the importance of saving the human species.

However, a more pressing concern was building among them that was going to seriously challenge the profound nature of their circumstances. This currently pretty kettle of fish within the alien spaceship was unknowingly being threatened by a negative bodily reaction occurring within Mayor Bishop's guts.

The overconsumption of Alejandra's barbacoa tacos had wreaked havoc on the man's gastrointestinal tract, and he was now aware that no one had inquired if Baku's ship had bathroom facilities before they'd taken off. As panic set in, he glanced around to see if anyone could hear the loud rumblings coming from his stomach or if there was anything akin to a toilet or even some kind of a bucket to defecate into.

With no relief in sight, Mayor Bishop decided that he had no other choice than to try to release some of the internal pressure within him that was currently making him resemble the *Hindenburg*. But a risky maneuver such as this also came with further implications – the man most definitely did not want to shit his pants instead of just farting, and his concentration on this matter brought a glistening sweat to his forehead.

Stealthily, he moved away from the group gathered at the main monitor and gradually released his anal sphincters. This effort and his concerted preparation to stem whatever happened to come out, if more than just gas, was unfettered and made Mayor Bishop's face look like Marty Feldman attempting to deadlift the front of a Volkswagen bug.

Luckily, for him, only a harmless, sustained puff of flatulence came out. However, his victory was short-lived. The overwhelming aroma of a rank fart rushed his olfactory senses like a horde of General Santa Anna's troops storming the walls of the the Alamo, and he was aghast to confess that he'd just unleashed a silent but deadly fart on the small group in the very tight and enclosed space. This truth forced him to now contemplate whether Baku's ship had an adequate ventilation system as well.

With this deed done, Mayor Bishop found himself in a delicate situation. If he remained in the same spot, away from the group, and continued to fart – after all, once one passes gas like this, the rest of the stinky arsenal within wants nothing more than to get out and join their free brethren – the people he was sharing this chamber with would know, without a doubt, that he was the author of their distress. And he did not want that to happen. So he moved *toward* the group, slowly emitting his tootings like a crop-dusting plane.

Aware that he could not arrive with his poisonous clouds of sulfur and stay too long, for that would correctly indict him as the culprit, he made a comment to the gathering and then continued walking until he was next to Baku, who he then asked what the Palmetto Bug Monster was doing at that exact moment.

This juvenile ploy worked. Ira Morton, General Richardson, Usotsuki Shirinigatsuku, Eve Sanderborn, Bernie the cameraman, and Sarah Pretlusky were all suddenly engulfed by the foul fecal fog, and a round of strong reactions and accusations against one another followed.

"Omigod! Which one of you did that? That's horrible!" Sarah said, her fingers pinching her nose.

"*Hyakunichinoseppouhehitotsu,*" Usotsuki snarled. This Japanese proverb literally translates into "one fart in a hundred sermons," but it refers to the cultural belief that one mistake ruins everything. Mayor Bishop had most definitely ruined this moment in the alien's spacecraft.

The general, attempting to look like the flatulent aromas were not troubling him, commented coolly, "Well, I can tell you all one thing. I may have ordered the dropping of a lot of bombs during my military career, but I certainly did not drop that one! Plus, I can tell that that stinker was a civilian fart."

"Oh, General Richardson," Eve cooed through the face mask that she'd made with her hands, "are you *really* trying to say – with a straight face – that military farts smell differently than civilian farts?"

"Yes, ma'am, there's no debate on the issue. I've spent a lifetime among fighting men and among the civvies, and there are distinctive aromas to a warrior's fart. This effluvium, although impressive enough to be potentially used as a military weapon against the Palmetto Bug Monster whenever this crazy scheme of having a juvenile delinquent crawl inside the ear of the giant lizard all goes tits up, was, without a doubt, issued by a non-military person."

Mayor Bishop's rectum continued to release bits of pressure involuntarily, and the repeated psst-pssts being emitted from his backside were so persistent that it was as if his ass was trying to get the attention of the other nearby bottoms, both human and alien. Luckily for him, the alien android he was standing next to did not have a traditional sense of smell.

The Neanderthal was watching the group of discomforted earthlings around him with a look of concern. He addressed them: "I am sorry, earthlings, I don't really have a nose, so I cannot smell what you are all reacting so negatively to. However, my environmental sensors do indicate elevated levels of nitrogen (N2), followed by hydrogen (H2), carbon dioxide (CO2), oxygen (O2), methane (CH4), and hydrogen sulfide (H2S) in my spacecraft chamber."

"No kidding, mac!" the cameraman yelped, "I can barely breathe. Holy cow, what an absolutely horrible smell."

"Don't mind the stink, Bernie. Just keep filming what's happening on the monitors."

"Yuh, you don't have to worry about me, Eve. I'm a professional. There's nothing going on out there right now, but I've got the camera aimed right at the monitor, and we're gonna get the shot when something changes, babe. I'm just worried that the green clouds from those killer farts are going to film up the lens and block the view."

It was at this instant that Mayor Bishop released more pressure, but this time, it was not the same kind of subtle sound to quietly attract the attention of the other rear ends in the spacecraft. It was a full-on rectal utterance of an audible, "Hey there!"

Baku stared straight at Mayor Bishop. "Oh, I might not be able to smell, but I definitely heard that, earthling. Why are you making noises from your rectum in that manner?"

The resulting uproar from the group, complete with cursing, wild allegations, and threats aimed directly at Mayor Bishop, caused the small man to blanch. And while he couldn't deflect the blame or their anger, he resorted to stating the cause of the stomach issues.

"I think I ate too many barbacoa tacos."

"Huh, I thought you were frequenting the taco truck a little too often," Bernie said, with a small motion to express his feelings without upsetting the camera aimed at the monitor.

"And now we need to all pay the price," Eve stated coldly.

"Can we crack open a window, please! I don't think I can stand another minute of being gassed like this," Sarah nasally retorted as she continued to pinch her nose.

Ira Morton, who had been seemingly unaffected by the flatulence and was continuing to stare straight at the main monitor, suddenly spoke passionately. "What's the big deal? Yeah, it smells pretty rank in here – get over it. My grandson is down there encountering god knows what. Maybe he's in a much worse condition than having to endure the unpleasant aromas of Mayor Bishop's upset stomach. Gustav – here, take a couple of antacids and see if that helps. I always keep a pack in my breast pocket."

The older man's severe remarks made everyone go quiet. He was right – Bugsy probably had it worse – and the declaration of this fact made them all embarrassed for their initial immature human reactions.

"I will set the ship's life-support system to filter out the negative elements and refresh the chamber with more fresh air," Baku declared.

This caused the group to smile and turn back to look at the monitor. All except General Richardson, that is. He continued to scowl at Mayor Bishop while shaking his head in disbelief.

"For Pete's sake, what were you thinking, man? Don't you know that Montezuma's Revenge is the main aim of all Messican food, you bug-eyed ninny!"

"I am in love with Alejandra Fuerte."

This surprising effusion from Mayor Bishop's mouth was as impressive as the ones he'd been issuing from his backside, and the entire group, except Bernie, who kept his camera focused on the monitor, turned once again to look at him.

For the second time, there was something akin to a shared moment of sentimentality among them. In a world that was teetering on the brink of destruction, the beautiful exchange between a grandson and grandfather and now the mayor's stark admission of love felt for a virtual stranger caused the percolation of new feelings within them. It certainly seemed ridiculous in these circumstances to have an inkling of hope in the dark, emotional, primordial soup currently brewing in their hearts, but that was exactly what was happening.

Alas, for the second time in so many minutes, this chance to address something deep and weighty in the human condition was interrupted by more pressing matters. All at once, the spacecraft chamber was filled with the flashing of red lights and the blaring of alarms. Baku, still seated at his computer, began typing frantically. His fingers were moving so furiously over the keys that it almost appeared that he had sprouted extra digits and had even grown spare appendages.

"What in Sam Hill is going on, alien?" General Richardson inquired with some concern. His booming voice could be heard over the wail of the alarms.

With a face full of concentration, Baku responded out of the side of his mouth, "The Palmetto Bug Monster is on the move. It's coming this way. Fast."

Eve said haltingly, "I thought that it was still fending off the military attack some distance away from us."

Baku disregarded this statement with a sound that resembled a mini-sneeze. Without looking over at her and the rest of the group, the Neanderthal spoke more to his monitor than to the earthlings. "The Haag superweapon has completely obliterated all of those fighting units confronting it and, somehow, has picked up the exact location of our lizard. I'm not sure if it was the temporary de-camouflaging to allow Bugsy to get inside that did it, but the cockroach has now no doubt about where it is. It's making a beeline straight here...very, very quickly."

"What are we going to do?" Mayor Bishop asked wholeheartedly, but his sphincter was unable to contain another burst of methane. He looked about sheepishly to make sure that no one had heard his newest fart.

Disregarding the question and the noticeable reaction of the group to another creeping sulfur bomb from the mayor, Baku leaned in to speak into the microphone. "Bugsy, Bugsy! Hurry up and make some kind of connection, my boy. The Palmetto Bug Monster's on its way here and it seems armed for bear. You need to get He-Knew-Pat-Sajak into a defensive posture immediately! If you don't, all will be lost. Bugsy, Bugsy...come in, Bugsy. Do you hear me? You've only got a very short time before all hell is going to break loose. The bug sees you. I repeat, the bug sees you! And it's coming in for the kill at a very high rate of speed. Bugsy? Bugsy? Please respond."

The intercom stayed resolutely silent. Baku, in an effort to remove all other noises in case the reply to his impassioned pleas was spoken too softly, turned off all of the alarms and buzzers, and the earthlings and the singular alien aimed their ears up to the speaker to try and discern any reply. In this tense and muted environment, there was nothing to diffuse the sound of the mayor's latest anal salvo, and strangely, the man's flatulence made the unmistakable pronouncement of the exact sentiment that each entity in that alien spacecraft was feeling at that very moment: "We're so fucked."

鯛も一人はうまからず

tai mo hitori wa umakarazu

Eaten alone, even sea bream loses its flavor.

Although brief, the initial psychic exchange between Bugsy and He-Knew-Pat-Sajak had oddly put the teenager more at ease. There was something in the creature's persona, revealed instantly in those loud but comforting thoughts, that made everything feel better. While Bugsy found himself physically unable to move in the tight confines of the lizard's ear canal, which meant that there was no way he could even think of turning around and getting the duck out of Fodge, these potentially overpowering truths were becoming nonissues. For reasons that remained unclear, all of the young man's anxieties were now evaporating, leaving behind only the finest dust of uneasiness. On top of that, the passage of time had ceased to exist for him. As a result, his own current situation and his emotions were becoming nothing of consequence. Strangely, he was focusing more on the condition of his host than on his own needs.

The depressing truth was that Bugsy was now fully aware that He-Knew-Pat-Sajak was toast. Somehow the teenager could intrinsically sense the extent of the pain that the giant gecko was feeling from the countless wounds that it had incurred during the first battle with the cockroach. Even worse, he was now cognizant of just how much it had convinced itself that it wasn't going to be able to carry out the rest of its mission. Being exposed to the creature's deep melancholy was too intense for Bugsy, and he closed his eyes and felt the waves of the lizard's sadness saturate his being like the electromagnetic radiation of a microwave oven streaming into a frozen burrito at a 7-Eleven. The teenager was about to be overwhelmed by it all, but then he gathered himself and thought only positive thoughts. If he was going to have any chance at turning this whole thing around, he needed to cut through the oppressive grief of the creature and try to buoy the spirits of their partnership.

I'm here to help. We can get through this if we work together.

Who are you?

I'm Bugsy. What's your name?

My handlers call me Moog.

Do you want me to call you that?

No. I don't like it. Makes me sound like a burp. What do your people call me?

Here, Bugsy decided to give a quick discourse to explain the most common of the current monikers used to describe the creature, including He-Knew-Pat-Sajak, gecko, and lizard. He'd hoped that the explanation of some of these names would make the connection clearer between the earthlings and the entity that they all hoped would be their savior, but that was not the immediate result. Instead, a sustained and deeply awkward silence followed. Bugsy waited patiently for some kind of a response, but when none came, he finally broke in with a question.

Do you want me to call you by any of these names?

No. I don't like any of them. They are stupid. They are not me.

Well, do you have another name that you prefer?

Yes.

What is it?

Do you promise not to laugh?

I promise.

The last thing I heard my Shxtor handlers call me as they placed me into the volcano was that I was Planetary Engineered Defensive Rescue Organism 0-20223. As I went into suspended animation to await the arrival of the Haag weapon, I decided that I liked the acronym of that designation, P.E.D.R.O., and I began to call myself Pedro. It is the name that I've referred to myself as long as I've slumbered.

Okay, I will call you that. Hello, Pedro. I'm Bugsy. Nice to meet you.

It's nice to meet you, Bugsy. Now, can you explain why you're inside my ear?

Bugsy told Pedro about Baku's arrival, the inexplicable delay in the Haag superweapon, and the untimely expiration of the larval creature designed as a psychic conduit to the android handler. Trying to sound calm and confident, he went on to add that, due to their own apparent psycho-emotional connection, it was decided that it made sense for Bugsy to crawl inside Pedro's ear to establish contact, and that, using the wireless headset he was wearing, Baku could still guide Pedro to defeat the Palmetto Bug Monster. He stopped for a moment to see if his host would be enthusiastic about this plan, but all that the creature gave was something akin to a sustained mental sigh.

I can't win, Bugsy.

Sure you can. With Baku's help, you and I will be able to dispatch the giant cockroach.

No, I can't win. Somehow, while I waited for the Haag superweapon to arrive, I overcooked. I came out of the volcano too old to do much of anything. You can probably sense that I do not possess enough strength to win this battle.

Plus, you saw it with your own eyes when the giant bug mocked me openly as it kicked my ass. Now that we're connected, you definitely can feel exactly what I am feeling. I'm gravely wounded, very, very tired, and I know in my heart of hearts that I'm unable to complete my one and only mission – to save this planet. Bugsy, I've failed, I'm a failure, and I have let your species down. I'm sorry, but that's the real end of this whole story.

No, no, Pedro! We can keep hiding right here and let you continue to recover. And once I start communicating with Baku, he might have some ideas how to rejuvenate you quicker and how we're going to win this battle. You gotta have some faith, my friend.

Just then the headphones sprang to life with Baku's panicked pleas and the dire news that the Palmetto Bug Monster was closing in on them. Having grown accustomed to having a psychic conversation with Pedro, Bugsy struggled to find his voice to talk with the android, but ultimately he did.

"I'm here, I'm here! I've made contact with Pedro and we're awaiting orders as to what to do next."

There was the sound of raucous cheering in the background as the gang in Baku's ship celebrated the good news that Bugsy had survived the trip and made a connection with the gecko.

However, Baku's own response was full of incredulousness. "Who the hell is Pedro?"

"That's what He-Knew-Pat-Sajak prefers to be called. I can explain it all later, but now you need to start instructing us on what to do next. What should we do, Baku?"

"Get the Moog...He-Knew-Pat-Sajak...Pedro—whatever it's calling itself these days—out of there immediately. The giant cockroach is bearing down on you. Somehow, it can now see you and is coming right there to put an end to this defender of the planet. You're in a horrible location to put up any kind of fight in this valley here. Get that big lizard to stand up immediately and run away! Go anywhere you can, but you can't continue to lie there. Tell the Moog that that's a direct order."

Bugsy conveyed Baku's message to Pedro. However, there was no rise in optimism in the lizard's thoughts. In fact, its depressive feelings seemed to grow.

I told you, it's hopeless. I can't just get up and run. I'm too tired and in so much pain. I'm unable to do what the android is ordering me, Bugsy. It isn't possible. Plus, I'm not sure that I can move and keep camouflaged at the same time anymore. Once I stand up, everyone will be able to see me.

Come on, Pedro. Let's try. Okay? Try to stand up. Please. You can do that. Once we're standing tall again, Baku can tell us where to go next to get some distance between us and the cockroach. We just need to get you up first.

Okay, I'll try.

To Bugsy, the inherent feeling of rising up into the sky as the massive lizard got to its knees and then stood up was akin to a very smooth elevator ride. His interior altimeter told him he'd gained about fifteen stories in elevation, but it hadn't been too jarring an event. There were some sudden serious side effects, however. All at once, the young man could feel all of the intense pain that this maneuver had caused Pedro and, at the same time, he was able to "see" what the lizard could see. One moment he was staring at the black curtain of the darkened space of his confined position, the next he had the view of the overwhelming vista of the Alaskan landscape that Pedro was now standing in – albeit with a hazy filter over everything that the teenager attributed to the lizard having a bad case of cataracts. The combination of these powerful sensations was almost intolerable for Bugsy, and he struggled to keep his wits enough to ask Baku what to do next.

"RUN! Get that lizard the fuck out of there," the android hollered. "The bug is right around the next river bend and charging its way toward you. RUN!"

"Which direction?"

"Downriver, Bugsy. The Palmetto Bug is coming from upriver. It cannot catch up to you two. Hurry, hurry! If it gets a hold of you and the Moog now, all is lost."

地獄に仏

jigoku ni hotoke
Buddha in hell.

The group stared intently at the main monitor. If they weren't in the middle of such an earthshaking set of circumstances, the views of the surrounding landscape would have been quite soothing. The Yukon River broiled brownish through the stout gauntlet of frequent delta-like islands, and the pristine and lush river valley was full of forests of dwarf birches, willows, aspen, and spruce. The topography of the land went quickly from the flattened areas carved by the river up to the elevated plateaus and then higher into the tall and imposing mountain ranges that ran alongside the Yukon like the gutter guards of a mammoth natural bowling alley. No, if they weren't keeping track of a planet-destroying giant cockroach as it neared the Earth's last hope, the direly wounded gecko, the group could have been easily lulled into calmness by the placid scenes being shown on the screen.

As correctly forecasted by Pedro, as soon as he started moving away from the approaching cock-roach, he lost the ability to use his camouflage anymore. The group exclaimed distressed sounds as the giant lizard suddenly appeared while it began fleeing from its opponent. For if they could see it, then the cockroach and the military were now able to see it as well, and that was not a good thing.

"We've got to do *something*!" Ira Morton declared urgently.

"We can't do anything. It's totally up to them to help themselves." Baku answered back.

"You're sure this ship doesn't have lasers, alien?"

"It has no offensive weapons, General Richardson."

"And what does it have to defend itself?"

"It has shields, general."

"Shields?" General Richardson reacted as if the android had said that it had onions.

Baku was irritated at having to answer these inane questions, and he began speaking to the group in a patronizing tone. "Yes, shields. While traveling through interstellar space, it's kinda necessary to create an impermeable barrier between your spacecraft and the objects, both inert and offensive, that might collide with the hull and do harm to its integrity. It pays to have some protection, duh. So we have shields to keep us safe. *Nobody* likes to go BOOM!"

"We're not a bunch of idiots, Baku," Mayor Bishop sniped. "General Richardson was just inquiring about whether we could do anything to help Bugsy escape."

The Neanderthal sighed heavily and stared down at his feet. He shook his mane of hair and then looked back at the group, but smiled as he addressed them. "I know that. I'm sorry. I shouldn't have lost my cool. Let me start over. So, General Richardson, yes, we have shields. But not just simple shields. The Shxtor scientists devised some of the strongest shields in all of the galaxies, capable of repelling nearly any space debris or aggressive pulsar attacks. One time, on the other side of Gherrardia, I once piloted a Shxtor scientific research ship through an Altoonian war fleet in the middle of a nefarious asteroid field. If it weren't for my presence of mind to deploy the shields at the precisely right moment and then exhibit my otherworldly skills at the helm, I'm not sure that—"

"For the love of Pete, Baku," General Richardson roared, "I'm asking if your ship's shields would be able to survive a direct impact with the bug?"

Baku grinned soothingly. "Oh, don't be alarmed, sir, we are quite safe from anything that the Haag superweapon could throw at us in this ship. It cannot see us, and even if it did get lucky enough to fire at us with its ray blaster or swing at us with its arms, it couldn't penetrate the defensive shields. We have nothing to fear as long as we stay inside this ship and keep the shields up."

Usotsuki aggressively pointed his long, slender index finger at Baku like the tip of a samurai's katana. He placed his feet in the stance of *hassō-no-kamae* as he snarled with emotion, "You're missing General-san's point, Baku-san. As we say in Japan, *kōgeki wa saidai no bōgyo* – attack is the best defense.

What would happen if you drove this ship right into the Palmetto Bug Monster like a weapon? Would we survive?"

The android's jaw literally dropped once he'd comprehended the Japanese cryptozoologist's question. He'd never thought to use his ship as some kind of an instrument of attack, but now he tilted his head as his internal processor scrambled to figure out the correct answer.

"Yes! The odds are quite in our favor that, using this ship's superior technology and my substantial expertise at piloting it, we'd be able to tell the tale after a direct collision with the creature. I mean, we would be thrown around like popcorn inside it, but the ship would definitely survive."

"Then let's do it!" Bugsy's grandfather implored.

"Well, Mr. Morton, that's an easier task to talk about than actually do," Baku explained with a wag of his shaggy head. "Likely we'd survive, yes, but we could do real damage to my ship. Since this craft is vital for the survival of this planet, not to mention the survivability of yours truly...and all of you, too, of course...I'm not sure it is the most prudent plan to endanger it in any way."

Eve Sanderborn stopped narrating the scene for the filming and motioned Bernie to turn his camera from the monitors showing the fleeing gecko and the approaching cockroach to aim it directly at Baku. She intoned in her reporter's voice, "So, Mr. Baku, with the last great hope for Planet Earth, He-Knew-

Pat-Sajak, barely able to escape the approaching, murderous Palmetto Bug Monster, which seems ready to pounce and eradicate it, what do you propose to do? Now, please speak up, for all of the inhabitants of this planet are listening to what you intend to do next to save them. Are you going to use your ship as a weapon as has been suggested, or are you going to sit here in the aforementioned safety of your ship and watch that giant menace take care of the one thing stopping it from decimating this entire planet?"

The Neanderthal looked deep into the endless chasm of the lens peering at him and he started to say something, but he inhaled deeply and looked at the rest of the group as they watched his impromptu interview with a sustained interest. He peered at the monitor showing the approaching insect and then over at the one with the fleeing reptile on it. He grumbled low, "Okay, let's prepare ourselves to fly my ship into the Palmetto Bug Monster. I don't know what we're going to accomplish, but here we go. We're in for one helluva bumpy ride, folks, to say the least."

Baku's ship, still cloaked, stealthily descended to nearly ground level and then, with its rockets flaring, shot up toward the Palmetto Bug Monster's head. And like an invisible spiked strike from an invisible ball-and-chain flail wielded by a giant, invisible version of Hayo van Wolvega, the spacecraft caught the giant insect under the chin – well, to be biologically accurate, under the labrum and mandible – and delivered a devastating punch. Unseen and unexpected, the mighty blow caused the giant cockroach's head to snap up with such force that the creature was knocked off its feet and backward. Like a boxer who'd just had his clock cleaned by an uppercut, the insect lay there on the ground and appeared to even have been knocked out.

Inside the spacecraft, Baku had shouted out his instruction to assume crash positions just before he'd begun the strike, so the group had been able to get themselves into places to brace for the impact. However, the force of the collision had been such that they'd all been thrown together, and their writhing and tangled bodies, would have, if this all had happened under a much more positive sexually heightened encounter, resembled some kind of Roman orgy. In this case, the group endured the awkwardness of literally being thrown together before they then started to peel themselves from the knot of humanity they'd become, straighten their clothing, and return to view the monitors. These all revealed that the Palmetto Bug Monster was currently lying on its back and was too stunned to get up.

The sight of this brought about a series of heartfelt cheers, but General Richardson broke the sounds of celebration by saying emotionlessly, "Hit him again, android."

"But, General, that attack drained my ship's shields. They are only at three-quarters strength right now. Another such blow would take them down to half strength or lower. We'd become like a sitting duck without enough protection."

The general's eyes narrowed into slits as he roared, "Dammit, tin man, hit him again! We've got a chance to finally stop this menace before it destroys this planet."

Ira Morton, who, due to his advanced age, had suffered more than the rest from the jarring effects of the crash, struggled to stand erect as he attempted to loosen a spine that had seized up from the whole affair. He looked at the monitor aimed at the cockroach, and this revealed that the creature was now shaking its head in a gesture that indicated that it was regaining its bearings. The older man pointed at the screen as he addressed the group. "We should wait until it starts to stand up, General. Then we could bring the spacecraft down onto its head from above and hit it like a blackjack."

The Neanderthal became suddenly angry, and his expression was fierce and slightly scary as he snarled, "You earthlings aren't fully understanding what you're asking of me. If I bring this ship down and smash it into the Haag's head, I won't be able to stop its downward momentum enough and we will likely strike the ground, thus weakening our shields even further. They could get so perilously low, there'd be no guarantee that we'd be able to survive even the meekest attack from the monster."

Ira spoke defiantly. "But Bugsy needs our help. Anything we can do to buy him and the lizard time to recover helps our situation, right?"

"Not if it endangers us all. That is faulty reasoning, as far as I see it," Baku declared firmly.

"I agree with Ira," Mayor Bishop added. "Nothing else has seemed to cause that bug the pain that we've just inflicted on it. If we hit it again, we could disable it enough to give He-Knew-Pat-Sajak and Bugsy a fighting chance."

Baku did a little twitching dance as he fought to contain his reaction. "Our demise wouldn't do anybody any good. I'm still needed to guide the Moog superweapon to defeat the cockroach. And if it's all up to wonderful me to pull this off, I kinda need to survive. Look. We've given Bugsy time to get the Moog away from the Haag. See how the lizard is already around the next bend and making good progress in a downriver direction? We've struck a powerful blow and we've been a good diversion. But we can't blow our whole wad on this, right?"

General Richardson looked over at the Alaskan bush pilot and calmly asked, "Sarah, do you feel confident that you could take control of the ship and smash us into the bug again?"

This stark question caused a sound similar to one of Mayor Bishop's farts to be issued involuntarily by the group, especially Baku, who looked crestfallen by what the military man was inferring. He openly challenged the general. "Are you really suggesting such a distasteful and unchivalrous act as mutiny, General? Hard to believe that a military man such as yourself is prompting an act of insubordination like that."

General Richardson rolled his eyes as he spoke directly to Baku. "We wouldn't have to resort to any of this if you'd just do what we're asking, alien."

"Sorry, General, none of this sounds like a request."

"Are you getting all of this, Bernie?" Eve whispered to her cameraman.

"Oh, yeah. It's all on film, babe."

"The Palmetto Bug Monster is starting to get up!" the Japanese cryptozoologist announced loudly, pointing at the screen.

The group turned to see that the cockroach had recovered enough to get onto its knees. Ira stepped forward and pleaded gently, "Please, Baku. Another hit would do it even more harm. Please."

The Neanderthal clenched his teeth and growled in frustration, "Everyone needs to grab hold of something sturdy. This time is going to be much worse than the first one. Prepare yourselves for one helluva fender bender, earthlings. Whooee!"

The cloaked ship shot down toward the ground and hit the cockroach on the back of the head like a massive unseen cudgel, knocking the insect face down onto the ground. Unfortunately, Baku's prediction was highly accurate, and the spacecraft caromed from the impact and continued downward into the trees and crashed upon the earth. In this process, the group experienced the effects of not only one collision, but two. They were thrown together into another pile of bodies, but this time, buzzers went off, the lights of the chamber flickered, and even some sparks and smoke were released into the air around them.

As luck would have it, General Richardson found himself with his face fully planted in the cushiony cleavage of Sarah Pretlusky. And while the dirty old man was thoroughly happy to be in such a delightful fleshy haven, the silver metal pendant hanging off a delicate chain around the woman's neck, which he'd first seen during their scuffle outside of Circle, intrigued him even more. He grasped this object in his hands, identified that it was some kind of whistle, snapped the links easily, and then sat up and blew hard into it. Oddly, no discernible sound came out, so the general assumed that it was broken, but he tried to send another breath through it to make sure.

The improbability of this moment requires several questions to be asked: Why did this Alaskan bush pilot have a silver dog whistle around her neck? And why did General Richardson feel so compelled to take the whistle and blow into it?

It turns out, Sarah Pretlusky was the proud owner of a wolf-dog, and she used the dog whistle she wore around her neck to help manage the nearly wild animal. While it was still too unpredictable to live freely inside of her house, she'd built an outside enclosure that connected to her basement in such a way that the animal could get out of the weather when needed. It always responded well to the ultrasonic tweets from the dog whistle, allowing her to feed and train it whenever she needed to attempt to do so.

As to why the old military man snatched the whistle and blew into it, perhaps it was just muscle memory from his extensive military training. As soon as General Richardson came eyeball to pendant with the whistle around Sarah's supple neck, he was no longer in the enviable position of having his face smothered in a woman's breasts in an alien spacecraft that had just collided with a space monster. Suddenly, instead, he was on the battlefield and required to signal to his distressed troops. He was hoping that they would form ranks again after the concussive explosion they'd all experienced and initiate the needed counterattack on the enemy, but the soundless tootle of the silver whistle had sobered him up enough to realize the futility of his actions.

However, the act had not been entirely a futile exercise. During the earlier series of tumultuous tumblings, Baku had inadvertently flipped the switch to the external speakers of the spacecraft, and General Richardson's exhalations on the dog whistle had been transmitted directly at the Palmetto Bug Monster. Even though none of the group was a trained entomologist, they each would swear that the wounded giant cockroach emitted a cry of great pain from the emissions of the silent whistle.

So, while Baku struggled to get his heavily damaged ship disentangled from the tree branches and back up into the sky again, he began talking a blue streak to no one in particular. "What the hell just happened? If I didn't know better, I'd say that the blast from that odd whistle just injured the bug. That can't be possible. My sensors identified the sound of the whistle to be in the twenty-three to fifty-four *kilohertz* range. Shxtor scientific knowledge has no reports of ultrasonic sounds in this realm having any impacts on these creatures, yet that whistle seemed to have really hurt this one."

General Richardson excitedly held the whistle in front of him and said beseechingly, "Lemme do it again, alien. Another blast from the whistle could finish it off."

"Let me get my ship out of harm's way first, okay, General? According to my instruments, the shields are now down to less than twenty percent, which would not even be strong enough to protect us from a collision with a chickadee at this point. Also, the cloaking apparatus has been damaged and could fail at any moment. If this happens, we would be instantly revealed to the monster and to any of those earthling eyes circling us right now. And my propulsion system reactor has sustained a debilitating blow. Forget trying to strike again with the silent whistle. We quite literally might not be able to stay airborne or remain hidden from view."

The spacecraft labored to get to an altitude of several hundred feet and then hovered uneasily in

place. While the android worked furiously at his control panel and attempted to carry out the long list of
needed repairs, the group, sensing that now was not
the time to act like a collective gadfly, turned their
attention to the monitors again. On one, the Palmetto Bug Monster continued to lay face down on
the ground as it made jittery motions with its limbs.
These revealed that the creature had been deeply
hurt by the two physical assaults with the spacecraft
and the one unintentional sonic attack. On another screen, the now-visible He-Knew-Pat-Sajak continued to progress downstream at a good clip. The
group sighed loudly that they had somehow helped
the situation, even if it left them in such a perilous
condition.

Sarah Pretlusky sidled over to Baku and cleared
her throat. "Is there anything I can do to help? I can
patch together any flying machine with nothing
more than bailing wire, duct tape, and chewing gum.
Maybe I could be of some use."

Baku's first reaction was to disregard the woman's offer, but then he paused for a moment before
directing her to the cloaking system computer banks.
He began guiding her as to how to repair these while
he continued to pilot the ship. Seeing this, the rest of
the group, except for Eve and Bernie, who remained
at the monitor and continued to film and narrate the
scene outside, came over to offer their assistance.
Serendipitously, they all had expertise with mechanical objects – be it the military hardware of the Army,

the trucks of the Tok Road Commission, the Japanese computers needed for monster hunting, or the aged vehicles and buildings of the Parker House – and they were immediately put to work repairing the damage to the spacecraft.

About an hour later, Baku announced that they were out of danger. All damage had been temporarily fixed with impromptu patches and amateur tinkerings, and even though it now appeared that the Palmetto Bug Monster had recovered from its injuries, they congratulated one another for helping to right the ship. The chamber was free of smoke and sparks, the strength of the shields had begun to build, the cloaking device had been maintained, and the navigation and propulsion systems were nearly back to normal.

With disaster averted, Baku said confidently, "I think it's time to hit that SOB with another whistle blast. To purely satisfy my scientific curiosity, of course."

As he lowered the hovering ship down a bit to get closer to the now standing cockroach, General Richardson, who'd continued to hold on to Sarah's whistle as if it were now his, stalked over to the main control panel. The alien flicked a switch and nodded at the venerable military man, who puckered his lips onto the silver metal cylinder and then blew into it until his face reddened. No sound came out of the whistle, but the cockroach let out another sustained scream of agony.

This time, the Palmetto Bug Monster struck back. Without warning, the insect's vast abdomen glowed brightly and then it fired a blast of white-hot energy straight at Baku's ship. The powerful direct hit was like an electronic tsunami that smashed the vessel violently and undid all the hard work that the crew had just done to fix the damages.

The sounds of buzzers and alarms, numerous sparks, and smoke refilled the chamber as Baku screamed out the precariousness of their situation. "Shields are down to less than ten percent, which means that a spitball could take us down, the cloaking system is kaput so the cockroach and the rest of the world can see us clear as day, and the reactors are teetering toward going offline. I have to take care of getting those stabilized or we are lost. Sarah, take the controls! Make it hard for the Palmetto Bug Monster to get a bead on us"

Without hesitation, the female bush pilot started a series of evasive maneuvers and the rest of the group sprang into action to attend to repairs again in those areas of the ship that they'd been working on before. Although the situation appeared to be dire, the response of these earthlings in the face of this crisis bespoke a more veteran crew.

"The monster is looking straight at us," Eve reported loudly. "Now that we are uncloaked, it can see us and it's getting ready to fire again at us!"

Turning his head while his hands continued to scramble over the wires and components of the propulsion system, Baku mused, "I don't know how it found us like that for its first shot, but now that we're visible, we are one blast from becoming a dust cloud."

"The fuck we are!" Sarah snarled. "I've had enough of this shit. We're getting the hell out of here."

Baku shrieked out his concern. "What are you doing? We barely have enough power to control—aahhh!"

Sarah let the spacecraft drop steeply until it had built up great speed and then she powered the rockets to blast the craft just over the treetops around and past the giant cockroach, up the raised riverbank, and into the surrounding mountain valleys. Thrown off their feet by the forceful motions of the craft, the earthling group all remembered enough of her flying skills from their initial terrifying flight up to Circle to not panic. Baku, regrettably, was ill-prepared for any of this. His sole response was similar to someone riding the Comet rollercoaster at the Crystal Beach amusement park in Fort Erie, Canada, which was hardly a dignified reaction for an advanced android of alien design.

"The Palmetto Bug Monster is starting to follow us," Eve announced to the group.

They all looked at the monitor and saw that the cockroach had become thoroughly preoccupied with the now-visible silver spacecraft and was giving chase to it. Instead of continuing on down the Yukon in pursuit of the gecko, the huge bug was clambering to get inland to hound after them. Leaving the relative flatness of the river valley meant that the creature was struggling more to make any headway through the thick trees of the forest and over the elevation changes of the wilderness area.

Baku, who was still focused on making the necessary repairs, spoke to the group. "This is really fascinating. It looks like we've angered the creature enough by wounding it that it wants nothing more than to get its hands on us...if Haags had hands, that is. This has never happened before. The creature is completely disregarding its prime mission to get some retribution on us. It's like we've hurt its feelings, and it won't rest until it gets at us. Perhaps it will continue to do this and let Bugsy and the Moog heal up before it's time for the big, fated, final battle."

Usotsuki scratched his stubbled chin and looked from the monitors over to Sarah. He spoke calmly, but authoritatively. "Slow down a little, Sarah-san."

"What?" Baku screamed. "No, no, no, we can't turn and fight, not now. We're still in too much of a weakened state. We cannot take another hit."

General Richardson shook his head. "We're not going to turn and fight, alien. We're going to make ourselves into the perfect lure. The crazy Japanese gangster is right. If we slow down, shake our shiny ass, and get the monster's complete attention, we might just be able to take the bug into the thick of these mountains and make it hard for it to get anywhere else."

Baku swung his arm to gesture at the monitors showing the giant cockroach starting to chase them. "Well...unless it opens its wings and flies right at us to take care of business! Then it's game over for us."

"No, Baku, they're right," Ira remarked. "We need to make it so that the monster keeps pursuing us. If we slow down and make sure that it sees us, and maybe even hit it with some sonic blasts from the whistle from time to time, it'll continue to try and get to us. We can use these mountains as a good place to sneak and snipe at it, and thereby give Bugsy and Pedro even more time to escape. Sarah's made a career of using these valleys and rivers as places to dip and dodge and stay off the radar."

Baku spun to look at the group before expressing his complete vexation with them. "Do I need to remind you all that we are completely visible to *everyone* right now? If a missile were to be fired at us by some trigger-happy pilot of one of those jets circling the area, our shields aren't up to fending off that kind of attack. Whether the cockroach gets us or an air-to-air missile hits us, we can't be waltzing around these mountain peaks like we're totally safe. We're not, and you're all forgetting that fact."

Sarah put her hand on the alien's arm, and the gesture seemed to pacify him somewhat. Her voice was soothing when she said, "Don't worry, Baku, I'll keep us out of the monster's reach while I scan the skies for any incoming missiles. You guys focus on fixing this ship while I keep the cockroach's attention.

It's so full of piss and vinegar right now and wants so badly to be able to get at us – we've just gotta keep it preoccupied enough that it doesn't remember to go after Bugsy and the lizard. I've got this."

Baku grimaced. "Alright, earthlings, we can try your plan. But I do have one question for General Richardson."

"Fire away, alien," the military man said with supreme confidence.

"Why *haven't* the military planes sent a barrage of missiles toward us yet? I mean, they can see us as clear as day."

General Richardson smiled when he heard this, and he let his fingers start scratching his nose. "I cannot rightly say why at this moment, alien. However, the fact that they haven't yet lets me know that there must be a military strategy in place that our sudden appearance and our current behavior doesn't infringe upon. In other words, we are useful to the big overall plan. I guess we'll know as soon as we are no longer part of it. I can't guarantee we won't be facing a missile attack at some point, but I'm guessing we just need to worry about the monster...for now."

Baku soaked in the man's words and then he announced to the group, "I need to communicate with Bugsy to tell him what's happening."

He went over to the microphone and spoke into it. "Hey, Bugsy, we've got the Palmetto Bug Monster following us right now. You two need to continue down the river until you get to the town of Eagle and then take the Taylor Highway south. That open and semi-paved road will give the Moog a better surface to make good speed. Tell it to enact the Recovery Protocol as you go, if it hasn't done so yet."

"He really prefers to be called Pedro," responded Bugsy's voice.

Baku looked at the speaker as if it had just punched him and then he leaned in toward the microphone. "What? I don't care what it wants to be called! Just make haste to get as far as you can and we'll try to lure the cockroach into the mountains to buy some more time. Then we'll need to figure out a way to bring the two superweapons together for their battle somewhere that's far enough away from people."

"Is my grandfather okay?"

"Yes, he's fine."

"That's good. I'm fine, too. Talk to you soon. Good luck."

相変わらず

ai kawarazu
Together, unchanging.

The United States of America was currently a real mess. It would be easy to pull up the imagery of some flaming culinary metaphors – perhaps some flambé dishes like bananas Foster or cheese saganaki – to aptly describe the present state of the Union, but that might be more akin to reaching for the literary low-hanging fruit. For while some of the flames from the Palmetto Bug Monster's rampage were indeed still burning, or at least smoldering, the reason that the nation was reeling from it all went well beyond dealing with the literal and the physical realities of what amounted to an alien invasion. No, if one were being entirely honest, the good ol' USA now most closely resembled a pitted green olive.

The meteor carrying the Palmetto Bug Monster may have landed nearly six hundred miles from the actual geographical center of the "Lower 48," which is twenty miles north of Lebanon, Kansas, but many citizens viewed its impact crater to be in the very middle of America. By a somewhat faulty logical progression, Vincennes, Indiana – a town that many Americans still needed to look up in an atlas to pinpoint its location on the Wabash River – was now seen as being a vitally important site within the heartland of the country. Hence the town's vaporization by the cockroach's space rock was considered to be a devastating strike at the very core of the nation.

The Palmetto Bug Monster's disastrous trek to Indianapolis and then up to Chicago was comparable to General William Tecumseh Sherman's "March to the Sea" during the American Civil War. The sixty-two thousand Union troops under the Ohioan general had cut a two-hundred-and-eighty-five-mile-long swath of destruction across the Confederate state of Georgia, from Atlanta to Savannah, as they embarked on their scorched-earth campaign of "total war." The singular Palmetto Bug Monster, on the other hand, left a wide lane of total annihilation that ran two hundred and seventy-three miles from Vincennes to Indy to Chicago – plus another thousand miles from Chicago up to the Canadian border. Perhaps the alien creature's ability to inflict damage might have been much more complete than a bunch of smelly, ignorant, and illiterate Northern soldiers, but both actions had cut the country to the very core.

Additionally, with the news that there were now two monsters and that they were duking it out in faraway Alaska, most Americans used the perceived respite in an attempt to comprehend what had actually happened to them. But as they regarded the almost ineffable wreckage of two of their major cities

– which now both more closely resembled the state of Hiroshima and Nagasaki on Alfred Hitchcock's forty-sixth birthday – and saw the incalculably high death toll of civilians as well as were bombarded with the ever-increasing casualty lists from the military, they turned their attention onto Washington, D.C. to get some kind of relief from the leaders there. Regrettably, there was nothing positive happening in that city, so their sense of hopelessness only increased exponentially when they saw the unchecked chaos going on in the nation's capital. It would be an understatement to say that there was a real hole running through the middle of most Americans these days.

The President, seen by many before this crisis as a weak man who was too much of a pacifist to adequately serve in the office, had virtually disappeared from view. After his staunch refusal to use nuclear weapons, which he'd voiced during his last news conference to the nation, he'd either voluntarily barricaded himself inside the White House or had been imprisoned there by the apparent forces that were attempting to take over. In the absence of a recent visual sighting of the man or even a verbal acknowledgement of his existence, a whole slew of rumors abounded unchecked, including that the President himself was an alien.

Other furphies were that the FBI had been tasked with finding the missing First Lady. That the CIA had been ordered to attempt to design some kind of mind-control device to turn the giant cock-roach into their slave weapon of mass destruction. That Congress had dissolved into nothing but a cesspool of self-serving and fraudulent individuals who were scrambling to save their own asses, assert themselves for personal gains, or get themselves away from the dangerous place that the capital had become. That alien soldiers were now active in the conflict. That the governors of all fifty states had been told that they were now on their own, as the federal government was too overwhelmed and fractured to be able to respond and be helpful in any way. And that the Joint Chiefs of Staff were now in charge.

This last rumor turned out to be the most true. With the President no longer acting as if he were the leader in any way other than in title, these mili-tary men had essentially assumed control. They were spearheading the defense of the country against the alien monster invasion and actively communicating their plans with the American public as if they were the top dogs. So, by default, they were the ones with the chest candy who most everybody now thought of as the big kahunas. The members of Congress and some of the other checks and balances of the Amer-ican governmental system were so intimidated by the big and lethal stick that this collective of senior uniformed leaders carried that they quickly conced-ed whenever there were any disputes. Not only that, they frequently tripped over their own feet in their retreat to get out of the way of these powerful and grizzled veterans.

The Chairman of the Joint Chiefs of Staff was now the former Chief of the Army, Eduardo "Fast Eddie" Newman, and this robust and powerful four-star general looked large and in charge as he stepped in front of the camera and held his widely watched press conference after the fight between the Palmetto Bug Monster and He-Knew-Pat-Sajak. Using very colorful, yet hazily detailed, charts and maps, he outlined how the entire state of Alaska was now under martial law. All travel to and from the state was strictly forbidden, the media was currently being restricted to the point of an all-out blackout, and the U.S. military was in absolute control of enforcing these new rules. He quickly added that such radical measures had been enacted to turn Alaska into a killing chamber that could deal with the alien cockroach once and for all.

With the U.S. armed forces amassing along the Alaska Highway as an immovable wall, the cockroach was, the general boasted, pinned in. Not only that, but the concentration of the Canadian Army, the Royal Canadian Air Force, and the Royal Canadian Navy gathering on the border between Alaska and the Yukon Territory created an eastern flank. To the west, General Newman pointed out how the immense buildup of Soviet weaponry in their Eastern Military District had created another framing flank. Looking very confident, the new supreme leader of the U.S. announced that these huge and powerful armies were now positioned in such a way to be like the jaws of a massive pincher closing down on the cockroach to crush it.

Pundits of American military strategy noticed that the general had not made any mention of either using nuclear weapons or the status of the giant gecko. The omission about the nukes was taken as being evidence that somehow the President was still sitting so tightly on the control of these armaments that the Joint Chiefs of Staff hadn't gotten their hands on them...yet. The implications of the resulting need to forcibly wrestle these weapons of mass destruction away from the President of the United States caused those in the know to shake their heads with worry that the country had somehow come to a watershed moment that it couldn't return from.

The non-admission about the giant gecko was more challenging to stomach. The fact that the general hadn't put a bullseye onto the back of the alien lizard seemed to be alarming to many, mostly because it implied that the military still saw the creature as a viable hope for stopping the cockroach. This seemed ridiculous to most people, especially after watching on national television the creature getting the stuffing kicked out of it by the giant cockroach. Most fully expected that the Palmetto Bug Monster was going to ultimately track down He-Knew-Pat-Sajak once again and easily rip it to pieces without breaking a sweat...before turning its attention fully back onto destroying the human race.

The only slim hope to hold fast to for many was that the military would drop an atomic bomb on the cockroach and the lizard while they were fighting and take care of two problems at the same time.

知らぬが仏

shiranu ga hotoke
Not knowing is Buddha.

Bugsy could sense that Pedro was about out of gas and ready to collapse, but he urged the giant gecko to keep going until they were right outside of Eagle, Alaska. Baku had directed them to catch the origin of the Taylor Highway here, and now that they were close enough, it seemed like a safe place to take a little rest. He suggested to Pedro that it was time to re-camouflage and curl up on the largest river island off from the town. It was big enough to accommodate the one-hundred-and-fifty-foot-tall lizard, and with the creature blending into the background, they would be safe from the prying eyes of the locals and, more importantly, from the military jets that were prowling the skies.

Bugsy just hoped that his grandfather and the gang could keep the cockroach preoccupied long enough to get them time to rest and recuperate. If Pedro could heal just a bit, maybe with Baku's help they could defeat the Palmetto Bug Monster. It was all a lot to hope for.

I'm tired. I need to sleep.

Okay, Pedro, take a little snooze. Oh, Baku wanted me to re-mind you about enacting the Recovery Protocol. We need to get you back into fighting shape.

I've already started the healing procedures, but it won't matter...not in the end.

Get some rest. We'll figure out what happens next when you wake up.

Bugsy didn't expect any more thoughts to come from his humongous host, and he lay in the dark silence and let his mind wander. The lizard's eyes were closed and he'd obviously fallen asleep, so there wasn't much to do at the moment except think. However, after a little while in this quiet darkness, Bugsy started to get fatigued as well. It had been a stressful stretch of days and he'd not been able to get enough rest. Staying awake wouldn't serve the team, so he let himself drift off. He didn't know if he and Pedro would share dreams as they slept or not, but the prospect of seeing what an alien superweap-on dreamed of intrigued him. He hoped it wasn't go-ing to be too scary, surreal, or sexual, but he couldn't control any of that.

When Bugsy awoke, he could see that Pedro had his eyes open, and that the sun was rising. He had slept very hard, and in spite of the perceived discomfort of being crammed in the terminus of the ear canal of a giant alien gecko, he could not complain about his night of sleep.

You snore.

Do I?

Yes, your heavy breathing sounds were all I could hear in my ear all night.

Sorry.

It's okay. I actually found it rather soothing to hear that someone was with me. I must admit that I've felt quite alone since coming out of the volcano.

You're not alone anymore, Pedro.

No, I'm not. Well, Bugsy, what do you think we should do now?

Baku said we should head toward the Taylor Highway to make our way south.

The lizard raised its head and looked over at the small Alaskan town on the banks of the Yukon. Bugsy could see for himself the buildings and the streets of Eagle, but he sensed that Pedro was concerned about hurting anyone as he made his way through the town. This continuing philanthropic quality of the creature made Bugsy smile.

If you can tiptoe through the streets and around the buildings, Pedro, I bet that, once we're on the road, it will get easier to move quickly without doing any harm.

Hopefully, it's early enough that we won't encounter too many of your kind. I do hope that I can regain enough of my balance and dexterity to not be too clumsy. I'd hate to slip and crush someone or do unwarranted damage.

Just take your time. My grandfather says that more harm happens when he's rushing to get things done. Sure, we're in a little hurry, but we also don't have to rush and make some costly mistakes.

Remember, once I start moving, I will no longer be able to stay camouflaged. I'm still too hurt to do both at the same time anymore. I am going to be a slow-moving and very visible target again.

I know, Pedro. Don't worry about all of that. Just take your time.

The giant lizard stood up and stretched. It easily crossed the river tributary to get into the heart of Eagle. As it tightrope-walked its way through the town's narrow streets, Bugsy felt just how wonky the animal's balance truly was. It struggled to keep its feet from catching on things, and there were several times when the immense creature tottered awkwardly enough to risk falling down. But they ultimately made it to the edge of town without any major incident. Once on the cleared space of the open road, they were able to make their way quickly.

After a mile or so, Pedro cursed to himself. Bugsy wasn't sure what he was trying to say.

What?

I just get mad at how my body is rebelling on me.

Is this part of what you called your "overcooking" while you were waiting for the cockroach?

Yes. I have some memories from before I came to your planet, but they're so distant and faint as to be near invisible to me now. I know that there was a time of my life before I was put into the volcano, but so much changed while I was hidden in there, and now I'm old without having ever enjoyed a youth. It causes me to be angry all the time.

My grandfather, too, calls himself a grumpy old man.

Yes, I get that. But he might be that way because he remembers the days he was more able. For me, I don't have a clear recollection of ever being young. I just know that all of the simple tasks I'm attempting to undertake these days – like sneaking through a sleeping earthling town – shouldn't be so hard for me. Whereas your grandfather probably has many memories of being a virile younger version of himself and being free to love, fuck, and fight with vigor, I don't. There is no earlier version of me that I can remember, just this old and useless husk that exists nowadays. And because I know that I won't be able to defeat the Haag – the frustration from that realization is all-consuming, Bugsy.

We'll get through this, Pedro. You'll regain your strength, and then Baku will be able to guide you on how to defeat the Palmetto Bug Monster. I truly believe that we all can help you accomplish your mission.

When? Where? Instead of running away, I should be heading straight toward the cockroach to fight it. But I'm scared, Bugsy. I know I shouldn't say that, but it's true. I'm scared to fight it because I know that I can't beat it, not in my current condition.

But the bug is truly all alone. It's got no one supporting it. You've got me, Baku, and a big group of supporters who are doing whatever they can to help. You're not alone, Pedro. You've got a whole team in your corner.

What if that's not enough?

Bugsy found himself in the unenviable position of being the main cheerleader to a cognizant giant entity that was rightfully doubting itself. Through his intimate psychic connection with Pedro, it was now clear to him that the lizard was indeed too wounded, too frail, and too unconfident to defeat the Palmetto Bug Monster in a head-to-head battle. To continue blowing smoke up the creature's ass and keep issuing baseless encouragements that were one shade away from blatant lies would only make things worse. Holding to false optimism was like trying to get to and capture a loose beach ball on a lake during a windy day – it took more energy to keep trying and failing than it did to give up. One thing Bugsy had learned from the hardships from his parental abandonment and the bullies at school was that hard truths might be more difficult to soak up, but there's something powerful in being allowed to process the reality you are actually in.

What if the role you're supposed to play in the destruction of the cockroach is a supportive one? What if you're not actually supposed to be the star?

Explain.

Let's say that you and I engage the Palmetto Bug Monster, but we make it so that someone else can kill it. Isn't the main goal to kill the creature and save the planet? Maybe you can beat the bug by yourself, maybe you can't. But what if you could wound it or hold it down in such a way to expose one of its vulnerable areas to the military forces of Earth at the right time, and they could apply the coup de grace? You might not get the outright credit for defeating the creature, but isn't a win a win?

There was a brief delay in the creature's response to this last thought. Bugsy was nervous that he'd been too honest with Pedro, but he could begin to discern a differing type of emotion starting to percolate within the lizard. To call it optimism would be overambitious, but it was clearly a new emotion. He was unsure whether giant alien geckos could grin or not, but he imagined that if he could see Pedro's mouth currently, it would be smiling. Regardless of any of this, Bugsy could tell that their pace had suddenly picked up.

You are absolutely right, Bugsy. A win is a win.

石が流れて木の葉が沈む

ishi ga nagarete konoha ga shizumu.
Rocks will flow, and leaves will sink.

Eve Sanderborn knew that she needed to stay focused on the monitors and continue to narrate the amazing footage that Bernie was capturing, but she could not help herself from looking over at the group of people and the alien that she was sharing this spacecraft command center with and feel a warmth in her body that she quickly attributed to a growing sense of admiration. As an ambitious news reporter, she was well aware that she had sunk her teeth into the story that would make her career and carry her for the rest of her life. As a young woman, still in her prime and capable of feeling emotions that she often suppressed or shoved to the side to maintain her pursuit of greatness, she knew that she was experiencing something that, even though it was going to change *everything* for her professionally, was really going to change her *personally*.

During the previous twelve hours, Baku's ship had maintained a tense game of cat and mouse with the Palmetto Bug Monster. While successfully evading and baiting the beast, a subtle but powerful transformation was occurring within the ragtag group – this odd collection of individuals was becoming a real team. With all of the damage sustained from the two collisions with the cockroach patched up enough to proceed without worry and the infuriated bug now entirely obsessed with chasing them deep into the tricky, twisted mountainous area, the seven earthlings and one alien android had stopped acting like a captain and his idle guests and had started to become a supportive, united, and collaborative team.

Baku and Sarah were like the crew of the infamous Pan Am Flight 50. But instead of flying a Boeing 747SP over both poles of the Planet Earth, these two took turns flying the spaceship around treacherous mountain peaks fast enough to escape all of the ray blasts and violent foreleg strikes from the cockroach, but slow enough to keep the enraged giant creature enticed enough to keep following them. Baku learned from Sarah how to hug the ground and use the terrain as a tool of evasion. Sarah learned from Baku how to hyper-focus and move her fingers across the control panel in a blur of efficiency. Together, spelling one another whenever the other got tired or frustrated, they kept the monster at bay as they brought it into a landscape that was harsh enough to cause it to have to struggle and fight to keep up its impassioned pursuit. Although it was hard to tell if the alien cockroach was truly fatiguing or not, the image on the monitors of the bug seemingly slipping and tripping as it kept coming after them into the Alaskan wilderness made the group smile cruelly with satisfaction.

General Richardson was no longer issuing orders as if he were in charge. Instead, he had taken on the role of monitoring the military forces that Baku was observing. He'd made it abundantly clear that he wasn't going to help with the injuring of any personnel or the damaging of any American weapons, but with his vast knowledge of military strategy, he'd quickly discerned that the U.S. Air Force seemed content to let the cockroach and the now-visible alien spaceship play out this ridiculous game of tag within these unpopulated mountains. He identified – correctly, as it turned out – that the big plan was to drive the cockroach south and west into a massive armed trap waiting for the creature there, and as long as the UFO led the monster toward that, they weren't going to waste any of their missiles to attack it. Scanning a map, he advised Sarah and Baku to guide the ship and the pursuing insect in the direction of Chicken, Alaska, which he calculated would be an ideal location for the final battle.

Usotsuki was in charge of keeping his eye on the Palmetto Bug Monster's behavior and keeping the pilots apprised whenever it appeared that the cockroach was losing interest in them and starting to refocus on the location of the gecko. Sometimes he'd yell out that they needed to do a little *gion-odori*, which he explained was his way of saying that they needed to "shake their booty" a little more to keep the giant creature interested enough to continue chasing them. Several times, he had asked General Richardson to blow into the dog whistle to wound and anger the cockroach some more, but although the gruff military man was more than willing to do this until his face resembled a beet, the effects of this strategy seemed to be waning the more they employed it. The Japanese cryptozoologist worried that the Palmetto Bug Monster was growing immune to the pain from the ultrasonic whistle, the outcome of which would have dire consequences upon their plans to continue to lure the monster in the right direction.

Ira Morton assumed the role of the main communicator with Bugsy. Most of this entailed his describing what they were each currently doing and thinking, but a lot of it became the idle banter that they'd enjoyed as grandfather and grandson. Their back-and-forth dialogue seemed to relax them both enough to keep the situation from overwhelming them, and the infectious sound of the older man laughing at something that Bugsy had said lightened the mood in the entire alien ship. Ira would convey some of the highlights to the group, and the crew members would send messages of encouragement back.

The overall sense was that their current circumstances paralleled one another in an eerie way – the teenager and the gecko were bonding together just as efficiently as the humans were connecting with the alien android and his spacecraft.

Even Eve and Bernie's roles had changed. No longer were they journalists solely attempting to capture the story that they imagined would save their careers. Seeing how much the group in the spaceship was now gelling as a fighting unit, they had become more like chroniclers of a huge, life-changing event – like a beloved uncle with an Eastman Kodak Super 8 camera recording an important family function, or a filmmaker documenting something that was at risk of never happening again. The impact of this was that the rest of the crew now felt unifying vibes coming from the two journalists instead of the divisive emotions of their earlier self-promotion, and that only continued to focus them all on the task at hand – leading the Palmetto Bug Monster to its demise.

Mayor Bishop found his role to be the provider of hospitality. Without any prompting, he'd shed the slightly ridiculous aviator leather cap and had begun to flutter around the group in an attentive manner. He'd never thought of himself as a professional innkeeper, but now he slipped into making the effort to ensure that each member of the team was taken care of during this momentous endeavor. He'd thought far enough ahead to ensure that some snacks and drinks had been loaded onto Baku's ship before they'd taken off from the Parker House, and he now distributed these with an extra wide Marty Feldman-like smile and a silly curtsy whenever someone was looking like they needed a boost. He'd quietly conversed with the alien android to figure out some kind of waste management, so they had what amounted to a working toilet, and no one more than he was happy to finally have a place to take care of this business. He even lovingly tucked in those who were needing to take a quick rest, using some alien fabrics as makeshift blankets and pillows.

Mayor Bishop went around the control center of the spacecraft with an efficiency that made his helpful actions and supportive comments almost unnoticeable and assumed. And like all good hosts, he did all of this without stopping to get a compliment or praise – he was just like some kind of hummingbird flitting amongst them and taking care of everyone.

It was General Richardson who broke this growing spell of optimism and goodwill within the shared chamber. He had begun shuffling the paper charts that Baku had printed out for him with motions that were almost violent, and then he announced to the group, "Well, ladies and gentlemen, we've run out of runway. We've kept the bug's attention focused on us for a long time, but we just now entered the Chicken Creek tributary and it's a straight shot down from here to where the kid and the gecko are waiting. It's time to let Bugsy know that we're on our way."

Ira spoke into the microphone to inform Bugsy that there was no more time to prepare. The final battle was nearly at hand.

Bugsy's response was quick and strong. "We are ready for it."

Almost on cue, the Palmetto Bug Monster appeared to realize that it was now within striking distance of its hated opponent. Instead of fixing its attention on the spacecraft anymore, it headed purposefully down the creek bed without hesitation. Baku and Sarah brought the vessel down toward the monster for one last attempt to distract it, but it only wanted to get to the gecko. Without as much as a foreleg swing or bio-ray blaster shot, it sped past the shimmering alien craft and trudged southward with a singular focus.

Inside the ship, there was the stunned silence that occurs when there's been such a painfully clear loss of purpose. All of the crew now looked at the monitors to see the giant cockroach acting like an eager shark following a trail of tuna blood as it approached where the wounded gecko and Bugsy waited, and each of the crew wrangled with the emotions of their newfound helplessness. This was so paralyzing that they risked just becoming a mere monument of idleness floating in the sunny Alaskan sky.

Mayor Bishop now moved dramatically as he tried to awaken them out of their stupor. Looking just like Marty Feldman as the over-attentive bodyguard in *Sex with a Smile*, he passionately implored the group, "Hey, guys, snap out of it! We did what we could to give Bugsy and Pedro enough time to heal up and get themselves ready for this. Thanks to us, that stupid cockroach not only felt some pain, it had to make it through the toughest terrain it's ever had to travel through. We wounded it and I think we tired it out a little – these are really good things that might help defeat it. Now we need to shift back into being the fully supportive team for this final confrontation."

"The odd-looking little man is right," General Richardson agreed. "We need to resume our duties to ensure that the cockroach dies here and now. Baku, you need to cloak the ship again and take us up to a vantage point where we can see what's going on and can help win this battle."

Baku helped Sarah to engage the cloaking device and started to guide the ship toward the best vantage point, but he kindly called over to Bugsy's grandfather, "Mr. Morton, I'm sorry to be the one to say it, but you need to say goodbye to your grandson now. It's time for me to do my thing and guide the Moog to victory. And I know it's hard to admit, sir, but we need this all to end."

The group looked at the old man as the truth of the matter hit him and the swelling melancholy overwhelmed him. He nodded feebly to them and then spoke into the microphone. "Okay, Bugsy, I've got to sign off now. Baku is going to start sending the strategies for defeating the cockroach. Know that I love you, boy. I'm proud of you."

Eve chimed in, "We all are, Bugsy. All of us in this spacecraft and all of humanity – we all are grateful to you for what you're trying to do. I hope that you can feel all of our support coming your way!"

Bugsy responded that he could feel that support from them and that he'd talk to them once the cockroach was a stain on the bottom of Pedro's feet. He sounded very confident as he said he'd await Baku's directions. Then he went silent.

Baku's cloaked ship flew high up above the town of Chicken and hovered unseen in place. General Richardson asked for the alien to hail the United States military forces on the radio. The startled reaction to hearing directly from the alien ship was a series of nervous questions about what the UFO wanted and where it currently was.

The general grabbed the mike and began speaking in an authoritative voice.

"This is General Buchanan Richardson of the United States Army, and I am aboard the alien spacecraft with six other humans and an alien android. We've been working hard to get the cockroach here so that the gecko can fight it and destroy it. Henry Kissinger has given me the authority to pursue these ends, and I want to relay to him that it is time for one-stop shopping. All military units need to be pulled back to a distance that will keep them safe from whatever happens next."

There was a bout of uneasy static on the radio as a response to this announcement. Then the meek voice replied, "Roger that, General Richardson. I will alert my superiors and Mr. Kissinger about this matter and we will take the appropriate action, if possible. Thank you, sir."

"And if you haven't already done so, it's time to evacuate all of the citizens of Chicken. There's going to be one helluva dust-up here in just a few moments, and no one needs to be nearby for that."

"Roger, General. The town is empty. Hopefully the gecko can take care of the bug this time."

The general nodded as he said into the microphone, "It'll give it the old college try, that's for sure, soldier. I will be in contact in the future, whenever that's possible. General Richardson out."

The group exhaled with relief that the general had been able to make contact with the military forces around them and that He-Knew-Pat-Sajak would be given the chance to defeat the Palmetto Bug Monster without becoming a target. General Richardson looked at them with a comforting expression on his face, but his thoughts were much more conflicted. He was grateful that, for the first time in this whole campaign, the radioman appeared to recognize his name and had acknowledged Kissinger's role in the mission, and the general hoped that he'd been able to dispense his thinly-veiled coded message that it was time to use nuclear weapons on the monsters as they fought. This was clearly a time when it was best to kill two birds with one stone.

口は災いの元

kuchi wa wazawai no moto
The mouth is the source of disaster.

Bugsy and Pedro could now hear the Palmetto Bug Monster trudging toward them, roaring and hissing loudly as it crashed through the woods and houses on the banks of the creek. Bugsy could sense that the giant gecko had tensed up for battle, but there was a renewed streak of confidence to the lizard's movement as they made their way to the far end of the gravel runway at Chicken Airport to await the bug's arrival. General Richardson had passed the recommendation through Baku that the airport was the best site for the final battle, and it made a certain amount of sense that, if two giant alien creatures were going to tussle to the death, the wide-open spaces of the facility would even the playing field.

However, the next set of commands from Baku caused Bugsy an uneasy moment. The alien android directed that the Moog should start answering the Haag with its own high-volume responses because riling up the enemy monster could be a key to victory. Bugsy didn't relay this straight to the gecko because he thought that it was wrong on two levels.

First of all, he'd made it abundantly clear that Pedro didn't want to be called the Moog anymore. And secondly, he'd learned during all of those countless confrontations outside the high school combating Jerry Zumquist and his thugs that a silent response was a much better way to throw off an overly verbal opponent. In spite of wanting not to get in the way of a victory, Bugsy felt compelled to push back on the order.

"Mr. Baku, please refer to him as Pedro. He doesn't like the sound or meaning of Moog, and it will make him more inspired to fight if you call him by his preferred name. Also, I've found it far more effective to leave a bully guessing as to what you're thinking as they come near you, especially when they are talking trash. It unnerves them."

Baku made a sound that was like an electronic blip and then he responded curtly, "The Moog is a Moog. It doesn't matter what we call him. And, Bugsy, these are monsters designed to combat one another to the death, not a bunch of moronic teenage earthlings with raging hormones who are getting ready to rumble. Just pass on my command to the Moog and don't waste time arguing."

Bugsy was now fuming with anger, but he knew that Baku's last jab had been correct. It wasn't the time to second-guess any orders; it was the time to do everything needed to defeat the threat. He prepared to swallow his pride and just pass on the message to Pedro, but he'd forgotten just how tightly the two of them were now joined.

Thank you for sticking up for me, Bugsy. Apparently my android handler doesn't understand me or respect me as much as you do. That's okay. We're in this to win this. But I agree with you, it seems silly to respond to the bug's insults.

What's it saying? I can feel that you're getting angry at it.

It just said that my mother must have copulated with a bunch of ugly creatures to create something as hideous and weak as me. Oh, and that, if given the chance, it'd love to copulate with my mother as well.

Not to sound ignorant or insulting, Pedro, but did you even have a mother?

Huh, good point. I'm not actually sure. If not, it's certainly making an ass out of itself right now, isn't it?

Uh, yep, it sure is.

Baku's voice suddenly came through the headphones, and it sounded perturbed and grumpy.

"Bugsy, you simply cannot overrule an order. You need to tell the Moog everything I say to you. It is imperative to our success. Got it?"

"Yes, Mr. Baku. Pedro and I talked about it, and he agreed with me about the effectiveness of not responding. Plus, the cockroach was talking about his mother just now, and since we aren't even sure of whether there was a mother involved with Pedro's creation, it is rather silly to be insulting—"

"Stop talking, Bugsy. No more talking! Your job is to not talk from now on. You need to listen. Can you see out of the Moog's eyes?"

"Yes, I am able to see and hear everything he can."

"Good. Do you see that the cockroach is crashing through the village center on its way to you? The fight is here and now. You need to realize your role in this. Stop talking, just listen. With the larvae, I send my thoughts to them and they advise the Moog on what to do. They are genetically modified to understand the Shxtor language and there is a direct line of communication from my android cerebral processors to the brain of the Moog. But you don't speak Shxtor, Bugsy. I'm going to be speaking a completely alien language to you, and you're going to have to relay things you don't comprehend directly into your own thoughts. If you miss anything that I say because you're questioning the orders, there will be the potential for the winning strategy to be lost in translation, and we will lose this fight. Do you understand?"

"Yes."

The Palmetto Bug Monster was now at the other end of the runway, and it continued to be loud and antagonizing. The cockroach was an impressive specimen, and Bugsy could understand why Pedro might be a bit intimidated. But as he peered at what Pedro's rheumy eyes were taking in, he could not help but notice that the bug was sporting a new swollen area under its jaw and on the back of its head. He could also sense a slight sluggishness to its movements that hadn't been there when he'd witnessed the first fight in Circle. He'd always done a visual inventory of the gang as they approached him before a fight at the high school, and he was veteran enough of these types of quick appraisals to think up some optimistic thoughts before this battle was to begin.

Pedro, did you notice the swelling around its jaw and head?

Yeah?

I think that the gang in Baku's ship wounded it and tired it out for us. We can use that to our advantage.

I'm ready.

Me too.

Bugsy relayed to Baku that they were ready, and the android replied, "Okay, here we go."

The Palmetto Bug Monster began to smash its forelegs together menacingly and then it advanced toward the spot where He-Knew-Pat-Sajak stood. The headphones sprang to life as Baku began to speak quickly, and Bugsy found himself suddenly confronted with the task of having to repeat Shxtor back to Pedro. He'd half-expected that this was going to be akin to being in the huddle of a football team and getting the play called in a series of code words and numbers – like how the Pittsburgh Steelers' coach Chuck Knoll had called a pass play "66 Circle Option" before the infamous "Immaculate Reception" – but what came through his ears was much more akin to the spoken African language of Khoisan. A series of clicks, sounds, and indiscernible words were issued quickly, and he had to repeat them verbatim back in his thoughts without having any idea as to what was being said. He fought to remember the sequence and then he echoed it back to his gigantic host.

Pedro reacted almost immediately to the command. The giant gecko set off quickly toward the cockroach, which assumed a defensive stance. About halfway down the runway, the Palmetto Bug Monster's belly began to glow, indicating it was about to shoot its ray blaster. Pedro instinctively dove into a controlled duck and roll that was supposed to avoid an incoming blast and end up with the lizard in a position to spring up and land the first blow in the fight. Unfortunately, the movement did not go as fluidly as was intended, and Pedro did something comparable to an awkward somersault and flop. The end result had him lying helplessly on his back with his feet toward his opponent.

The Palmetto Bug Monster did not hesitate. It lunged forward and thrust the sharp tip of its right foreleg's arolium through the gecko's shoulder, piercing the skin and driving the point straight through and into the ground. Meanwhile, it used its left foreleg and midleg to start battering Pedro's head with repetitive blows. Bugsy could feel the impressive force of these inside the giant gecko's skull, but he was nearly blinded with pain from the penetrating wound in his host's shoulder. Their psychic connection was now transferring the sensations directly between them, and Bugsy had to struggle to not lose consciousness.

Baku's voice came through the headphone with another series of odd sounds and words in his next command. Bugsy fought through the excruciating agony to remember the order well enough to repeat it back to Pedro. The gecko's response was to move his legs into what should have been a successful attempt to throw the cockroach off in a judo-like movement, but the giant bug anticipated the maneuver and the gecko's legs were not quick enough or strong enough to avoid the blocking move that the Palmetto Bug Monster implemented. Instead of throwing their opponent off of them, they were further pinned. All the while, the cockroach continued to smash the gecko in the head with some very effective strikes.

When Baku spoke again and Bugsy conveyed the command, Pedro swung his tail in an attempt to swipe the cockroach's feet out from underneath it. Once again, the Palmetto Bug Monster anticipated this strike and spread its wings in such a way as to catch the tail and hold it. The muscles in the gecko's tail cramped up and the cockroach had yet another anchoring point to hold its foe down while continuing to deliver more vicious blows to its head and face.

Bugsy panicked. He'd never allowed himself to become so compromised during a fight as they currently were, and the pure fear of being helpless caused him to forget promising not to speak/think anything while Baku guided them through the battle. He could not help himself – he just thought that they needed to get out of this position.

Spit at him, Pedro.

The gecko did this, and although the Palmetto Bug Monster moved quickly enough for the sputum to miss its eyes, the acidic glob hit the cockroach in the joint between the foreleg and the thorax and began to burn and cause the insect discomfort. The tender spot of the underarm area was thinly armored and the creature obviously felt this pain.

Make your hands into fists, Pedro. Strike straight up with both of them. Use the ground to give you more force for this double punch. We need to get this asshole off us. Strike now!

The giant gecko thrust its two clenched fists straight up into the Palmetto Bug Monster's body with enough strength that it dislodged the embedded end of its foreleg and got the insect off balance from the shock of the attack. With their opponent now reeling and stooped slightly lopsided, Pedro was able to free his legs and bring them up into the cockroach's mid-thorax area to flip the creature up and over his head. The ground shook as the insect thudded down, but it quickly scrambled to get upright again. Meanwhile, Pedro struggled to stand, but the pain from his damaged shoulder made this difficult. With a great deal of agony, he got himself up and turned to face his menacing foe.

Baku came through the headphones with another string of Shxtor clicks and words. As soon as Bugsy had passed these on, the giant gecko set off in a near-sprint to jump at the cockroach. Regrettably, the lizard was leaning too far forward when he attempted to do this and the movement was awkwardly slow. The Palmetto Bug Monster easily moved aside and raked its razor-sharp tarsal claws across both sides of the gecko's neck, causing deep and bloody wounds that were so painful that Pedro's knees buckled once its unsuccessful charge was done.

Without pausing, Baku directed another order to Bugsy to give to the injured lizard. After passing on to Pedro this round of directions, the teenager helplessly watched as Pedro spun right around and made another run at the Palmetto Bug Monster. Once again, the effectiveness of this measure was

compromised by the dubiousness of Pedro's balance and his currently impaired state. The cockroach
easily sidestepped the assailant, again employing its
sharp claws to add another series of ghastly wounds
to the gecko's neck as it rushed headlong past its
intended target. This time, the injuries were so debilitating that the massive lizard fell to his knees, while
the cockroach began to emit sounds of its revelry.

Pedro, we've got to get off of our knees. We're too vulnerable
in this position. While the bug's whooping it up back there, we
need to stand and get moving. If we can get the jump on it, we
can retreat a little and go somewhere to recover from this fight.

I'm losing too much blood...I'm so weak. I can't run anywhere.

Come on, we've got this. Let's get up.

Pedro labored painfully to get back on his feet,
but once this feat was accomplished, he didn't have
enough strength to do anything more.

With its Moog opponent seemingly powerless
to attack it again, the cockroach savored the win
by kicking dirt and rocks at the gecko to signify the
thoroughness of the humiliating defeat.

It was in the middle of this juvenile display that
Baku spoke over the headphones with another Shxtor directive given in an urgent voice. When Bugsy
relayed this message, he secretly hoped that it meant
that they were going to get out of harm's way to lick

their plentiful wounds. But when Pedro attempted to take an aggressive step toward the bug, he knew that they were being ordered to head once more into the breach, and he yelled his disapproval aloud as the Palmetto Bug Monster's stomach suddenly glowed brightly.

The insect's ray blaster produced a beam of energy that hit the massive gecko like a powerful sledgehammer blow. This lifted Pedro off of his feet and drove him backward toward the other end of the runway. The wound from the strike became flaming hot, and both Bugsy and Pedro screamed in pain as they flew through the air. Then everything went black and quiet.

イタチの最後っ屁

itachi no saigo-pei
The weasel's final fart.

In a mere matter of moments, the once-unified crew inside of Baku's spacecraft had quickly dissolved into an unruly mass of chaos. While watching the second resounding defeat of the giant gecko by the colossal cockroach, each human member of the group had formed a very strong opinion about the apparent mishandling of the situation by Baku, and they began voicing these all at the same time. The flood of their directed animosity was too much to bear for the alien android, and instead of remaining cool and collected in the face of such overt criticisms, he lashed out at any and all challengers to defend himself.

Simply put, the former unified Alaskan dogsled team inside of the alien spaceship had been instantly transformed into a pack of wolves that had begun to turn upon itself.

"Oh-ho, you've just killed my grandson!" Ira ranted.

"Yes, Baku-san, I'm a little confused. You've been exhibiting a little too much *chototsu moshin* for my tastes. You were making the gecko act too much like the *kaiju* Anguirus in *Godzilla vs. Gigan* when it kept charging recklessly at its enemy. The lizard was definitely not up to that task."

"I agree with the Japanese gangster," General Richardson scoffed. "Even General George S. Patton understood that it was reckless to send his troops straight into the fray each time. Although not often, 'Old Blood and Guts' would sometimes demonstrate that he knew that there were times to attack the enemy's flank or to take a retreat when necessary. You've been reckless with that near-useless lizard today, android."

Bernie began filming Baku as Eve took up a more aggressive reporter's stance and spoke into her microphone. "Yes, Mr. Baku, do you think that any of these charges leveled against you today are justified? Were you too aggressive in your strategy? Did you put the lizard and the teenager within it in danger with your reckless tactics?"

The Neanderthal glanced at the monitors in what looked like a stupor of confusion before he focused his eyes onto the lens of Bernie's camera and – although highly unlikely that an alien android can feel such volatile emotions – looked ready to blow his top.

"Reckless? Reckless? Raise your hand if you've ever guided a Moog to victory over a Haag. Go ahead, raise them up high."

The android stopped talking and dramatically looked around the chamber as if he were seriously searching for someone with their arm raised. He pantomimed this so well that the other group members also scanned around them to see if there was someone present who they'd missed. When he was satisfied that he'd made his point, he put his hands on his hips, tilted his head, and remained silent for a moment so that this truth could soak in with the earthlings.

"No? No one other than yours truly has ever defeated a Haag? Hm, that's funny. I'd assume that means that only one of us has the necessary expertise to critique or judge the outcome of this fight. And, guess what, earthlings, as an android handler of a Moog superweapon, I'm undefeated. Me and the 1972 Miami Dolphins football team, we've both got a record of seventeen and zero. So you can take all your mean-spirited and ignorant comments and shove them up your—"

"I think that I just saw He-Knew-Pat-Sajak move!" Mayor Bishop announced loudly. He'd remained staring at the monitor showing the giant gecko flat on its back. The steam and smoke still rose off the singed front flank of the creature, but the mayor pointed at the twitching finger pads of the lizard as evidence of life.

The general stomped his foot hard onto the floor. "It doesn't matter, you wide-eyed pathetic little man, the cockroach is going to soon end this juvenile savoring of its triumph and then it's going to finish the lizard off. This battle is over, thanks to the caveman."

Baku gave General Richardson the middle finger and then began yelling into the microphone to get Bugsy's attention. The lack of any answer hit the group like a punch in the solar plexus because it signaled that Bugsy might be critically injured...or dead.

"Oh-ho, you've just killed my grandson!" Ira repeated.

The android started to answer this charge with another strong rebuttal, but when he saw that the older man was now sobbing with his face in his hands, his expression softened into a look of bewilderment. His fingers continued to move about the control panel, but he was now shaking his hairy head and muttering to himself.

"We could hit it again with the ship. Our shields are up to full strength."

The way that General Richardson said this caught everyone off guard. His statement was not given out as a gruff executive command or an impassioned plea of desperation, but sounded much more like someone suggesting which television show the group should watch. His suggestion seemed to be one that the group agreed with, and they all began nodding at Baku, who vented air out of his mouth and let his lips flap loudly.

"No, we cannot do that. The ship's computers have analyzed the data from the last couple of days, and they've come to the conclusion that the cockroach has somehow become immune to the whistle blasts and, even worse, learned how to track this ship even while it's cloaked. If we try to bash the Haag in the head again, it would not only be able to avoid our strikes, but there's a likelihood it would shoot us out of the sky or knock us to the ground and crush us."

"It could give Bugsy enough time to wake up and get the lizard back into the fight," Sarah declared powerfully.

General Richardson sneered. "This fight is over. It's time to come up with a Plan B. I think I need to make a plea to Washington to fire a nuke or two while the bug is too busy dancing with joy here to resume its destructive ways again."

The stark reality of the general's comment caused all in the spacecraft's chamber to go completely mute. The truth of the situation, albeit one that was hard to stomach, was that they were out of any easy options. They gazed at the monitor showing the Palmetto Bug Monster as it continued to roar, hiss, and shimmy-shimmy-shake, and they each had to accept that the general might be right.

Baku hit the control panel with his fist. "Dammit, how did *this* happen? I've never lost. Never. I mean, it was obvious that this Moog wasn't in prime condition because of its long-delayed deployment, but these moves have never failed me. I just don't get it."

Mayor Bishop, who was still intently watching the prone gecko on the monitor, turned slightly to face Baku. His face looked just like Marty Feldman when his character Igor first met Dr. Frederick Frankenstein in the movie *Young Frankenstein.* He spoke to the alien, but his voice was soft and unthreatening. "How long did you say that you and He-Knew-Pat-Sajak were waiting for the arrival of the Palmetto Bug Monster?"

"About fifty thousand of your Earth years, according to the computer logs."

The mayor brought his hand up to his chin and cupped it in thought. If possible, his eyes widened even further as an idea struck him. With almost a tone of glee, the man began to speak again. "So all of your victories were fifty thousand years ago, too, right, Baku?"

"Obviously. I was asleep during that whole time."

Mayor Bishop's face changed to show that he was processing something. He asked another question. "Do you know why there was such a delay in the Noosbit weapon arriving on our planet?"

Baku made it clear that he didn't. "No, my computers have been unable to get that information to me as of yet. Without talking to someone in the know, the gap in timing and the reasons for it are unknown to me."

The television reporter aimed her microphone at the innkeeper. "Mayor Bishop, why is any of this important to talk about right now? I mean, look at the scene out there. I hate to say it, but what does it matter why or how we got here?"

Eve's question was another journalistic inquiry to attempt to get the best response for the camera, which was now filming the diminutive man.

"Yes, this is all a waste of time," General Richardson snipped. "What we don't need to do now is debrief, we need to figure out how to stop the goddamn cockroach!"

"Wait a second, General-san. Mayor Bishop-san may have a point here. I think he's trying to say that we find ourselves in the same circumstance as what happened in *Godzilla vs. Mechagodzilla*. In that movie, an alien race has learned how to defeat Godzilla and they build a powerful robotic version of him to do that. Don't you see? There's a chance that the Noosbits have had fifty thousand years for their computers to analyze the defeats of their superweapons and for their scientists to make some improvements. Baku-san is performing like he hasn't missed the last fifty thousand years, but he might be facing an improved enemy that has updated its tactics."

"Yes, Usotsuki," Mayor Bishop cheerfully commented. "That's what I just realized. Not only has the giant gecko been acting like a shadow of its former self, it's been facing some kind of an enhanced opponent that may have been prepared to employ new methods to win the battle. On top of that, I think Baku might have been using outdated strategies without knowing it. Imagine if General George Washington had been resurrected to help fight the war in Vietnam – it'd be absurd to think that his tactics at Yorktown would have ever worked if used during the Tet Offensive."

General Richardson gasped loudly. The military reference that Mayor Bishop had just employed hit its mark with him. If this all was true, it didn't matter whether the lizard woke up or not. The truth was, the situation was now doomed. He needed to get on the radio to speak with Washington immediately.

"Okay, Baku, patch me in to the U.S. military on the radio again. I need to inform them of the gecko's defeat and how it's now imperative that a nuclear strike is launched immediately to take care of this threat. We're out of options."

The group remained planted in place as they each individually mulled over the implications of the general's comments. Although they may have wanted to debate some of his conclusions, there was no getting around the fact that their situation was as dire as he'd described. Without any dissent, Baku began working on the control panel to hail the military for the general, but all his attempts came back with nothing but static. After a half dozen unsuccessful tries, the group settled back to looking at the monitors. On one, the Palmetto Bug Monster was still roaring, hissing, and kicking gravel and dirt in celebration. On the other, the unconscious He-Knew-Pat-Sajak lay flat and unmoving on the far end of the runway.

Mayor Bishop turned slowly to face Baku and then he asked timidly, "What were you referring to when you told Bugsy to remind the gecko about the Recovery Protocol?"

"The Moogs are all genetically programmed to be able to enact some repairs to their bodies when needed. It cannot work miracles, but it has gotten many a weapon back onto the battlefield. Unfortunately, this Moog has already used its one emergency measure, and that means there's nothing else it can do for itself."

"What about this ship?"

Baku whipped his head around to stare down Mayor Bishop. "And what do you mean by that, Mayor?"

"Well, I was just thinking about the fact that most vehicles driving around Alaska usually have a first aid kit in them, just in case of emergencies. Ira, you must have a first aid kit in your truck, don't you?"

"Oh-ho, of course. Town truck, so it's got to have one of those. I've had to use it many a time – on myself and sometimes on someone I'm helping."

Mayor Bishop was now nodding like he was listening to music. "And Sarah, you must have one in your plane, right?"

"Hell yeah. You never know when you'll need it."

Baku frowned mightily as he spoke. "I am not sure what you are asking, earthling. We are too far away from your vehicles or planes to get the first aid kits out of them. Are you injured? Do you need health care?"

General Richardson struck the palm of his left hand with his right fist. "For such a supposedly advanced alien android, you sure are dumb as a fencepost sometimes, tin man. What the bug-eyed dwarf is asking you, Baku, is, does this ship have some kind of first aid kit for the superweapons you oversee?"

"No, I told you all that I don't. We only have the Recovery Protocol embedded in the creature's genes. They get only one, and this Moog has used it up."

Mayor Bishop made an impressive gesture to point out the scope of the command center. "I understand about all of that, Baku. But it doesn't make sense to have this kind of set up for an advanced spaceship that monitors and helps guide these giant lizards to victory, yet not have some way to use the ship to supply first aid to them whenever needed. Our primitive trucks, planes, and military vehicles cannot be better prepared than this intergalactic scientific vessel, can they?"

"Mayor Bishop-san is right. There must be something in here that could help the *kaiju* heal."

Baku put his hands onto his hips. "There isn't. And I should know. I've been the captain of this spacecraft for most of my missions before this one."

Ira Morton started moving his lips, talking to no one but himself. He looked as if he were looking for something down low on the floor, but then his gaze shifted quickly to Baku. His face was shimmering with a good idea.

"You've never needed it before, Baku. As you said earlier, you're seventeen and zero. Each time you've been a handler in one of these situations, it's probably been quick work for you and the monster under your control. The strategies you've been using today most likely have worked so wonderfully, you haven't needed to resort to any kind of first aid kit. Maybe you just had the creatures enact the protocol to heal themselves, if they happened to get a little wounded during their aggressive attacks, and that always worked. But it's highly unlikely that the Shxtor scientists didn't outfit this ship with some way to help them heal if needed – a first aid kit."

Baku sounded less sure as he responded, "No, I'm telling you all, I'm pretty sure that there is nothing aboard this ship that can help."

"Have you ever asked the ship's computers, Baku-san?" Usotsuki inquired.

"Noooo, I haven't. But I'm fairly certain—"

Eve implored, "Mr. Baku, this might be the right time to do so, no matter what."

The android looked at the reporter and saw the concern in her eyes. The rest of the group was scrutinizing him as they waited for his response.

Baku looked up at the ceiling and asked his question. "Hey, ship computer! Do we have anything on board that could help the Moog heal?"

This question was followed by a series of blips and beeps. Then an emotionless computer-like voice boomed over the intercom. "This spacecraft, a model F-117A, is equipped with the Mkultran Drone. This aerial drug dispensary system is designed to be able to administer medications directly into the Moog superweapons. These therapeutic pharmaceutical products are designed to quickly help the weapons heal if they are gravely injured during a battle. Field tests have shown positive results, but the effects may be short-lived."

Baku recoiled at the news. Then he shouted up at the ceiling again. "How is it that I've never heard about this?"

"You've never asked before, Captain Baku the Marvelous."

"How many drones do we have, computer?"

"Each F-117A is equipped with one for each mission."

"Well, I'll be damned!" General Richardson yelled as he slapped his leg with his hand. "Fire that fucking thing posthaste, android!"

Baku waved the man off, but then he looked back up at the ceiling. "Computer, what is the most effective way to ensure that the drone will reach the target?"

There were some more computer calculation noises, and then the speakers blared with the reply. "The ship must be directly overhead of the injured Moog for the procedure to work with the highest level of success."

Baku motioned for Sarah to join him at the control panel, and the two began immediately pushing buttons and moving levers. Baku leaned in toward the female Alaskan bush pilot and spoke authoritatively. "If I am right, Sarah, as soon as we start any kind of motion with the ship, we're going to catch the attention of the Haag. Your job is to help me avoid the ray blasts as it starts to unleash them in our direction and continue to keep our shields up."

"Roger that."

And just like that, the crew of Baku's ship was unified once more. Even as the Palmetto Bug Monster began firing at them, and their flight toward the gecko was made bumpy with near-misses, the seven earthlings and the one alien worked together as a singular entity to get close enough to the giant gecko to shoot it full of drugs.

起死回生

kishi kaisei
Revival from the edge of death.

Bugsy groaned. He hadn't been fully knocked out by the power of the ray blast, but he'd been stunned enough to have blacked out for the briefest of instances. He now shook his head to clear the cobwebs and tried to focus on whatever Pedro was currently gazing upon. When he saw nothing but the big Alaskan sky, he immediately inferred that they'd been blown right onto their back by the immense blast, but he also knew that he and Pedro had both lived through the attack and were conscious. The fleeting thought that his lizard host had died with his eyes open did buzz through his thoughts, but then he sensed that, although gravely – and possibly lethally – wounded, Pedro was not dead...yet. He could hear the thunderous sounds from the victory dance that the cockroach was doing, which shook the very ground they were lying on, and he could sense that the creature was gloating with arrogance over his victory in the one-sided fight.

Bugsy's mind, still reeling from the head-pelting by the cockroach and its bombastic blast, was clearly lagging behind its normal functioning speed. It took him a few minutes to evaluate the situation to decide what needed to happen next, but, like baseballs hitting the spinning rollers in a JUGS Curveball Pitching Machine, his thoughts started whizzing around with way too much mustard. Their current reality – helplessly lying on their back in the middle of an ongoing fight to the death with a superior foe – caused Bugsy to urgently attempt to get Pedro's attention.

Stand up, Pedro! We've got to get upright again. The cockroach is coming to finish us off!

I'm done, Bugsy. I...can't go on.

Come on, get up! Just stand up. If we can get off our back, we're still in this fight. We only have the slightest of chances to survive, but we definitely don't have any just lying here. Get up!

What does my android handler say that we should do?

The mere mention of Baku incensed Bugsy. He had not been a fan of the strategy that the android had used throughout the fight, and his levels of frustration and even contempt were running high and causing him such a palpable anger that the gecko could feel it coming from his little passenger, and it sparked enough emotion to repeat his question.

What does my android handler say that we should do?

Sorry, big guy, he's been silent. I haven't heard a peep out of him since we got blown to smithereens.

Then what do *you* think that we should do, Bugsy?

I think you need to stand the fuck up, Pedro. Right now!

The giant gecko rolled onto its side and started to get up. The charring on the front of his body from the ray blast, the puncture wound in his shoulder, the deep gashes on his neck, and the overall painfulness resulting from getting the shit kicked out of him made this endeavor excruciatingly difficult. But after a couple of unsuccessful attempts, the giant creature got its feet underneath it and stood up to face the still-celebrating cockroach. Although he was teetering like a stiff breeze could knock him down at any moment, Pedro was standing.

Reach out to the android, Bugsy. We need to know what he wants to do next...if I'm able to do anything, that is.

Bugsy was hesitant to follow through with this request, but he could sense the feelings of utter defeat that Pedro was experiencing, and he figured that the creature needed guidance in this moment, even flawed guidance. He called out to Baku to ask what to do next.

Finally, Baku answered him, but instead of sending another series of chirps and indiscernible Shxtor words through the headphones, he commanded Bugsy to tell the weapon to stay put. Furthermore, he yelled out the direction, "Stand still."

As Bugsy imparted this strange behest to his host, he looked out of Pedro's eyes and saw that the Palmetto Bug Monster was now coming in their direction, all the while shooting its ray blaster up into the air in a seemingly random pattern. Although he couldn't be sure, he wondered if the creature was firing at Baku's cloaked spacecraft. His first instinct was to try to get Pedro to spring into action to help the airborne group survive the cockroach's attacks, but he remembered the plainly powerful message that Baku had just delivered. They were to stay put and stand still, and he reminded Pedro that that was what they were going to do. It was as they watched the scene in front of them that they both felt the sharp jab of something into Pedro's rear end.

Ouch!

What the hell was that?

I just got stung, I think.

Does the cockroach have the ability to send out stingers at its opponent?

I dunno, but if it does, I'm already dead. The poison's already in my system.

Do you feel bad from it yet?

Uh, no. Actually, I'm feeling a little better suddenly. Whoa, I'm feeling a lot better, actually.

Really?

Yes. If I didn't know better, I would say that someone just gave me a shot of something to help me heal.

Bugsy watched as the Palmetto Bug Monster now turned its back on them and continued to fire its ray blaster up into the sky at an unseen target. He could only assume that Baku's ship had come close, fired some kind of medical dart into Pedro, and then fled the scene. The cockroach had finally seemed to run out of enough vitriol to keep blasting away at something without success, and Bugsy hoped that this indicated that the gang had escaped harm. When the Palmetto Bug Monster turned to face them, Bugsy knew the fight was once again back on.

As Bugsy awaited Baku's voice to come over the headphones, he thought back to the series of commands given throughout this battle. He'd played enough games of Hūsker Dū? with his grandfather to notice that Baku's orders had been the same series of clicks and words. Bugsy might not have been able to understand or speak Shxtor, but he knew that Baku had pretty much repeated the same thing, over and over. There was no other conclusion to come to than that they'd been directed each time to make an aggressive charge right at the cockroach. This strategy had only resulted in Pedro receiving a series of debilitating wounds that had weakened him to the point that he'd been helpless to avoid the cockroach's ray blast. Bugsy stayed silent, but his agitation toward Baku was increasing by the moment.

What does my android handler say that we should do?

He hasn't been talking very much, Pedro.

Perhaps you should reach out to him, Bugsy. To get our next orders.

Second verse, same as the first...

If Pedro understood the reference to the 1965 song, "I'm Henry the Eighth, I Am" by Herman's Hermits, the creature did not let on. Instead, he simply repeated his request to reach back out to Baku to get the next direction for the fight. Bugsy had been quietly attempting to stem his growing anger with Baku, but he needed to make sure that Pedro felt comfortable and secure in the leadership that was guiding him. Through clenched teeth, Bugsy hailed Baku to get the next command.

After an uneasy moment of no response, the android's voice came across the headphones, but its tone was now much different. It actually sounded a bit defeated.

"Well, Bugsy, the truth is, I don't have another command for the Moog."

"Goddammit, he prefers to be called Pedro!"

Baku's exhalation was so strong that Bugsy expected the breath to mess up his hair around the headphones. When the android spoke again, his voice was tainted with humbleness.

"Okay, I don't have any good commands for... Pedro."

"What the hell are we supposed to do now?"

"Listen, Bugsy, it's come to my attention that I've been actually using outdated strategies so far. Apparently, that cockroach has been engineered to be an updated version of the superweapons I was programmed to defeat. And we can all see the results of that discrepancy, right?"

"That damn bug is getting ready to blast us out of existence, Mr. Baku. We need to do *something*."

"It is beyond painful for me to admit my shortcomings, Bugsy, but I think that the Moo...Pedro would be better served by someone else."

"Who?"

Bugsy could hear the rest of the group in the background as they all offered up their suggestions of which one of them should take over as the strategist for the battle. Baku forcefully rebuked them all and they grew silent. Then he started speaking through the headphones again.

"Listen, Bugsy, it has to be you. You've bonded with the creature to the point that you are far more qualified to figure out how to help it defeat the Haag. I know it's a lot of responsibility, but it's all in your hands now. You're in charge."

Somehow Pedro could deduce what had been said between Baku and Bugsy, and he thought an encouraging message was needed for his young earthling passenger.

Okay, Bugsy, *you're* in charge now. I know that you can do this, my friend. So, what should we do?

We definitely need to use a different playbook. The one that Baku was using was sending us repeatedly into a bad situation. This is no longer a battle between alien superweapons, Pedro. This is a fight against a bully. And I know how to do that, that's for sure. Open your mind, my friend.

Whenever there is a shared psychic connection between two entities, letters, words, and sentences are not required to transmit specific ideas and thoughts. Yes, a type of mental conversation can occur using those, but there are other times when all that is needed to be dispensed can happen in a kind of mental outburst. If a picture is worth a thousand words, a 4-D mind movie, complete with all of the emotions, smells, sensations, sights, tastes, and all of the other accouterments, is worth all of the words necessary. With such an intense intellectual share-all such as this, everything that is known and needed to be imparted can be viewed in one nova-like exposure.

Bugsy was attempting to do this right now with Pedro. He opened his mind to hand over the full extent of his kung-fu knowledge from the lessons from Master Chui and to give the gecko each and every surviving memory from his fights with the boys of Tok. In a nanosecond, Pedro knew all that there was to know. He could recall the moves and the strategies Bugsy had used to survive the schoolyard fights and, ultimately, how he'd put an end to the bullying. He could feel the range of emotions that made up Bugsy, and the creature had a new, stronger sense of understanding about the personal philosophies of the young boy. He comprehended how Bugsy had taken on all of the conflicts he'd ever faced in his short life. In the process, Pedro and Bugsy merged into a united fighting machine.

The timing was perfect. The cockroach was moving in such a way as to indicate that it was positioning itself to finish off its near-dead opponent. There was an outpouring of overconfidence radiating off the giant bug as it stalked toward them, but since the battle up to now had been nothing but a string of defensive moves designed to neutralize all of the lizard's aggressive attacks, the Palmetto Bug Monster shifted its body in such a way that it betrayed its barely hidden desire to bait its opponent into making the next wrong first move and then applying the final death blow.

Should I charge, Bugsy?

Nope. It's expecting that.

Are we giving it a healthy dose of *Wu Wei* then?

Here, Bugsy raucously laughed. He hadn't done this in a long time, and the expression of mirth in such a dire situation brought something akin to the rays of a rising sun to the both of them. There was no way for Bugsy to know it, but his laughter had been as powerful a medicine as whatever had just jabbed Pedro in the *derrière*. The combination of those two elements suddenly energized the lizard.

Yes! Stand still, Pedro. Show nothing yet. Be a statue.

We wait for the cockroach to make the first move?

We do. And whenever it does, it'll give us the opening that we need.

Their inactivity was working to confuse the cockroach. While the Haag was never going to be called overly intelligent, the fact that its opponent was no longer charging at it made the gears in its head turn and grind. The result of this was clearly a turgid sense of uncertainty.

Should I strike now?

No, let it get a little closer. It can't help itself, Pedro. It's just about here. When it's within striking distance, you need to feign an assault. Move in such a way as to make it think that you're rushing in for close combat again. Every time we've done that, it's been ready for our attack. But if you can get it into that particular defensive stance again, you can then hit him with your tail. If you whip it around and smack him under his own defenses, I think we can finally get a good blow in.

I don't know if I can pull any of that plan off, Bugsy. I'm in such pain...I'm still feeling so weak.

I know, buddy. I know that you're hurting. But if we can get one or two blows in and cause that cockroach some pain, we can change this fight. We've been giving it an easy target with predictable strategies. Let's see how it handles some unexpected moves. We need to stretch this fight out and see if we can do our part. And remember, a win is a win.

I remember.

Get ready. NOW!

The gigantic gecko made a motion as if it were going to charge once more, but pulled up as soon as the cockroach deployed its same defensive stance. With the cockroach's forelegs and midlegs in this heightened position, Pedro's sudden surprise spin move resulted in a successful strike of his massive tail right into the insect's midsection. The force of this blow might not have been at full strength, but it caught the Palmetto Bug Monster so off guard, the insect fell backward onto its hindquarters.

The spin move had caused Pedro a little dizziness, and he staggered unsteadily as he regained his bearings. But Bugsy was quick to direct him for another strike.

Pedro! Get ready to do a flying side kick. Wait for the bug to start to get to its feet. When it does this, we need to take off running and propel ourselves into it before it gets fully steady.

Your expectations might be far beyond my current capabilities, Bugsy.

It doesn't have to be pretty, big guy. We just need to put our body weight behind another blow. We're trying to win this fight, for sure, but we're also attempting to get the bug really frustrated and angry. An opponent in this state starts fighting two foes – the enemy and itself. Once the bug finds itself in this situation, it will be prone to make mistakes. Now, get ready.

As Bugsy had correctly forecasted, the Palmetto Bug Monster turned quickly to stand up. As it did, its eyes seemed to blaze red with anger. Before it could get its feet set, however, the giant gecko moved as fast as a rifle shot and launched itself into the air with its right foot extended directly at the insect. The flying lizard, which weighed nearly the same as the USS *Missouri* battleship, hit with enough force to send the cockroach flying. The Haag did two backward somersaults and came to a stop, face down on the runway.

Pedro had crashed down to the ground like a solid oaken plank, and the pain from this awkward landing and the great exertion from the flying kick caused the giant gecko to be unable to arise again.

Pedro, get up. We've gotta keep after the bug. We've got it on the ropes.

I can't move right now, Bugsy. My back feels like it's about to snap in two.

Maybe we should do the cat-cow yoga pose. It could help.

You're joking, right?

Master Chui is a fan of using yoga to improve flexibility, Pedro. He constantly talks about how a warrior needs to be able to move freely to fight properly.

We're in the middle of a fight, Bugsy. I'll look like a complete idiot if I suddenly start doing what you're thinking of having me do.

We're currently lying flat on our back and are unable to move. We already look bad.

That's true. Okay, I'll give it a try.

Pedro labored to turn slowly onto his side and then onto all fours. Slowly he curved his lower back and brought his head up, tilting his pelvis up like a "cow." Then he brought his abdomen in, arched his spine, and brought his head and pelvis down like a "cat." Meanwhile, the cockroach was shaking off the effects of the powerful kick and was regaining its footing again.

Let's do that one more time, Pedro. I can feel that it loosened you up a bit.

Uh, the cockroach is coming at us, Bugsy. And it looks like it's ready for another round of fighting.

Well, you better hurry then. And remember to breathe.

This is *utterly* ridiculous, but I've got to admit that it's working. My back definitely feels better.

Don't lose concentration, but look over there. Do you see those two airplanes and the small fuel truck on the other side of the cockroach? They must have been abandoned when this place was evacuated. We could use them. I've got an idea how we can get a quick blow in and slide over there to get them. Ready?

Yes.

The lizard got into a sprinter's stance and took off running as if a starter pistol had just gone off. As it barreled straight toward the Palmetto Bug Monster, it picked up a substantial amount of speed. The cockroach prepared itself for the assault by spreading its legs wide. Just before they were to collide, the lizard bluffed that it was about to leap high to tackle its opponent around its head and neck, but when the bug lifted its arms up to defend that region, Pedro instead performed the perfect slide of a baseball player attempting to steal third base. With its foot pointed forward, it slid straight through the space made by the insect's widespread legs, simultaneously delivering a stout punch to the abdominal plate between the creature's cercuses as it did.

The cockroach seemed to be confused by this attack and pained by the cheap shot, and as it turned to locate its opponent, the gecko came to a stop, stood up, and reached down to grab the two small bush planes that were lying helter-skelter on the grass beside the tarmac. With as much force as he could muster, Pedro threw these like they were *shuriken*, Japanese throwing stars. The planes struck the cockroach, and although they didn't penetrate its armored shell of chitin, they lodged into the creases of the creature's midlegs. While the Haag was distracted by these projectiles, the giant gecko bounded over to the nearby fuel truck, grasped it like a football, and then threw it at the cockroach, which continued to attempt to shed the still-attached planes.

The old Ford fuel truck sailed through the air and smashed violently against the cockroach's head. The toss had caught the creature off guard and the antiquated vehicle shattered into many pieces and spilled its contents over the bug.

Before Bugsy could guide the gecko to make the next move, the enraged Palmetto Bug Monster spread its two sets of arms wide to reveal the head of a hidden projectile, and this shot out from its concealed launch pad. There was some kind of fleshy tether that streamed directly out from the cockroach's interior and that kept the missile connected with the bug. This tethered dart shot by Pedro's head, but then acted just like some kind of gaucho bolo as it wrapped around the gecko's neck several times. Before any attempt could be made to clear this off, the bug's chest lit up as if it were made from an array of electric light bulbs. Some kind of violent energy ran through the fleshy strand and directly into the gecko. Pedro screamed in pain as he convulsed from whatever was being directed into him, but then he went lifeless and fell to the ground.

The cockroach unwound this body part from around the motionless lizard's neck and slowly retracted it back into its body like some kind of power cord. The cockroach then threw its forelegs and midlegs up into the air and roared a victorious hissing howl up toward the sky.

Two United States Air Force F-16 Fighting Falcons suddenly screeched down from the clouds and launched a barrage of missiles at the celebrating cockroach. These all hit home, and the resulting massive explosions ignited the aviation fuel in the two bush planes still lodged in the body segments and the petrol from the obliterated fuel truck. The cockroach was immediately engulfed by an intense blaze. The jets launched another strike, adding to the pyrotechnical display, and then they set out with the afterburners firing to get away safely.

While the intense fire would keep the cockroach busy for a moment or two, it was clear now that it wasn't going to incapacitate it. The lizard had been bested, the fight was over, and the military was getting ready to throw everything it had at the cockroach. If that, like the giant gecko, failed to stop the Palmetto Bug Monster, there was now officially little to no hope for the human species' future.

会者定離

esha jouri

Those who meet must part.

The President of the United States was currently hiding within the secret presidential bathroom in the middle of the underground tunnels that ran under the White House. These top-secret subterranean passageways had been constructed during the Truman Administration, when the iconic building had undergone a massive, down-to-the-studs renovation of the antiquated living quarters of the chief executive. During this ambitious project, it had become clear that, now that the nation was busy treading water in the middle of the nasty Cold War, the amenities of the place not only needed to be modernized, but many of its features needed to be essentially nuke-proofed.

With the edifice stripped down to nothing more than its vaunted facade, no one took too much notice that there were also some other large earthmovers and a team of workers digging and building something away from the main structure. Officially, the public was told that the sewer and electrical systems needed a major upgrade, and hence the need for so much excavating and pouring of concrete.

It had been Harry S. Truman, always the keenly practical Missourian, who had also suggested that if the leader of the free world was going to head down into the sunken tunnels underneath the grounds of the White House as a last resort to outlast the nuclear winter, he would probably need a place to piss and shit. And, taking it a step or two further, if this haven was going to be the likely location of some kind of last stand, it not only needed to be designed to be absolutely impregnable, it should be outfitted to be a fully supplied bunker as well.

Because of this directive, the restroom had the thickest walls of the entire underground survival complex, an imposing bomb-proof door that locked from the inside, an impressive pantry to supply the occupant for months, and an almost air-tight secrecy about its existence. Only those in the most inner circle of the staff knew anything about it, and they had been forced to swear they'd die with the knowledge.

Bess Truman had decided to decorate this super-secret lavatory. The nickname that the president had given the First Lady was "the Boss," and she took on that role as the interior designer for this fortified restroom. She'd been a behind-the-scenes supporter of the White House project and she was actively planning how the newly designed rooms in the living quarters were going to be furnished and decorated to tie the past together with the future. But, with the bunker bathroom, she decided that the room needed to be a vestige of home. So she'd demanded that an exact copy of the loo in their Independence, Missouri, house be built.

As a result, the water closet in the survival bunker underneath 1600 Pennsylvania Avenue had a baby-blue toilet, sink, and bathtub, pink patterned wallpaper, blue shag carpeting, and lots and lots of chrome. Although there are no official records of whether the First Lady ever went down to the secret bathroom to feel sentimental about her hometown or not, she certainly designed an intimate space capable of doing just that.

The current President of the United States was now locked within this bathroom, and he was safe and sound. None of the panicking staffers, congressmen, cabinet members, intelligence agencies, or even the Joint Chiefs of Staff who were looking for him could find him. They weren't sure if he'd run off, been killed, or was just hiding, and they were unable, in spite of great threats of bodily harm and even execution, to get his location out of anyone who worked in the White House. It became clear that the staff either didn't know where their boss was or they would willingly go to their grave withholding that information. The exact whereabouts of the President was anyone's guess, and since there were now two alien monsters duking it out in Alaska, playing a game of hide-and-seek with the man seemed like a colossal waste of time at the moment.

That's not to imply that the President presently resembled a giggling, self-congratulatory child down in the safety of the best hiding spot in the world; the veteran statesman had been on one hell of an emotional roller-coaster ride during his time in there. This bathroom, which reeked of 1950s nostalgia, had been an ideal location for deep self-reflection, and the man had done nothing else but review the events leading up to this moment over and over, and he had metaphorically whipped himself for his role in it all.

He was proud, though, of the way he had reacted publicly to this whole horrible ordeal. At first, he'd been able to put on a brave face with the arrival of the cockroach. He'd even seemed fully prepared for the arrival of an alien monster seemingly hell-bent on the Earth's destruction. To the surprise of everyone around him, he'd been almost optimistic about a quick end to the conflict in those early days, and, even more noticeable, he'd begun preaching optimistically that the giant cockroach was going to be just the kind of trauma that could launch the planet onto a new and lasting course for peace.

Not everyone had been pleased with him. As the gigantic bug rumbled its way through Indiana and then decimated Indianapolis, the man had lost many fans as he'd continued to offer up encouraging soundbites and hopeful anecdotes. Then, when he was heard uttering a completely inappropriate comment as he watched the news footage from the destruction zone, the diagnosis that he'd lost his mind was set in stone.

Regrettably, the President had said under his breath, "Well, you *do* have to break a few eggs to make a good omelet."

Next, his discovery that the First Lady had skedaddled had broken his heart. Whatever bravado or certainty he may have been holding went right into the circular file as soon as he was notified that she'd gone missing. There'd been no evidence of any kind of a sinister abduction; supposedly she'd willingly packed a suitcase, walked out the door, and voluntarily gotten into a VW bus with two elderly men, one of whom appeared to be her old flame, Henry Kissinger. The air of calm determination around the woman that afternoon meant that no one had dared intervene. She had seemed like she was headed on vacation with a couple of friends, and since there was some kind of giant space insect currently pulverizing the Midwest and getting ready to exterminate their species, many in the Secret Service had to admit that they'd barely noticed the First Lady's strange choice of travel.

In spite of this, the President had continued putting all of his energy into working to get the essential parts of the executive, legislative, and judiciary branches and their families to safety, maintaining the appearance of being calm, cool, and collected, spouting hope and optimism, attempting to keep everything functioning in Washington, and effectively blocking the war hawks from getting their hands on the nukes. He'd seemed like a man on a mission, but it had been during this stretch of time that he'd actually begun to lose faith. Like one of Macy's Thanksgiving Day Parade balloons with two big holes in it – one from the appearance of the gecko and the other from his wife's departure – the man had outwardly begun to show that he was deflating. Unbeknownst to *anyone*, this had been due to the fact that he was beginning to accept responsibility for the whole shit-show.

The surprise visit from the blue Noosbit ambassador a month earlier had been like some kind of peyote dream. Having an alien representative show up next to his presidential bed to wake him up to have a chat in the middle of the night had been so surreal that the President fought bouts of all-encompassing self-doubt throughout the entire encounter and afterwards. But there'd been no way to deny that there was an extremely short, blue-skinned ogre of an alien straight from a fairy tale tapping him on the shoulder with its stubby blue index finger and calling his name. Surreal or not, this encounter was real.

The torrent of outpourings that flowed from the creature had overwhelmed his residual sleepiness or overt skepticism, and he'd sat up and listened to everything coming from the alien's mouth. It had identified itself as a Noosbit emissary and then proceeded to tell him that its cloaked spaceship was currently on the White House roof, undetected and invisible to all known early warning systems that ex-

Put a Bug in Your Ear (Mimi ni mushi o ireru)

isted on the planet, and that all of its weapon arrays were pointed down directly at the President. The little blue extraterrestrial then announced that any attempt to call out or signal for help would not go well.

The goal of this conversation, the Noosbit claimed, was for the President of the United States, and *only* the President of the United States, to learn about what was soon to occur on the planet. After this information was dispensed, the intergalactic envoy said that its job on Earth would be done. It promised that it'd get right back into its ship and fly off to the next planet to give a similar preemptive tip to the leaders of that unlucky world on the Noosbits' shopping list.

After the President had nodded that he'd understood the rules, and the implications of his breaking them, the little blue alien continued to divulge details in a rapid-fire manner. An immense creature of destruction, which it called "the Haag," was approaching Earth and it was going to provide a make-or-break moment for the entire earthling species. If they could unify to fight the threat and defeat it, the Noosbit promised that there'd be a lasting peace among their many populations. If not, then the monster would do its darnedest to massacre every single inhabitant of the planet before the Noosbits came in and enjoyed the smoldering wreckage that the creature left behind it for them. Nothing personal, just the cost of doing business with the Noosbits.

Here, the alien had added what the President considered to be an unnecessary fact. According to him, the Noosbits had been doing this little song and dance quite successfully for a very long time, but after their home planet had sustained a sinister surprise attack by a barbaric race called the Shxtors, their planetary reclamation program had to be put on hold while their civilization rebuilt itself from the pile of ashes they'd been reduced to. And rebuild they had! It might have taken them many, many millennia to come back from the edge of extinction, but they'd not only just recently started sending out their monster superweapons once again into the galaxies – for the betterment of the people on the targeted planets, after all – they'd even gotten a chance to modify and improve them greatly. The event that had nearly destroyed them had turned into a chance for them to grow even stronger.

When there was no response from the President to this announcement, the ambassador went on to issue two little caveats. The first was that the President could not tell another living soul about this meeting, or about the approaching monster, or about any of the other details just conveyed to him. If he did tell *anyone*, the Noosbits would know, and they'd unleash another monster onto Earth. And another. And another. The humans had the slightest of chances to defeat one monster, but none against multiple versions. All the President had to do was keep his mouth totally closed.

The second caveat was that under no circumstances should the earthlings use nuclear weapons.

The little blue alien warned that the Noosbit super-weapon would actually feed off the energy of such a blast, and it would only strengthen and grow even more devastating if these weapons were used. No, if the humans were to win this one, which they really could, their only choice was to unite and use conventional weaponry.

With their short one-sided meeting over, the Noosbit did a strange gesture to signify the end of their talk, and then it vanished into thin air. There were no sounds in the following moments – no science-fiction zap of transportation or teleportation, no shrieking *whoosh* sound effect from the takeoff of the alleged spacecraft on the roof, and no noises whatsoever to indicate that the Secret Service or any of the White House staff had seen or heard anything out of the ordinary. The only thing that the President could clearly make out was the gentle snoring of the First Lady, who was sound asleep in her own bedroom down the hall.

As soon as he'd heard this one soothingly familiar resonance, he'd been tempted to head to her room and share everything with her. But the alien had been clear as day about what would happen if he told another soul, and the President had taken its warning to heart. He couldn't tell *anyone* else, so he had headed downstairs to go straight to the Oval Office in the West Wing to pretend that he'd had another bout of insomnia. He had a lot of planning to do.

That's why, by the time that the meteor had come screaming down through the atmosphere and vaporized Vincennes, Indiana, the military was strangely prepared for something big. Sure, there were many throughout the nation who had been shocked and openly critical of his sudden, seeming about-face from being a peacenik to becoming an advocate for a quick buildup of heavily armed forces, but everyone had certainly been grateful that there were plenty of jets, artillery pieces, and tanks at the ready when the giant cockroach had started laying waste to everything in its path. The presidential cabinet had also wondered why their boss was suddenly reaching out to the leaders of other nations – both friend and foe – around the globe to ask for help and to prepare them for when the fight came their way, but the man had been wholly convinced that the battle for the planet could be won and that a lasting peace would be established afterwards.

The combination of the news about the appearance of He-Knew-Pat-Sajak and the subsequent abandonment by his wife had been the straws that had broken the camel's back. No longer capable of acting like an energetic and hopeful leader, the President had begun to sit behind the Resolute Desk and sob silently. When the Joint Chiefs came into the Oval Office and essentially took over the government, the President of the United States had sadly acquiesced and slunk off. In the disharmony that followed, no one knew where he'd gone, and no one could find the nuclear codes.

The real reasons for why he'd sought the sanctity of the hidden potty was not something he could address – or defend – at the moment, but his solitary time there had given him the chance to come to grips with the fact that he'd been duped by the little blue Noosbit visitor. He hadn't told another living soul about the visit or the shared prophecies, yet there was another alien monster on the scene. It was clear that he'd taken the alien's threats too seriously and, in the process, had hampered Earth's defensive effort. Not that that would have given the residents of the planet a real fighting chance – he now correctly assumed that the game that the alien had really been playing was the sadistic planting of false hopes and the subsequent crushing of spirits that accompanied the annihilation of the conquered worlds. If nothing else, it was obvious to the president that these Noosbits were some cruel motherfuckers.

Although no longer able to partake in the Situation Room meetings or get any updates from the intelligence communities, he'd been watching the small black-and-white television that was in the bathroom, and he had a generally good idea of what was happening. The Palmetto Bug Monster had flown to Alaska and had soundly defeated He-Knew-Pat-Sajak, but the lizard had supposedly rallied and was now fighting the bug again to help the planet. It was also clear that the Joint Chiefs had decided to turn Alaska into the location of their last stand. With the proximity of Russian and Canadian forces, the President had to assume that they were part of the plan, and he smiled that his species had unified enough to come together to attempt to defeat the threat.

Buoyed by this assessment, and by the fighting spirit that the persistent gigantic gecko kept exhibiting, the President came to the decision that he'd sat on the sidelines long enough. He grabbed the armored briefcase with the nuclear codes and started unlocking the bathroom door. It was time for him to get back into the game and make amends for all of his recent transgressions.

酔生夢死

suisei mushi

Get drunk on life, dream of death.

The command chamber in Baku's ship was eerily silent. Other than the usual noises coming from the control panels, monitors, and computers, there were no other sounds. The seven humans and one alien android were all staring at the monitors in a state of shock. Mere moments earlier, they'd been cheering for the gecko when it had seemed to be suddenly winning the fight; they'd been almost laughing when they had watched it do some silly yoga moves that had seemed overtly sexual in nature; they'd been shrieking when the weird snake-like weapon shot out of the bug, wrapped around He-Knew-Pat-Sajak's neck, and then apparently electrocuted the lizard; and they'd even given a feeble celebratory squeal when the air strike that the general had called in ignited the cockroach in flames. But as efficiently as if Baku had opened up the life-support vents in his ship and sucked all the oxygen out of the interior, no one was able to breathe a word as they now stared at the image of the lifeless body of the gecko on the screens.

It was Ira Morton who broke the noiselessness by scurrying over to Baku's control panel and yelling into the microphone, "Bugsy! Bugsy! Are you there? Come on, boy, talk to me!"

When no answer came, the others looked anywhere but over at the elderly man, and their faces took on a look of acknowledgement, for they all knew that the teenager was dead inside the dead gecko. As they dealt with a different series of emotional responses, General Richardson suddenly glared at Baku. It was clear that his moment of personal sadness over what had just taken place was now being shoved aside by the military tactician part of his personality.

"Okay, alien, what the *hell* was that?"

Baku looked over at the general and his mouth started moving in such a way that expressed it was going to start issuing an explanation, but nothing came forth. He seemed to be a caveman who was just realizing that he didn't have the ability to speak, but given the true nature of his mechanical interior makeup, it was clear that his circuits were probably overloaded by what had just taken place.

Undeterred, the general repeated himself. "What the *hell* was that, Baku?"

"I...don't...know..."

General Richardson advanced a step and bellowed his outrage. "How could you not know? You are supposed to be handling this situation. You have a seventeen and oh record, like you bragged earlier. Are you saying that you've never seen this before?"

"Bugsy! Bugsy! Are you there? Come on, boy, talk to me!" Ira repeated. His voice was rising in pitch and volume with his growing panic that his grandson was, in fact, deceased.

"The *gokiburi* has definitely either adapted or has been improved," Usotsuki said thoughtfully to the group.

"Well, how could that be?" the general queried with his usual blunt force.

The Japanese cryptozoologist took on a thoughtful pose as he explained. "Fifty thousand years is a very long time, General-san. That's plenty of time to improve weaponry. Remember how shocked the American pilots of the Flying Tigers were when they first encountered the *Mitsubishi* A6M *Zero* in 1940? Baku and He-Knew-Pat-Sajak...er, Pedro, had been asleep for a long time. We've been assuming that the Noosbits were, too, but it now appears that they've been quite active during that time, making important changes to their superweapons to win these battles. Between using a new playbook and having new weaponry, Baku, Bugsy, and Pedro have been like cavemen fighting against a Patton tank."

The mention of Bugsy's name caused another peristalsis of sadness to grip the group. While most just faced the monitors again and fought back tears, the general, ever the pragmatist, continued to attempt to figure out how to defeat the monster. He demanded an answer. "So where does that leave us? Are you telling me, alien, that the human species is completely fucked?"

"I'm afraid so, General Richardson. The Moog... Pedro...was the only weapon in my quiver. With its defeat, I have nothing left to offer. And here I was, believing that I was the great hope for your planet, and now I'm nothing. How could I have fallen so deeply in love with myself over the last fifty thousand years? I am nothing special. I'm a failure."

This moment of self-pity from the alien was too much to add to an already overpoweringly bad situation. Instead of acting like an agent of adhesion for the collection of individuals within the spacecraft, Baku's comments were more like the ceasing of the gravitational forces keeping them in their synchronized orbits. They were each cast out onto their own pathways, and mayhem ensued.

Ira yelled out loudly, "Stop talking like my grandson is dead! You don't know that he's dead, so stop acting like he is. He and the gecko might stand up any minute and start fighting again."

The blonde reporter, who was concerned that her tears were ruining her mascara, walked over to the elderly man and gently touched his elbow. "The evidence, Ira, says otherwise. Bugsy's not responding to you, the gecko is down on the ground, and the flaming aviation fuel on the cockroach has nearly burned itself out. It breaks my heart to say this aloud, but even if your grandson and the gecko are just gravely injured, it's now only a matter of time before the Palmetto Bug Monster finishes them off. We've been filming this whole thing, and the camera never lies."

"Actually, cameras lie all the time, Eve," Bernie said with a grimace.

Eve shot her cameraman a look that seemed to demand him to shut up, and then she gently added, "I just don't think that this is the time to believe in fairy tales. As bitter as it is, we need to accept reality."

Mayor Bishop stood taller and acted like he'd just had a good idea. "We should use this ship as a weapon again. We could smash into the cockroach a few more times. Maybe we'd get lucky and could hit it until it's dead."

Baku grunted as his hands continued to work the control panel. While he did this, he commented, "We'll be dead long before it is, Mayor Bishop. Even if we could land another lucky blow, the creature can now hear us well enough that we'd only get one shot. It'd have no problem detecting us and getting us."

Mayor Bishop's face took on a hopeful smile. "We should at least try. Bugsy was willing to try."

General Richardson bristled. "Do you have a death wish, you little wall-eyed motherfucker? What we need is a nuclear strike right now."

Mayor Bishop wasn't ready to back down. "And how are you going to do that, General? We've heard you try and try to get in touch with anyone and everyone to call in a nuke strike, but you haven't gotten a single response. It ain't coming, mister!"

Usotsuki stepped forward. "Plus, General-san, do we really want another Nagasaki, another Hiroshima, here in Alaska? Nuclear weapons might defeat the creature ultimately, but what will be left of our planet afterwards? If we're trying to save this place, do we really want to do that by ruining it?"

The general spit out his words at Usotsuki with venom. "Spoken like a true leftist anti-nuke looney bin that all you Japs have become."

Sounding more like Toshiro Mifune in the movie *Midway*, Usotsuki snarled his rebuke. "*Watashitachi no ikari wa genkai ni tasshimashita!*"

This translates into "We've reached the limits of our anger!"

Sensing that a fistfight between the general and the Japanese cryptozoologist was about to break out, Sarah turned to Baku. "Could we start distracting the cockroach again? If we were to uncloak ourselves now, we could try to use the ship to lure it back into the wilderness again."

The alien shook his wooly head. "A biting fly cannot stop a rampaging elephant, my dear. The Haag weapon knows that it's won. It won't be enticed to follow after a harmless spacecraft now that it has no opponent to defeat. No, it'll resume its primary mission of eradicating all of the creatures of this planet. I'm afraid that there's no way to stop it now."

The speakers suddenly crackled to life. "Grandfather...are you there?"

Ira leaned in to speak into the microphone. "Oh ho, thank goodness, you're alive, Bugsy."

"Yuh...barely."

"Is the gecko alive?"

"Yes. But...Pedro's not conscious."

"Can you snap him awake, Bugsy?"

"I'm trying, Grandfather. But I don't think I can before the cockroach comes over to finish us off. We may be toast."

"You've got to keep trying, you must..."

Baku's hand moved like a snake striking and hit a button to turn off the microphone. The group gave him baleful glares for doing this, but when the alien tucked his chin against his chest, they knew some very bad news was coming their way and they braced to receive it.

"I turned off the mike because Bugsy cannot hear what I have to say. I've got the worst news to relay, and there's no sense in sugar-coating it. I sent some of my reconnaissance drones to land on the Moog and attempt to give him some mild electrical shocks to wake him up, but they detected something quite troubling from the wounds on his neck. That fleshy lasso that the cockroach hit him with did send a surge of debilitating energy into the Moog, but it appears that it also injected some kind of poison into him. A quick analysis of the toxin reveals that it is *quite* powerful – strong enough to affect both the host and the passenger. Sadly, it's going to be fatal... for both Bugsy and the Moog...er, Pedro. So, even if the boy can awaken the creature and get it to put up a futile, feeble fight, they're both good as dead."

The news was yet another blow that the group in the alien spacecraft had to endure, and this one stunned them so badly that no one could react. In that very instant, they resembled figurines in a Madame Tussaud's wax museum, each caught in their own personal moment of pain, anger, and disbelief, all the while frozen in space and time.

Mayor Bishop broke the trance by speaking up. "Perhaps we could shoot another Mkultran drone to counteract the poison."

Before Baku could remind the group that there'd been only one such emergency recuperating shot, and before General Richardson could insult the man again, Ira Morton asked his dreaded question. "Does Bugsy know?"

Baku looked down at the control panel. "If he doesn't right now, he will whenever he can get Pedro awake. The Moog superweapons were designed to have a strong ability to self-diagnose damages and wounds. It's only a matter of time before it senses it has been poisoned and lets Bugsy know that he has too."

"Turn on the mike again, Baku. I need to talk with my grandson. I need to get my chance to say goodbye to him."

負けるが勝ち

makeru ga kachi
To lose is to win.

Bugsy had never been knocked unconscious in his life. He'd fallen during rambunctious moments of his youth and had nauseating feelings from the painful impacts, and had even seen stars, but he'd never blacked out. Even in his multiple fisticuffs with the thugs at school, he'd never been knocked out. It was a new experience. He'd expected it to be highly unpleasant, but this had been so quick and so thorough that it had skipped any steps of pain and anguish and gone straight to the velvety darkness and the soothing peacefulness of a deep sleep.

No, being out for the count hadn't been too bad, but now the teenager was finding waking up to be the shits. He was trying to shake the myriad physical and emotional effects of the trauma he'd just endured, but he was agonizingly slow in recovering. He could sense that Pedro was still alive, and he set about to wake him up.

Pedro, wake up! Hey, Pedro, wake the fuck up, buddy!

There was no answer. He had tried a couple of more times, but got no response. In desperation, he had called out to his grandfather on the headset, and the man replied. Their short conversation had helped make him feel a tad better, but it had been cut off so curtly that he knew that the microphone had been turned off for some reason that could not be any good. Without being able to see out of Pedro's eyes to view what the cockroach was doing, and unable to awaken his gecko host, he felt it was futile to attempt to get back in touch with his grandfather, and he renewed his efforts to get Pedro to respond to him.

Pedro! Pedro! Wake up!

No response.

Bugsy felt utterly alone and suddenly very scared, and he was unable to keep his mind from letting out what amounted to a primal scream. This was not a clever ploy on his part. It was the reaction of someone truly feeling a profound sense of desperation. However, this mental howl actually reached Pedro and caused the giant gecko to stir awake.

Bugsy?

I'm here, buddy. We're both still here. Can you open your eyes?

I can't see how close that fucking cockroach is to us.

I'll try.

The gecko fluttered its eyelids and then opened them up, and Bugsy could see that the cockroach was smoldering from some sort of intense fire. He had no idea why the insect had been aflame, but it was clear that the creature was quickly recovering and getting ready to administer the final knockout blow to them. Bugsy had a wave of comprehension that, unless they could get to their feet, they were dead ducks.

Can you try to stand up, Pedro?

I don't know, Bugsy...I'm pretty weak.

Yeah, me too. But if we don't get up, I think we're dead.

While it was nearly impossible to fully censor their thoughts, Bugsy could sense that Pedro was doing his best to keep something from him. Finding out what that was wasn't as important as standing up. From his fighter's training, he knew that they had a slightly better chance if they could get upright again. So, instead of asking Pedro about what he wasn't telling him, Bugsy urged him gently to keep trying.

Remarkably, the gravely wounded massive lizard was able to roll painfully onto its side and slowly stand up. The towering creature, although upright, now swayed like a drunkard about to pass out. Bugsy could see that the cockroach had taken notice of this activity and was starting to saunter in their direction. By the nonchalance of the bug's body language, it was clear that it was already calculating what to do after it easily dispatched its foe.

What was that thing the cockroach shot at us, Pedro?

I...dunno. My kind has never seen that before.

Well, we survived it. We just have to get our wits about us. I think, if we can do that, we can get back into this fight and—

I've got some very bad news to share with you, and it hurts like hell to do this to you, Bugsy, because it's truly horrible news. But you need to know the truth. Whatever electrical energy the Haag just shot into us did gravely wound us, but that wasn't the worst part of the strike. I'm sensing that somehow that thing just injected a deadly poison into me...into us. From the wounds on my neck, I'm guessing that there were barbs on that fleshy skin cord and I think they shot fatal toxins into me. And now I'm passing them onto you. There's no other way to say this, Bugsy, but we're both finished. We're both as good as dead.

It was at this moment that Bugsy's grandfather's voice came back through the headphones. It was so different, so gravelly with grief, that he correctly assumed that the man already knew about the poisoning. If so, there was no need to pretend.

"So you know, huh, Grandfather?"

"About what?"

"That Pedro got poisoned just now by the cockroach. That I did, too."

"Baku just told us. He sent some drones to wake you guys up, but when they found the fresh wounds on the neck, they went to investigate them. They found evidence of the poison."

There was a sustained moment of silence as the pair digested the truth of the matter. After all, what needs to ever be said when someone finds out that there's actually no hope?

"I'm so, so, so sorry, Bugsy! I should never have let you crawl into that gecko's ear. You should be here, safe in Baku's spaceship, with me."

"Oh-ho, like you could have stopped me, Grandfather!"

The old man chuckled. "That's true. You've always been the one who was gonna do whatever needed to be done, no matter what. I've tried, believe me, to protect you from the harshest elements of life, but they've been a constant for you. From the very git-go, you've faced nothing but the grit and grind of it all. And I have to accept for the rest of my days the fact that I've repeatedly failed you, my boy."

The strength and conviction of Bugsy's response nearly knocked the elderly man back a step. "I'm not even going to dignify those completely asinine thoughts with any kind of reply, Grandfather. Pedro and I are going to save the world, and the fact that I can still say that with any certainty is because of you. You've been the one and only force in my life that has been unchanging, and I owe everything to you. I am here, in the ear of a space alien super-weapon, confident in the face of a creeping defeat, only because you helped me become the person I am today."

Ira looked around at the crew and threw his hands into the air as if to say, *What am I going to do with this boy?*

"So, Grandfather, Pedro and I need to figure out what we're going to do next. Whatever happens, know that I love you."

"I love you, too, Bugsy. Baku wants me to ask, what do you two think that you're going to do now?"

"I dunno. But I guess we both have less to lose now. I mean, the ending of our story is definite. Master Chui says that the most dangerous opponent is one that knows that they cannot win, for someone in that position will do whatever it takes to do the most damage. That pretty much sums everything up for Pedro and me right now. If nothing else, we want to get our pound of flesh from the bug."

"I don't want to hang up, Bugsy, but I think the cockroach is getting ready for its final act. You guys need to come up with some kind of a plan."

"Okay, talk with you later."

As he signed off with his grandfather and started to put his attention back on guiding Pedro, Bugsy ruminated over the last statement's accuracy. No matter what, he probably wouldn't talk with his grandfather ever again, and the impact of that admission was enough to give him a moment's pause.

Do you have a plan, Bugsy?

No. I just know that we can't wait for that damn bug to finish us off. We need to go down swinging.

Agreed. I don't know what kind of defense I can muster, but we've got to try...one last time.

Yes. I know it's insane to say, Pedro, but I never thought my life would end like this. No matter how bad things got, I've always hoped that I'd go out with a bang.

What did you just say?

No, I'm not saying that I've had suicidal thoughts during my life, but whenever I've imagined my death, from time to time, I've always—

No, Bugsy, what did you *just* say...exactly?

Um, that I've always hoped to go out with a bang. Why?

If it were possible for a gigantic space creature to psychically utter a gasp of astonishment through its thoughts, that's exactly what Bugsy experienced from Pedro's involuntary response. With such little time to spare, the giant gecko opened his mind up to his passenger, just like Bugsy had done when he'd dispensed the knowledge about kung-fu fighting directly into Pedro's mind. Except, in this case, Pedro shared the intensely personal secret that the Moogs had kept for themselves over time immemorial.

In that instant, Bugsy became completely aware that these creatures had somehow discovered how to psychically pass on a learned behavior through their very own genetic makeup. In the process, every Moog somehow gained an innate awareness in their DNA from the experiences of each of their predecessors. One of the multitude of truths that they passed down among one another was that they all had the ability to blow themselves up whenever their job was over. They had a built-in self-destruct button.

The details on how this had all transpired were hazy to Bugsy, but somewhere along the line of their existence, a singular Moog had come to the conclusion that a victory wasn't really a full victory for their kind. After all, whenever they bested their Haag foe, their android handlers immediately left them behind because the creature's job was done. Too big to transport anywhere, or too wounded to continue on much longer, the massive geckos remained behind as the androids were deployed to the next threat. But the surviving Moogs had all suffered as a result of this tactic. Some had been revered by the beings of the saved planet; some had been cast as villains and were fought against for the rest of their lives, but ALL had died alone. Regardless of their successes, they were assured of only one thing for the rest of their life: loneliness.

The self-termination option had given them a chance to stop this solitary suffering. With their one and only role fulfilled, they merely disappeared within the massive all-consuming explosion that their bodies generated. And thanks to the fact that it was purely a biological combustion, there weren't any negative levels of chemical, nuclear, or pollutive residue left behind when they did the deed. Sure, there'd be a vast physical scar upon the surface of the planet, which was regrettable, but they all viewed this as leaving a less-than-subtle message from each member of their Moog species that said, "I was here."

With all of this information imparted, Bugsy realized why his comment had unleashed this hidden memory, and what Pedro and he could now do with this information.

We can blow this fucker up?

Yes. We just need to start the countdown and then get close enough to the bug to hit it with the blast.

I've got a plan. But I have to call my grandfather first. We need to prepare the group for what's about to happen.

We don't have much time, Bugsy. The cockroach is nearly here.

Roger that. Saying goodbye in Athabaskan is pretty short. It's, "tha," which means see you later. I just need to say this to my grandfather and get Baku to back his spacecraft away from the potential blast zone.

Bugsy hailed his grandfather and they spoke all too briefly. They were able to exchange their last goodbyes quickly and the young man was able to convey to Ira that something BIG was going to happen that would take care of the bug. He directed Baku to keep his ship at a distance of at least three or four miles away, and then he hung up. He shook off the headset – he wouldn't ever need it again.

It's time, Bugsy. The cockroach is here. It's about to finish us off.

Start the countdown, Pedro.

We've got about a minute in Earth time. We just need to keep it close to us for that long.

I'm guessing that the cockroach won't use that bizarre snaky thing again.

I agree. It certainly doesn't need to poison us anymore. If I were a betting creature, I'd wager that it wants to finish us off with its own hands, so to speak.

You think it'll want to make the first move?

I do.

Perfect. When it does, I think we should use some Praying Mantis kung fu to affect its interior balance before affecting its exterior balance.

I'm not sure I'm up for doing anything too fancy, Bugsy. I'm beaten bloody, and I can feel the poison slowly taking effect. I can't promise that you'll get too much from me. But I think we can keep the bug close enough to us to blow it up.

Okay, let's just stand still until it moves against us.

That I can do.

Here we go!

The cockroach had stopped in close proximity to the gecko, which continued to stand uneasily in front of it. There'd been no indication that it could defend itself, and the sense of confidence coming off the bug was like a heat lamp. It uplifted its two sets of legs into a threatening pose of attack, but when there was still no response, the creature seemed to get confused as to what to do next. Whatever its intellectual capability, it now seemed to be pondering about how to dispatch its opponent. It had a plethora of choices, and it seemed uncertain of which one it wanted.

The gecko took advantage of this hesitation. On Bugsy's command, the massive lizard came to life and leapt onto the neck of the cockroach. In an effort to avoid the ray blaster, Pedro spun his huge body around to the back of the bug as he sank his claws into the bug's shell and activated his suction cup feet to stick firm. Although this attack hadn't caused any pain or damage, they were now adhered firmly to the back of the cockroach as if they were getting a piggyback ride.

The Palmetto Bug Monster writhed and spun, but it could not shake them off.

It's been an honor to get to know you
and fight with you, Pedro.

The honor's been all mine, Bugsy. Fire in the hole!

泣いて暮らすも一緒、笑って暮らすも一緒

naite kurasu mo isshô waratte kurasu mo isshô
Life is the same whether we spend it
crying or laughing.

The blast was unimaginably immense. The shock-waves from it had not only pushed Baku's vessel another three miles farther away from their already distant location, and had further drained and damaged the ship's shields, but the brightness of the explosion had forced the ship's computers to shut down all of the monitors to protect them from short-circuiting. The group had had no time to prepare for any of this, and they were viciously thrown about the chamber as the spacecraft was shot away from the epicenter.

Sarah was the first to get back to the control panel to stabilize the ship. Baku joined her, and the two feverishly worked to get the systems back up and working. The rest of the gang, some in great physical pain from the thrashing that they'd just taken, scrambled to help out where they could. Although they were far from being okay, their busyness helped alleviate the sadness and the fear they were all attempting to tamp down.

The monitors were still off, there was smoke and sparks coming from the panels in the ship, and the alarms were continuing to go off, but Ira Morton had a solid memory come to the forefront of his mind. He'd once read the 1945 interview with Lieutenant Charles Levy in the *Free Lance-Star* newspaper, and he'd been so inspired that he'd cut out the article and kept it in one of his scrapbooks. The 26-year-old amateur photographer from Philadelphia had ridden in the nose cone of the *Great Artiste* – one of the support B-29s sent alongside the *Bockscar*, the carrier of the Fat Man atomic bomb – to observe and record the mission, and he aptly described the moment the weapon exploded over Nagasaki:

> "We all grabbed our black welder goggles and slipped them on. Even though it was broad daylight, the flash could hurt your eyes. Then the flash came – sharp and brighter than double daylight itself inside our plane – and we ripped the goggles off again. We saw this big plume climbing up, up into the sky. It was purple, red, white, all colors – something like boiling coffee. It looked alive...we were all plenty scared."

Ira had this quote memorized from his frequent readings, and the words seemed exactly true to what they'd all just witnessed. With such an enormous detonation, he had to assume that his grandson was gone, and although his heart was shattered by this fact, he found solace knowing that the boy had been spared any suffering by the instantaneous explosion. Although this brought him not a sliver of happiness, it did lend a moment of peace.

Within a few moments, the crew had gotten the monitors back up, the ship righted, and all of their minor injuries taken care of and treated. Baku and Sarah piloted the damaged ship back toward the town of Chicken, and they got their first views from the fight scene. What they saw made them collectively struggle to control their breathing.

The devastation was complete. There was no town. There was no airport runway. There was no cockroach. There was no gecko...from which they inferred that there was no Bugsy. There was nothing. There was only utter decimation.

In the two-mile-wide bullseye, there was a massive crater and around it the circular pattern of an expansive area that was charred and treeless. Beyond that, like another ring of a circular target, a two-mile-wide swath existed where all of the trees that had not been vaporized had been knocked down and uprooted. Due to the force of the blast, the trunks all lay pointing away from the center like the cilia of an amoeba. Further out, all of the surviving vegetation looked as if it had been scoured by the high velocity winds of a hurricane or tornado.

Immediately upon viewing the scene on the monitor, Ira Morton broke down into a quiet sob.

There was no way to console the elderly man, and the rest of the group first looked at the images of the complete ruination of the environment outside and then over to the devastation of the man next to them. They all had anguished expressions on their faces, and these reflected the helplessness that they felt. There was nothing anyone could say or do which would quickly fix either.

Baku was the first to break the tersely hushed chamber. "I had no idea the Moogs were capable of doing that!"

Ira stopped his crying and his head whipped around as he snarled at the alien android, "It must have been their secret! Now it's your secret; you have to keep it for them, Mr. Baku."

The Neanderthal showed his disagreement. "No, whenever I'm debriefed about this mission, I'll have to tell the Shxtors about it."

"You can't do that!" Ira yelled at him in a rage.

The man's unadulterated anger startled the group, but the general forcibly addressed them all. "Hell, if we'd known that it could do that in the beginning, we could've asked the big lizard to hop up on the cockroach's back the first time they met and blow it up. Would've saved us a lot of time, effort, and worry. Not to mention a shit ton of United States servicemen's lives."

The group looked at General Richardson with contempt for being so callous. Eve spit out a sharp charge at him. "Don't forget, General, our friend Bugsy just died. Have a little heart, sir."

"Oh, no, I know that. The boy's a hero in my eyes, don't get me wrong. But that gecko turned out to be nothing more than a walking, talking, ticking time bomb. So there was no need to draw this whole affair out like this – it could have been over before it started. And Baku needs to tell his people to have their superweapons skip the stupid fighting part and just blow shit up. It'd be way more effective."

"Why is it so easy for our species to come up with the most effective ways of killing and not be able to ensure any happiness or health?" Mayor Bishop bemoaned.

"General-san, even the kamikaze pilots of World War II had the chance to experience life, albeit a short time, before they died. With these thoughts you're expressing, you're sentencing these Moog creatures to have none at all. They would be grown to just be walking bombs. Don't they deserve the opportunity to make the choice for their own end?"

Ira Morton's face went from an angry snarl to one of a look of pleading. "Mr. Baku, you *cannot* tell the Shxtors about any of this. You must keep their secret safe!"

General Richardson took up a Mussolini-like pose of defiance as he began his oration. "You bleeding-heart liberals are all full of bullshit! If I found out that any of my soldiers were keeping the information about how to secure a quick, surefire victory to themselves, I'd shoot them myself. It is Baku's *duty* to report this to his people."

Before anyone could dispute this last missive, Baku picked up the communication between the U.S. military command center and several American fighter jets sent to scout the blast area. He put these on the intercom so that the group could hear them.

"Candyman, Candyman, come in, Candyman. Please repeat your last message."

"Roger, sir. Apparently a nuclear strike was called and it has wiped out the area. The cockroach and gecko have been neutralized. I repeat, I repeat, the threats have been neutralized. It seems like 'Peacekeeper' finally gave permission to fry their asses."

The group inside of Baku's ship began to chirp like a bunch of Japanese bush warblers (*Horornis diphone*) in the shrubbery, piping out those birds' characteristic "uuuuuu-guisu" as they started talking all at the same time. Their separate voices intertwined to become one sound.

"It wasn't a nuclear strike!"

"There was no mention of Pedro or Bugsy!"

"They're taking credit for saving the day when they didn't!"

"Bugsy died for nothing!"

Eve stopped this mayhem by asking, "General Richardson, who is 'Peacekeeper'?"

The grizzled general snarled at her question. "That's the code name for the current President of the United States."

They all listened as the military radio crackled with responses and orders. The entire area was to be secured by the aircraft as ground recon teams who had been protected from radiation poisoning were deployed to determine the current safety levels at ground zero. There was one further order issued for the pilots to keep their eyes out for the alien space-craft that'd been spotted earlier being chased by the Palmetto Bug Monster, and the pilots were given permission to shoot down the UFO.

With these messages heard, everyone in Baku's ship recognized that there was no real reason for them to continue to hover near the site. Not only that, their safety was now being threatened by the U.S. military aircraft circling around their cloaked ship. The unspoken truth that no one wanted to ad-mit was that Baku needed to get the earthlings back to Tok before he took off to close down his lunar base and then return to his home planet of Shxtor for his inevitable debriefing.

With little fanfare, the alien android gently brushed Sarah's hands aside and began moving the controls. The monitors showed that the craft was moving away from the former location of the town of Chicken, Alaska, at a great rate of speed.

"Mr. Baku?" Eve asked gently.

"Yes, Eve."

"Could you please drop Bernie and me off in LA before you take everyone else back to Tok?"

"Yes, but why shouldn't we hit Tok first? After all, it's on the way," Baku pointed out.

The blonde reporter nodded at the alien android, but she looked over at Ira, who was sobbing silently again, and she spoke out soothingly to Baku. "We need to try to change the narrative by getting the real story over the airwaves as quickly as is possible. The world needs to know the truth...that Bugsy and Pedro saved the day."

"Ha! That'll be great for your career, right? You'll get all the glory by breaking the story first." General Richardson spit out his words, oozing with sarcasm.

Eve waved his comment off with her slender hand as she made her way over to Ira, who she wrapped an arm around to comfort. Without glancing up to make it clear who she was talking to, she uttered monosyllabically, "It's not about careers or glory. It's about the truth."

Bernie made a weird sound with his mouth before saying, "It won't matter, not in the end. The storyline's going to be that the President of the United States finally took care of business and defeated the alien threat. I can see the headlines now, 'The President Fries Chicken and Kills the Space Monsters.' We can supply the visuals to the story, but I guarantee the end result of our tapes won't be the releasing of any truth."

Baku seemed to grimace. His hands began scuttling over the controls. "I'll have you there in a few moments."

Instead of strategizing with Bernie about how to get their coverage of the events right onto the air and who they needed to approach to make sure that this all happened in ways to best promote their own careers, Eve continued to give comfort to the still-sobbing elderly man. She genuinely seemed to be consoling him as she whispered gently into his ear. Whatever she was murmuring was doing the trick, and he began to wipe his eyes and stop crying. By the time that they'd reached LA, Ira looked less like a distraught senior citizen and more like a defiant scrapper with a mission.

The others in the group were preoccupied with their own thoughts about what had just taken place, or with their own mental machinations as to what they were going to do next, but Bernie had watched the unusual behavior from Eve, and he had to admit that he was seeing the woman in a new light. Through the lens of the camera and during their time together, he'd recognized Eve Sanderborn as the quintessential creature of insincerity. But here she was, acting like a loving human being. If he was being honest with himself, Bernie would have to admit that he was feeling what almost could be called amorous affection for this new version of his colleague. He even smiled stupidly at her when she looked over at him, and he could have sworn that the powerful blonde had blushed slightly at the way he was glancing adoringly at her.

Their trip to LA was over in a matter of minutes, and Baku landed his spacecraft on the roof of the KTLA building. He uncloaked the ship and then opened the hatchway for Bernie and Eve. The group helped them transport their equipment down the gangplank to the rooftop helipad and then they took turns hugging one another. While General Richardson's and Baku's efforts were a bit stiff, the others squeezed the reporter and cameraman with unrestrained emotion. After what they'd all just gone through, their embraces reflected the true sense of camaraderie that had grown amongst them. Together they'd just experienced the near-end of the world, the defeat of the Palmetto Bug Monster, and the death of their friend.

Before the group could head back up the gangway to go back inside the spacecraft to start their trip to Tok, Eve loudly proclaimed, "For Bugsy!"

Ira Morton thrust his fist in the air, "For Bugsy!"

The flight to Tok was quick and very quiet. Each member of the group continued to reflect upon what was going to happen next. They were deep in thought, not to mention extremely tired from the intensity of the recent events they'd all lived through together. Baku brought his ship down gently and landed in its regular spot in the back parking lot of the Parker House. The monitors and the quick report of his drones gave clear indications that the nearby military units were now far too busy to worry about the cheap roadside motel, and there was a very low likelihood that their presence would be detected when Baku uncloaked the ship.

However, the cameras on Baku's ship did pick up a very odd scene outside. A vintage VW bus was parked next to the lawn chairs that the group had used as a lounge area before, and when the cameras zoomed in it was clear that Alejandra Fuerte, Henry Kissinger, and a disheveled First Lady were seated there, apparently awaiting the group's return. The spacecraft's uncloaking did not seem to cause this group of people any concern.

Baku shut off the ship's engines and the chamber grew noiseless. The hatch opened, the gangway shot out, and the group shuffled down it to the gravel parking lot. Their curiosity then gave their footsteps a new added spice as they all struggled to explain away what they were seeing in front of them.

"Ah, my friend," Kissinger announced in his thick German accent. "*Sie hast* returned victorious."

The general gave a quick salute. "As expected. But no thanks to you, you fucking goat!'

"*Ich hatte alle Hände voll zu tun,*" Kissinger muttered quietly.

"As I said before, Mr. Kissinger, I don't speak Kraut."

The First Lady, whose hair was muffed up and whose blouse was not buttoned in a very conservative manner, looked up and spoke in a voice that revealed that she wasn't fully encumbered by sobriety. "He says he's had his hands full. I think he's referring to me and to what we've been doing for...good god, how long has it been?"

Ignoring her, the general directed his attention solely onto Kissinger. "So why are you here now?"

"To drive you home, *mein General.*"

"To the Kennedy Hill Plantation Retirement Home?" The general's voice croaked with disappointment.

"*Ja, ja.* You're technically AWOL, General. We don't need any unnecessary attention, *richtig*?"

"But I don't want to go back there. I've had so much..."

The general didn't need to end his thought, and his words drifted off unresolved.

Kissinger carefully walked up to General Richardson and put his hand tenderly onto the man's shoulder. "Ah, my friend, the way I've heard it, Arlene Simmons has been missing you. *Deine Freundin* desperately wants to hear you again call her the adorable Vietnamese pet name you have for her. And your troops there need you, General."

The stern countenance that General Richardson had been exhibiting up to this point melted, and he smiled weakly at Kissinger. "They have all needed me, huh? It feels good to be needed. As my old friend Doug MacArthur said, 'Old soldiers never die; they just fade away.'"

"*Ja, ja, mein General.* We must be going. We have a long drive and many military roadblocks to navigate. The First Lady is riding shotgun, so you will have to be in the *rücksitz.*"

General Richardson shoved Kissinger's hand off his shoulder as if it were something foul. "Like I'd wanna sit next to you – you smell like sauerkraut.

I'll take the seat of importance, as is my stature in life."

The general turned to the group and gave them a dramatic salute. There'd been no threat of getting a farewell hug from the man, and they smiled at his heartfelt and respectful gesture.

Mayor Bishop sheepishly approached him. "General, I owe you an apology. I thought you were making it all up about Kissinger and the VW bus. I was wrong to doubt you, sir."

"Well, don't beat yourself up, you wall-eyed elf. I kept waiting for Gene Wilder, Terri Garr, and Peter Boyle to hop out from the shadows behind you during this whole time. Come down to South Carolina to see me some time. I'll make you an adjutant-chef in the Foreign Legion and give you a medal."

With that, the old soldier ambled off, opened the side door of the VW bus, and got into the back seat. Kissinger helped the First Lady to her feet, walked her unsteadily to the passenger door of the bus and got her inside. He shut the side door and then walked in his curious gait around the front and waved at the group. "*Auf Wiedersehen. Es war mir eine Freude, Sie kennenzulernen. Gut gemacht.*"

The group did not understand his German expression, but they figured it was some kind of send-off, so they waved as the Volkswagen bus started up and drove out toward the Alaska Highway, kicking up a cloud of dust as it went.

The number of their ranks was now down to Ira, Usotsuki, Mayor Bishop, Sarah, Baku...and Alejandra, and they blinked at each other as if to express their joint question as to what was supposed to happen now.

Mayor Bishop sapped this trance of uncertainty by addressing Alejandra, who was still seated in the lawn chair, nonplussed.

"What are you *doing* here, Alejandra?"

The little Mexican woman glanced up at him with a look of nonchalance, but her brown eyes were warm and intriguing. "When the *federales* closed down the state, I couldn't get any supplies for my taco truck – even at *el mercado negro*. I had no food to sell, but then I saw that no one was running this motel, so I started doing that. *¿Quién lo sabía? Me gusta ser una posadera.*"

"Huh?" ask Mayor Bishop.

"I like being an innkeeper," explained the Mexican lady.

"You've been here the whole time?"

"*Si*, I've been taking care of the place – the motel has been busy with all the *soldados* here. I've been waiting for you to come back."

"Me?" Mayor Bishop asked and he emphasized his question by pointing at himself and grinning broadly.

"*Por supuesto*, I knew you'd come back here...to me."

Mayor Bishop dramatically dropped to one knee and grabbed her hand. "Alejandra Fuerte, will you marry me?"

For such an unexpected moment, the woman seemed completely calm. She tilted her head back and forth and clicked her tongue. Then she responded, "*Lo pensaré.*"

"Huh?"

The Mexican woman smiled at him. "I'll think about it."

Mayor Bishop nodded furiously and replied, "That's good enough for me. Listen, as soon as you parked your truck in my parking lot, Alejandra, I started thinking about building a Mexican restaurant onto the motel. You could run it and cook for our guests. What do you think?"

"*Si*, we could make *mucho dinero.*"

"We could grow old together, taking care of the travelers...together," Mayor Bishop said with a Marty Feldman-like impish grin.

"*No pongamos el caballo delante del carro.* Let's not put the cart before the horse, but I think we would make a good team."

Mayor Bishop snapped his fingers. "Again, that's good enough for me. Let's chat as we walk back to the office. I'm bushed from this trip and I need to sleep, but I can set you up in a room."

Alejandra caressed the man's face. "I have been staying in your *dormitorio* while you've been away. I will continue to stay there, *mi cariño. Vamos.*"

"Okay. Sounds delightful. See you later, Sarah, Baku, Usotsuki, and Ira. When we get the restaurant up and running, you'll need to stop by for some *comida.*"

The Mexican woman, upon hearing the Spanish word used by the mayor, punched his shoulder. "*Que bueno mi adorable pizote.*"

Mayor Bishop hugged everyone goodbye, and he and Alejandra set off walking toward the office. Immediately they became engaged in a very passionate discussion. It was hard to tell if it was a love scene or a fight.

An Army transport truck rumbled by the motel, and Baku peered around at the parking lot. "Well, I've gotta get going before I'm discovered."

"Where will you go?" Sarah asked. Her tone of voice was like a veteran aviator asking another pilot what their next destination was going to be.

"I'm to head back to the Moon base and shut it down, then I've been ordered to return to Shxtor immediately. I'm not sure what's going to happen there, but if I were a betting android, I'd guess it's not going to be a happy ending for me. Apparently I am now obsolete. Them's the breaks, I guess."

"I want to go with you, Baku," Sarah declared.

Ira and Usotsuki both looked at the woman with shock on their faces. Baku just shook his head as he spoke. "Oh, I don't know about that, Sarah. There's too much uncertainty to ever suggest that you'd be okay to undertake such a journey."

"That's just it, Baku. I like you – you're amazing. I could learn so much from you! I know everything there is to know about flying a bush plane around Alaska. I want to go somewhere entirely new with someone I find very intriguing. I want a challenge."

Baku grimaced. "I cannot guarantee that the Shxtor scientists won't probe you."

"A girl needs a good probing every once in a while," Sarah said with an impish grin.

"I also cannot guarantee that they won't put you in a zoo."

Sarah took on an expression of mirth. "But I'd get to go to the Moon? And get to learn to fly a spacecraft across the galaxies? Both of those are worth the cost of possibly being probed or being put into a cage. Does your planet have something that will get me drunk?"

"Oh, definitely. I think you'll find Kukulcan wine will knock you on your ass."

"I'm in! Let's get going."

"Are you sure, Sarah?" Ira asked with some concern. "You may never get back here to see your family or friends here again."

"And I might. What if I were to present myself as an ambassador of sorts to the Shxtors? Perhaps they'll make Baku my guide to travel through the universe to approach other saved worlds as the Earth's representative. If so, I will get to see amazing stuff and be able to come back here. If not, I will still get to see amazing stuff on my way there. Even if Baku gets turned into scrap metal and I end up in a zoo, it's worth the risk."

Baku looked at her with widened eyes as he stuttered, "Uh, well, I'm not sure..."

The sound of some approaching jet fighters interrupted him and caused him to flinch. "They still have a shoot to kill order for my ship, so we should get going. I would love to travel with you, Sarah. But we need to leave right now."

Quick hugs were exchanged with Usotsuki and Ira, and then Sarah and Baku ran up the gangplank, the hatch closed, the ship was cloaked, and there was the mild sound and turbulence from the ship taking off. This had all occurred without detection, and soon the parking lot grew quiet again, except for the usual ambient noises that a roadside motel experienced in Alaska. Ira and Usotsuki were left looking straight up into the sky, unable to see the ship's departure.

"What will you do now, Ira-san?"

Ira smiled at the Japanese cryptozoologist and then looked out at Tok. "Oh, I'm gonna put all of my energies into making sure that everyone in this town knows that one of their own actually saved the day. As the head commissioner of the roads in Tok, I'll push to name some of our streets after Bugsy and Pedro. And I know a few Native artists who I will commission to create some big pieces of public art. I want a gigantic statue of He-Knew-Pat-Sajak to be placed in the center of town to remind us all that the giant lizard actually saved the day. Then, whenever it is deemed safe enough to rebuild the town of Chicken again, I will make sure that a smaller work is put there to celebrate the sacrifice that Bugsy made. I know that Eve and Bernie will try to get the real story out, but they're right – the truth will be bent to the wills of those in power. I'll fight my battles here in Tok."

The two men shared a moment of not talking, but then Ira pursed his lips and asked, "What will you do, Usotsuki?"

"*Watashi wa ima hōmuresudesu.* I am quite literally a man without a country. I cannot go home to Japan – the yakuza will kill me there. I cannot legally stay here in the United States – my name is on the government's 'naughty' list. I don't know what to do. Can I stay with you…for a little while?"

"Oh-ho, yes, you should definitely stay here in Tok with me. I've got room at my house, and I think it'd be good for me to have some companionship. I won't ask you to fill Bugsy's shoes, but I don't really want to be alone now."

"*Hai*, I would like that, Ira-san."

Ira Morton put his arm around the Japanese man's shoulders. "You could help me with the roadwork and I could introduce you to some of my wife's relatives. They would love to tell you those Athabaskan stories about the spirits and creatures of the woods. Plus, we could get you on the Athabaskan Network, and it would give you the ability to contact people everywhere about local mysteries. Life in Tok is not really like living in the rest of the U.S. – you can kinda disappear here. We're kind of our own Monster Island, if you know what I mean."

The Japanese cryptozoologist chuckled at this reference from the Toho Co., Ltd. movies and then enthusiastically answered, "*Hai*, I would love all of that."

The two men started walking slowly back to where Ira had parked his old truck. As the jets continued to scream overhead and the endless streams of tanks and heavy equipment rumbled down the nearby highway, their sounds overshadowed the beautiful Alaskan day and the noises from nature. Halfway to the old Dodge Power Wagon, Usotsuki began to loudly hum Akira Ifukube's symphony for the main title of the Toho Co., Ltd. movie *The War of the Gargantuas*, and this made him and Ira smile.

The motion of a very large raptor caught Usotsuki's eye and he pointed it out to Ira, who started watching it as well. A displaced brown and white Steller's sea eagle swooped down and grabbed a hapless marmot from the side of the road. As it flew off with the lifeless carcass of the rodent in its talons, the elderly man from Tok said confidently, "*Shouganai.* It is what it is."

終わり
owari
The End

著者について

chosha ni tsuite
About the Author

The facts about Sam Sumac are hazy, at best. Any details we have about his life come from his own handwritten autobiographical sketch, "Please Don't Forget to Pay the Debt." According to it, he was born in Buffalo, New York, exactly ten months after V-J Day, to an unwed Polish woman by the name of Ewa. While he never knew his father's identity, Sam describes his childhood as a happy one spent with his mother in a home in North Buffalo. He claims to have attended various local elementary, junior high, and high schools throughout his youth before enrolling in the State University College of Education at Buffalo for one year, where he majored in physics. He dropped out to enlist in the United States Army.

Sam contends he was conscripted as a tunnel rat during the Vietnam War due to being just over five feet in height. While those early days of his military training brought him some moments of happiness, his deployment to the combat of the war only damaged him. Although unsubstantiated, Sam alleges that he was a member of one of many of the companies of subterranean soldiers in the Củ Chi district who were given a cocktail of hallucinogenic drugs before heading into the tunnels to do battle with their North Vietnamese enemies. He believes that these induced narcotic highs led him to have many out-of-body experiences, which he repeatedly calls his "enlightenments" in his writings.

Sam attributed the combination of the violence of the war and these unauthorized military drug experiments as cause for his nervous breakdown. According to him, the stress of the tunnel warfare and the impact from the unstable narcotics caused him to be briefly institutionalized in a military psych ward in Phoenixville, Pennsylvania. Prone to fantastical hallucinations during this time – most involving alien invasions, time travel, the apocalypse, the oil crisis, psychic mediums, the Middle East, and the gruesome punishments of many of the people he held responsible for his ordeals (especially a Bill Buchanan from Kenmore, Washington, allegedly a special operative with the CIA who Sam blamed for the administering of narcotics to Sam's unit) – he spouted a nonstop string of prophetic stories and sagas. He says his mental health gradually improved with care until, ultimately, he was well enough to be discharged from the Army.

When he returned to Buffalo, he found out his mother had passed away sometime during his hospitalization. Devastated, he decided to settle in his former hometown. He rented a house in the same neighborhood of his childhood and began working as a salesman at a local shoe store. While this job might not seem too exciting to most, Sam reported he "had a thing for feet" and the work appealed to him deeply. During this time, while living alone and working full-time, his compulsion to write down the stories inside his head hit him. Sam spent every spare moment writing late every night and putting onto paper the bizarre delusions from his time in the tunnels and in the military mental hospital, and in the process, he created a series of science fiction stories.

He vividly describes not being able to contain the flow of creativity coming out of him. During these writing frenzies, he wrote without purpose or order. He merely transcribed all the imagery and characters as they came out. These manic periods never left him enough time to edit or to prepare a manuscript for publication before the next story needing to be penned demanded his attention. He aptly recounts how he felt like a faucet of stories which was unable to be shut off.

Then, one day, Sam Sumac disappeared. When his landlord went to check on him after not receiving his rent payment, there was no trace whatsoever left behind of the man. The police were called, but they quickly decided there was no evidence of foul play so no further official investigation was needed. However, it is still unclear – even at this point in time – what actually happened to Sam. He simply vanished.

Some would like to think he changed his identity and moved to another city to resume his writing in a new locale. Others have a darker interpretation. Regardless, whatever happened to him is just part of the mystery of Sam Sumac.

The world would have likely forgotten all about the man if it were not for several boxes belonging to him being discovered in a storage unit a year after his inexplicable disappearance. Due to the lack of an annual payment for the storage and the absence of any next of kin on his rental application paperwork, these unclaimed items were given to his ex-landlord, who, in turn, gave them to a fellow employee at the same shoe store where Sam had worked. When this individual opened the boxes and saw the chaotic state of their contents, he resealed them and put them in his garage, where they remained undisturbed for nearly twenty-five years.

Finally these boxes landed in the hands of a retired Episcopal priest who was asked to claim the possessions of his former parishioner who'd recently passed away. It was only then, when the boxes were re-opened, that the writings of Sam Sumac were once again exposed to this world.

Sort of.

These boxes were brimming with intermixed and disarrayed heaps of handwritten pages on different types of paper and were done with various writing implements. With no organization or order, the process of collating and transcribing them has been a maddeningly complicated and time-consuming endeavor.

Put a Bug in Your Ear was apparently written in the late 1970s or early 1980s, and this is the fourth attempt to get a Sam Sumac story into a completed format. *Piss & Vinegar, Ain't Nobody Here but Us Chickens,* and *Who Drew the Short Straw?* were the first three. It is hoped that, over time, more of his novels might eventually get reassembled and come out in print sometime in the future, but the Herculean effort needed to accomplish this makes the task an incredibly slow process.

So, sit back and savor these words from an unknown genius, Sam Sumac.

P. B. – February, 2015

AUTHOR PROFILE

The facts about Sam Sumac are hazy, at best. Many details of his life have not been corroborated. Supposedly, he was born in Buffalo, New York in 1946, where he lived with his mother until he joined the U.S. Army and fought in Vietnam as a tunnel rat. After the war, he suffered mental breakdowns, sold shoes, and wrote sci-fi novels, and then vanished without a trace. *Piss & Vinegar, Ain't Nobody Here but Us Chickens,* and *Who Drew the Short Straw?* were his first three transcribed novels. The Sam Sumac Association has been tasked with preserving this mysterious author's work for future generations.

Website: www.samsumacass.com

Instagram: @samsumacass

Facebook: @samsumacass

WHAT DID YOU THINK OF PUT A BUG IN YOUR EAR?

A big thank you for purchasing this book. It means a lot that you chose this book specifically from such a wide range on offer. I do hope you enjoyed it.

Book reviews are incredibly important for an author. All feedback helps them improve their writing for future projects and for developing this edition. If you are able to spare a few minutes to post a review on Amazon, that would be much appreciated.

Publisher Information

Rowanvale Books provides publishing services to independent authors, writers and poets all over the globe. We deliver a personal, honest and efficient service that allows authors to see their work published, while remaining in control of the process and retaining their creativity. By making publishing services available to authors in a cost-effective and ethical way, we at Rowanvale Books hope to ensure that the local, national and international community benefits from a steady stream of good quality literature.

For more information about us, our authors or our publications, please get in touch.

www.rowanvalebooks.com
info@rowanvalebooks.com